Sophie wanted to change.

But how could she change now? How could she tell him the truth regarding anything without condemning herself to prison? She couldn't. Not yet.

An uncharacteristic sense of hopelessness swept over her. She blinked back the sting of tears.

But he'd seen. "Sophie? What is it? What makes you so sad?"

She shook her head.

Clay remained seated, but took her hand and raised it to his lips. His warm breath and a soft kiss sent a tingle up her arm, and her breasts tightened unexpectedly.

A good man. An honest, straightforward man. He was as different from her as the moon was from the sun. And thinking of the two of them together was hopeless.

But she was weaker than she'd ever imagined.

Kiss me, she cried silently. *Kiss me and let me feel the beauty just for this one night.*

* * *

The Lawman's Bride
Harlequin® Historical #835—February 2007

Praise for Cheryl St.John

His Secondhand Wife
Nominated for a RITA® Award
"A beautifully crafted and involving story about the transforming power of love, this is recommended reading."
—*Romantic Times BOOKreviews*

Prairie Wife
Nominated for a *Romantic Times BOOKreviews*
Reviewers' Choice Award
"This is a very special book, courageously executed by the author and her publisher. Her considerable skill brings the common theme of the romance novel—love conquers all—to the level of genuine catharsis."
—*Romantic Times BOOKreviews* (4½ stars)

The Tenderfoot Bride
"Cheryl St.John once again touches the hearts of readers…. Not many readers will be able to hold back their tears as they reach the conclusion."
—*Romance Reviews Today*

CHERYL ST. JOHN

The Lawman's Bride

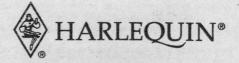

HARLEQUIN®

TORONTO • NEW YORK • LONDON
AMSTERDAM • PARIS • SYDNEY • HAMBURG
STOCKHOLM • ATHENS • TOKYO • MILAN • MADRID
PRAGUE • WARSAW • BUDAPEST • AUCKLAND

ISBN-13: 978-0-373-29435-0
ISBN-10: 0-373-29435-2

THE LAWMAN'S BRIDE

Copyright © 2007 by Cheryl Ludwigs

This edition published by arrangement with Harlequin Books S.A.

® and TM are trademarks of the publisher. Trademarks indicated with ® are registered in the United States Patent and Trademark Office, the Canadian Trade Marks Office and in other countries.

www.eHarlequin.com

Printed in U.S.A.

This book is dedicated to my readers.

Your letters and e-mails brighten my days
and encourage me.

Your pictures are posted around my work space to
remind me why I do what I do. When you tell me you've
read every one of my books, I'm honored. When you
say they're on your keeper shelves, I'm delighted. When
you share how a story touched you or helped you heal,
I'm humbled. Whether we've met in person, blogged
together, or live on different continents and will never
exchange a word, consider yourself deeply appreciated.

You are special to me.

Prologue

Morgantown, West Virginia, 1878

Dense clouds parted to reveal a slice of silver moon in the narrow gap of sky above the dark alley where the fourteen-year-old girl crouched beside a stack of crates. She wasn't afraid. No, there were plenty of things more terrifying than night. Darkness was a friend tonight, cloaking her in its haven of invisibility.

Adjusting her grip on the handle of her traveling bag, she glanced around and listened intently, making certain no one followed.

In the distance a train whistle blew, and her heart swelled at the promising sound. If she could make it to the station, she'd buy a ticket and be gone. It didn't matter where the train was heading. Freedom was an elusive place she could only imagine.

A pattering erupted as fat drops of rain struck the rooftops of the buildings on either side of the alley, pinging against every piece of metal and wood. Enough sound to muffle her steps, she thought with a surge of hope.

She straightened and took a step. A yelp startled her and she brought her free hand to her mouth to stifle a cry. The dog she'd surprised sniffed her feet then moved on. She took a deep breath, relaxed her muscles, and her racing heart calmed.

Determined, she grasped her bag and strode to the front corner of the building. Across the street in the yellow circle from a street lamp, she made out the word LUNCHEON painted in gold letters on an expanse of window glass and knew exactly how many buildings she needed to pass to move into the opposite alley. From there she could make her way to the edge of town. She stepped forward.

"Awfully late for a stroll, isn't it?"

Her heart dropped to her toes at the familiar voice. The black-shadowed figure of a man loomed out of the darkness. He moved in close, blocking her view of the street, thwarting her escape.

"Not the fairest of weather, either."

Around them stinging raindrops drummed on cans and crates. The pervading smell of dampened earth was strong. She couldn't breathe. Captivity did that to a person. Stole their ability to fill their lungs.

"You don't know what kind of trouble awaits you on the streets at night, Ogaleesha. There are far worse fates than your easy life."

Using the name given by her Sioux captors, Tek Garrett cunningly reminded her where she'd come from. She felt the hope that had buoyed her moments ago sink like a stone to the bottom of a river.

"I've ordered tea brought to my room. Doesn't that sound good? You'll be dry and warm in no time."

Her hand ached from gripping the handle of her bag with such intensity. What if she ran back the way she'd come? He would catch her and her situation would only worsen.

Garrett reached to take the bag from her, his fingers touching hers in an unspoken command until she gave up and relinquished her hold.

"Come, Gabriella. Let's get you inside before you catch a chill."

Thoughtful words. Caring, almost. She recognized the subtle threat all the same. The annoyance emanating from his lean body screamed a warning. The way he turned and gestured for her to move along the board-walk ahead of him left no room for choice.

Her legs felt wooden as she forced her feet to place one step in front of another and set a determined course for the hotel.

"Few young women enjoy privileges equal to yours," Garrett told her as they reached the building. He opened the door for her to walk into the foyer ahead of him. "You've had excellent tutors," he continued, nodding at the counter attendant they passed on their way to the stairs. "You'll be one of the most highly educated young women in the country. You own fashionable clothing and lovely slippers. I dare say you have hair ribbons and jewelry to match every ensemble. Wouldn't you agree?"

They reached the second-floor landing, and she dared a look at the lobby below, saying a silent good-bye to her last hope of freedom.

"Your speech is cultured and flawless. Quite different from when you first came to me."

She hadn't come to him. He'd bought her from a band of Sioux.

"You barely spoke English, as I recall."

During six years as a captive, she'd had little opportunity to speak her own language.

"I confess I'm hurt," he said, pausing in the hall outside their adjoining rooms. Moisture glistened on the shoulders of his fine black coat. "All I've done for you, and this is how you repay me?"

She studied a smear on the wallpaper to avoid meeting the chastisement in his eyes.

"I've been so patient." Those words came out as a thoughtful sigh. "Quite considerate really."

Turning, he fitted a brass key into the lock and guided her into his room. For the past two years they had traveled as father and daughter. He claimed the ruse was so that no questions would arise, but his true strategy was to keep her under his careful watch. Her door to the hall was always kept locked, and he held the only key.

"Perhaps you need more *attention*. A bit more of an *investment* in our arrangement."

Garrett set down her bag and shed his coat to reveal the same vest and pressed white shirt he'd been wearing earlier in the evening. He was twice her age but fit and dapper with razor-sharp cheekbones and an elegant square forehead. His hair couldn't be called fair or blond because of its dark undertones.

Reluctantly, she removed her damp shawl and hung it on the hook on the back of the door.

He bent to open her carpetbag and dumped its contents on the floral carpet. Two of her simplest dresses spilled out, followed by a book, a length of beads and a strand of pearls.

Holding the pearls in his palm, he straightened, studied them for a moment, finally closing his long fingers over the necklace.

"You wouldn't have gotten far with such a meager stash," he told her. "Not a wise decision." He leaned toward her to clasp the pearls around her neck, speaking against her ear as he did so. "Not wise at all. I haven't taught you *everything* yet. There is more... much, much more."

Another stone joined the first in that riverbed of hopelessness. He reached to her throat to unbutton her collar, then unfastened the row of buttons until he reached the waistband of her skirt.

Her heart thumped in her chest, but she held her anxiety in check, her expression revealing nothing of what she felt. *Show people what they want to see.* He'd taught her well. She conveyed regret and submission with her downturned eyes.

Garrett slid the shirtwaist down her arms, skimming his fingertips against her bare skin. "If not for me, you would be some man's squaw," he told her. "You would be cooking scrawny rabbits over a fire and suckling a squalling brat. If I hadn't fostered you, you'd be living with a mangy trapper who beat you over every small offense."

Garrett turned her around and unfastened her skirt, pushing the fabric to the ground in a silken swish of petticoats. "You should be grateful you've been spared all that. Grateful you're not down on Tucker Street, selling yourself to every drunk who comes through the doors with two bits."

She closed her eyes, fearing what he said was true. Anything was better than the things he described. She owed him for sparing her that kind of life. He'd always provided well and he was polite. He'd taught her the craft he considered an art, rewarding her when she learned and excelled.

"Plenty of other young women would be delighted to exchange places with you this very minute, Gabriella."

Even though she was a mere possession, Garrett was clever and handsome, well-mannered and clean. *She could be a lot worse off.*

Her life had been spared long ago, but spared for what? She'd gone from being a child to being a possession. The lessons she'd learned at the hands of the Sioux were as much a part of her as her dark hair and white skin, most importantly: *show no fear.*

She opened her eyes and met Garrett's, watched as he turned back the coverlet on his bed and beckoned her forward.

Yes. Her life could be a lot worse.

Chapter One

Newton, Kansas, 1887

What's a girl like me doing in a place like this?

She glanced into open doorways as she strolled down the second story hallway of the dormitory housing the young women who worked in Fred Harvey's elegant Arcade Hotel and restaurant.

Each from good families, the young ladies were of irreproachable character and had provided references and letters of recommendation to acquire their positions in the lavish hotel and esteemed restaurant. The irony of her presence here amused her.

Emma Spearman exited her room, closing the door behind her with a soft click. "Good morning, Sophie. Did you sleep well?"

"Very well, thank you. And you?" she replied.

Emma's bright smile revealed her pleasure. "I used to sleep in a lumpy bed with two sisters who tossed all night and stole the covers. My three noisy brothers were in a loft overhead. My nights here are *heaven,* thank you." She tucked her arm through Sophie's and said in a conspiratorial tone, "I will never admit this to a one of them, but I do sometimes miss my siblings. I'm taking the train home for a visit the first of next week."

Sophie smiled. A bed with two sisters and those noisy brothers overhead sounded like heaven to her.

"What about you?" Emma asked. "You haven't seen your family since you've been here, have you?"

So what was Sophie doing working and sleeping among people of good character? Well, she'd lied. Fabricated a background, established her own requirements and met her own standards. People wanted to believe her, so they did. She was attractive, well-educated, dressed smartly and spoke in a cultured manner. Her contrived references had been believable.

She was Sophie Hollis now, daughter of a Pennsylvania farmer, come to Kansas to broaden her perspective and earn money to tuck away.

"I'll be traveling east very soon," she thought up on the spot. "My father is remarrying, so I'll be attending the wedding."

"How exciting," Emma said. "A wedding!"

"Who's getting married?" Sophie's roommate Amanda Pettyjohn caught up with them, her pretty blond curls bouncing against her neck, her fawn-colored eyes sparkling.

Maybe she shouldn't have gone that far, Sophie thought belatedly. Mentioning marriage in this place was like dangling a juicy bone above a hungry dog's head. Everyone knew the young women working here were eager for husbands, but two years of service was required before a Harvey girl could resign her position. Each of them had signed a contract.

"Sophie's father," Emma told her.

"You didn't tell me." Amanda's tone revealed injury.

Sophie wasn't used to transparent displays of emotion. "I only got the telegram last evening. I didn't say anything, because I wasn't sure how I felt about it."

"Well, of course, you didn't. Your own dear mother could never be replaced." Amanda patted her arm as they reached the back stairs and started down. "I was devastated when my father remarried. At least you're grown and don't have to endure living in the shadow of step-siblings. Has your father known his new fiancée long?"

Sophie was in the process of inventing a reply when she was spared.

"There's a train within the hour," the starched and puffed head waitress of the dining room announced from the bottom of the stairs. "It's going to be a hot day, so you'll want your heavy chores completed early." The Harvey House employees called Mrs. Winters the trail boss for good reason.

"Yes, ma'am," Emma and Amanda chorused.

Mrs. Winters pointed an accusing finger at Sophie. "One more infraction by you, young lady, and you can pack your bags."

Sophie listened to the continuation of the tirade she'd endured at least once a day for the past month. Her kitchen and dining room skills were improving, for goodness sake. This was her first attempt at domestic chores after all, no matter what her references said.

The woman inspected each of them with a critical

eye. "Your morning duties are listed on the blackboard, ladies. Do them promptly. If the heat causes your clothing to become damp, change immediately. We must be prepared in case Mr. Harvey makes one of his sudden unannounced visits."

She turned and marched away.

Sophie watched her lumber into the dining hall. "Sudden unannounced visit sounds so much better than *sneaky inspection*."

"Did she refer to *sweat?*" Emma asked, mischievously covering her lips as though she'd said a curse word.

"Surely she knows Harvey Girls simply *glow*," Amanda added.

"Whatever did you do to make her take such a dislike to you?" Emma asked.

Sophie shrugged.

"Every man who comes in does a double take when he sees Sophie," Amanda told her. "Maybe the trail boss is jealous."

The three of them shared a giggle and, joined by coworkers, hurried to their morning tasks.

Clay Connor crossed his ankles and leaned back in his chair, the *Newton Kansan* and a cup of steaming coffee his only concerns in the world. Or so it should seem to the other occupants of the hotel dining room. On his left, an elderly mother and her son discussed the details of disposing of their husband and father's clothing and personal items. The son kept bringing the subject around to a land deed.

On his right, three merchants from Florence had several catalogs open and were bemoaning the fact that Montgomery Ward could offer items at a lower price than they could.

Straight ahead at the lunch counter, a slender fellow in a worn serge jacket folded his napkin and prepared to leave without paying for his dinner. The manager had sent for Clay when he'd first seen the man who met the description of someone who'd pulled the same stunt at another Harvey House in Wichita.

Without turning his head, Clay glanced out the window and confirmed that Owen Sanders, one of his deputies, was still out front on the loading platform. With the dining hall and lunch counter filled with Sante Fe passengers eager to return to their train cars and continue their journeys, a low-key arrest was imperative. Even though he didn't see a gun on the man, Clay wouldn't take chances with the well-being of innocent bystanders.

The patron under the marshal's scrutiny had seen the upside of forty. His clothing and shoes were well-cut and of fine material, but on the verge of shabby. With impeccable manners he finished his meal—breaded veal and vegetables, cheesecake and coffee—neatly folded the white linen napkin, and fished in his pocket as though searching for a tip.

The man waited until all the waitresses were occupied and the manager was out of sight before grabbing his hat and heading for the door.

Clay folded his newspaper, then nonchalantly rose to his feet and followed.

The fellow, settling a bowler on his head, was hell-bent on making a beeline for the deserted passenger car.

As his foot hit the first step, a pair of boots appeared on the metal platform above, and he looked up into the barrel of Deputy Sanders's Colt. As if to escape, he turned, but came up short against Clay's .45. Eyes as wide as silver dollars, he raised his lily-white hands above his head.

"What's your name?" Clay asked.

He didn't meet Clay's eyes, but glanced around with a feigned expression of bewilderment. "Er—gentlemen, is there a problem?"

"Problem is you forgot to pay for your meal back there."

"Oh! Oh, my." He started to lower one hand.

"Keep 'em in the air," Clay demanded.

His hand shot back above his head. "How careless of me. Uh. Let me just run back in and take care of my bill."

"Too late for that."

"But—"

"You just *forget* to pay for your breakfast in Wichita, too?"

"Well, I—I, uh—"

"What's your name, I asked."

"Willard. Willard DeWeise."

"Well, Willard Willard DeWeise, you'll be gettin' three squares a day in my jail until you have a hearing. Won't have to pay for *those* meals, either."

"You see, Marshal, I'm a bit down on my luck right now. I kept the tickets and I fully intended to repay the hotel when I could."

"Oh, you'll repay them. And you'll do your time. Never knew a man down on his luck who couldn't *earn* a meal along the Santa Fe. Got a bag in there?" Clay jerked his head toward the railroad car.

DeWeise nodded.

"Throw it out here."

Owen accompanied DeWeise into the car. Seconds later, the two of them descended the metal stairs and De-Weise dropped a scuffed leather satchel on the loading platform. Clay gestured for Owen to open it, and the deputy searched the contents. Shaving gear, a wrinkled but clean shirt, socks, and a packet of letters were its only contents.

Clay ordered DeWeise to place his hands behind his back and clamped handcuffs around his wrists. "Lock 'im up. I'll go talk to the manager."

Owen prodded his prisoner toward Oak Street.

Clay headed into the hotel.

Harrison Webb had followed Clay's movements and watched the interaction from a front window. Now he gestured for Clay to follow him back to his office.

"He didn't seem dangerous," Clay told him. "Small-time thief from the looks of 'im. He'll get a hearing, and the Wichita manager will have a chance to say his piece."

"We have to press charges," Harrison said.

"Rightly so," Clay agreed.

"Your coffee's on the house," the manager said, extending a hand. "Supper too, if you want to come back later."

Clay shook his hand. "I'll do that."

He exited the man's office just in time to collide with a young woman on her way through the pantry area.

The stack of plates she'd been carrying slid sideways, and Clay made an ineffective lunge to keep them from falling.

A mountain of white china struck the floor with an ear-splitting clatter, shards flying in every direction.

The lovely dark-haired waitress with whom he'd collided gaped at the pile of debris. "Shit, shit, shit," she sputtered.

The exclamation from such a sweet-looking young lady was a surprise that made him want to laugh. Instead, he pursed his lips and composed his expression.

Her shocked expression raised and her round dark gaze locked on Clay, then dropped to the silver star pinned to his shirtfront. Her attention slid to the .45 holstered at his hip.

The shrill whistle of the departing train seemed to jolt her into action, and she knelt to pick up pieces of china.

"Careful," he said, kneeling quickly and covering her hand to stop her. "You'll cut yourself."

She stared at his hand on hers, and his gaze followed, seeing his dark-skinned fingers over her smaller pale ones. She drew away as though he'd bitten her.

"This does it, Miss Hollis." A woman's harsh voice caught Clay's attention, and he straightened. The barrel-shaped kitchen manager glared at the young woman at his feet. "You had your last warning. This is the end of the line for you."

Miss Hollis stood and brushed her hands together, raising her chin and meeting the stern woman's accusatory glower straight on. For a woman so young and pretty, she sure had grit.

Sophie stared back at the woman who had it in for

her. She held no hard feelings for Mrs. Winters. The woman's position was at stake, and she'd given Sophie more chances than she should have. In most cases, the first mistake was a Harvey Girl's last.

The room she shared with Amanda wasn't the fanciest, but it had been adequate. Not only were three meals a day provided, but they were prepared by a gourmet chef. Looked like she would miss her favorite dessert tonight, that heavenly rich chestnut pudding made with cinnamon and red wine.

She wasn't afraid, just angry at herself for not being able to carry out her plan. She would have to move on and utilize a back up strategy. Luckless shame. She really liked it here. "I'll clean this up and then pack my things," she told Mrs. Winters. "I'll get a broom."

"Now wait a minute." The marshal had a voice pitched so low that a person felt its vibrations through the floorboards.

She and Mrs. Winters gave him their surprised attention.

"This wasn't the lady's fault." He gestured over his shoulder with a thumb. "I barreled out o' Mr. Webb's office right into her. She didn't see me comin' or have time to move."

When it looked as though Sophie wouldn't be sent packing after all, Mrs. Winters's expression revealed disappointment.

"I'll pay for the damages," the marshal went on. "It would be my fault if she was to lose her job because o' my two left feet."

Harrison Webb was now standing beside the marshal, staring at the mess on the highly polished wooden floor. "If Marshal Connor says so, it's a fact," he told Mrs. Winters. "This man's the law."

"Very well," Mrs. Winters said. "Just clean it up. There is another train arriving shortly."

"You will not pay for the damages, Marshal," Mr. Webb declared. "As you said it was an accident."

Sophie hurried to the back room for a broom, a dustpan, and a paper-lined crate. The sooner she got this mess removed, the sooner the incident would be forgotten. Just her luck for something like this to happen when Mrs. Winters was aching for her to make a mistake. Maybe she *would* use her three-day pass and travel while the dust settled. She'd already invented the story, she might as well follow through.

The marshal was waiting for her when she returned. She drew up short at the sight of him.

He reached for the dustpan. "You sweep. I'll dump."

She didn't let go. "You don't have to help."

"My fault." He tugged.

She held fast. "Not really. I was in too big of a hurry."

The man propped a hand on his hip and squinted down at her. "You arguin' with a lawman?"

His eyes were blue. A blue made softer and brighter by the color of the chambray shirt he wore. That silver star gleamed in a beam of light filtering in from the dining hall.

It was the August heat that stuck the high white collar of her starched black shirt to her neck and sent beads of perspiration trickling down her temple. She wasn't given to fits of nerves or emotion, but this was definitely more than a *glow*.

She handed him the dustpan.

Beneath the stiff white apron and black skirt that made up her plain uniform, her damp skin prickled. She was definitely going to have to change before she served customers. She knelt and picked up the largest pieces of china and piled them in the crate.

Marshal Connor hunkered down to gather a share of debris. The bay rum he'd used after shaving that morning was a familiar scent. She'd detected it on several occasions while serving him at the lunch counter. She'd always tried to make herself as inconspicuous as possible.

A waitress stepped around them on her way to the dining hall, craning her neck to watch. Sophie gave her a glare, and she hurried on.

The man beside her hadn't noticed the interaction. Sophie's sideways glance found a closely shaven dark square jaw, ebony brows and lashes. The hair that fell over his collar was the rich deep color of strong coffee. Perspiration rolled along her spine. Running headlong into the marshal certainly hadn't fallen into her plans for not attracting attention to herself. He glanced up and caught her perusal.

"Clay Connor," he said with a nod.

"I know. Sophie Hollis," she replied.

His blue gaze traveled across her face and hair before he turned back to his task.

They finished cleaning up, and Clay picked up the crate. "Where to?"

She wasn't about to tell him the waitresses' most well-kept secret. All accidentally broken china was smuggled from apron pockets to outhouse to keep the damages from being deducted from their paychecks.

"There's a rubbish bin out back."

She led him through the sweltering kitchen to the rear door. The dry Kansas wind plastered tendrils of hair to her damp cheek, but the air felt better than the confinement of the building. She pointed out the bin.

A piercing whistle rent the summer day, preceding the arrival of the one-twenty. She glanced at the watch she wore on a chain around her neck. Orders for forty-seven had been wired ahead and she had to be at her station in a clean crisp uniform when they arrived. "I have to go," she told him.

He dumped the crate and set it on the ground with a nod. "Sorry for the mess."

She shook her head. She had to say something. "Thank you. For helping me."

"Least I could do."

Gathering her hem, she ran for the back entrance, pumped a pitcher of water, and flew up the stairs to her room. After peeling off her damp clothing, she washed with a cool cloth and dusted herself with lilac talcum powder.

She was Sophie Hollis, and no one had reason to think differently. Boldness and confidence were convincing. *You are who people want to believe you are.*

A disturbing thought nicked her self-assuredness. Before today she'd remained inconspicuous, just one of the girls. Now the city marshal had taken notice of her. Had a good clean look. A good enough look to remember her. Good enough to recognize her face on a wanted poster.

Chapter Two

The marshal returned for supper. He was at one of Emma's tables, but Sophie spotted him the moment she carried a dinner tray from the kitchen. No worry. She had this role down perfectly. She knew her strengths, and being convincing was one of them.

The plate fiasco had been the highlight of conversation around the dining hall that afternoon. Sophie was weary of the looks and questions. These girls lived for a whiff of excitement, she told herself, refusing to become irritated.

"He's having the flank steak, sautéed mushrooms and a roasting ear, with cheesecake for dessert," Emma whispered from behind her as Sophie filled two cups from the gigantic silver coffee urn.

"I didn't ask," she whispered back. She hadn't had her own dinner yet, and she got a little testy when she was hungry.

"He's partial to that cheesecake," Olivia Larson said on her way by.

"I don't care." She looked over her shoulder to find the two females grinning at each other. "Very well, enjoy yourselves at my expense," she said lightheartedly.

After placing the filled cups on a tray, she carried them to her customers, two cattle ranchers who'd just had the filet mignon cooked in brandy.

Try as she might, she couldn't keep her gaze from drifting across the room to the marshal. He sat at a corner table where he could watch both the door to the street and what was happening outside the front windows.

He met her gaze and offered a nod.

Sophie quickly turned back to her table. "Are you gentlemen ready for dessert?" she asked.

"I am a man who appreciates sweets," the older of the two men replied with a wink.

"I'll have the applesauce cake," the other answered.

"And you, sir?" she asked the first gentleman.

"What's your favorite?" he asked.

"I'm partial to the chestnut pudding."

"Then that's what I'll have," he decided.

"I'll be right back." She carried the tray to the kitchen and asked for their desserts.

When she returned and set plates in front of them, her newfound admirer asked, "Do you like the opera, miss?"

"I do."

"Will you join me this Saturday evening?"

"I'm afraid I have to work the dinner shift," she replied easily. "It's kind of you to ask, however."

"Perhaps the following week."

She refilled their coffee cups. Enough girls had been

hired after her that she never had to work Saturday evenings unless she volunteered. "I'll have to see whether or not I'm on the schedule to work next Saturday evening."

As though encouraged, he smiled and picked up his fork.

She hadn't meant to encourage him. She wasn't interested in what he had to offer. All she wanted was to be in control of her own destiny, and being bound to a man wasn't part of that plan.

She attended to her other patrons and eventually returned to the coffee urns.

"What did he say to you?" Emma whispered.

Sophie glanced at the marshal who was finishing his cheesecake and a cup of coffee. "Who?"

"Charles Barlow. They say he's the richest rancher between here and Wichita."

"Oh, him. He invited me to the opera house."

Emma looked as though she would swoon. "You're the luckiest woman in all of Kansas." She fanned herself with the hem of her apron. "He's taken a shine to you, hasn't he?"

"He's a man," Sophie replied dryly. "Men take a shine to anything in skirts."

"When are you going to the opera?"

"I said no."

"What?"

"I told him I had to work."

Emma touched her fist to her forehead in a frustrated gesture. "Any girl here would give a month's wages for that invitation. Why didn't you say yes?"

"Because I don't want to go with him."

"Trade me tables."

"What?"

"Trade me tables. Maybe he'll ask me."

"Mrs. Winters would have my hide," Sophie objected.

"She's gone for the evening. Come on, why not? Give someone else a chance. I won't take your tip. *Please,* Sophie."

She didn't share Emma's passionate need to endear herself to a man, but neither did she have the heart to stand in her way. Sophie waved her off. "Go. They're ready for coffee refills."

Emma kept her squeal discreet, composed herself and picked up the pot Sophie had just filled and set it on her tray. With a determined nod, she headed for the table where the cattlemen sat.

Sophie observed as Emma greeted the ranchers. The Barlow man said something to her, and she blushed and giggled.

Shaking her head, Sophie wiped her hands and glanced at the table she'd traded for. Marshal Connor had finished eating and was glancing around for his waitress. Darn it. She gathered herself and approached.

"Would you like more coffee?" she asked him.

He glanced up at her. "No thanks. I'll be makin' myself a pot when I get back to the jail. I have work to do tonight."

"What kind of work keeps you busy in the evening?"

"I make a weekly report to the county court, one to the railroad, as well." He took coins from inside his leather vest and laid them on the table. "I have a stack of papers this high on my desk that I never seem to get through." He held his palm a foot above the tabletop.

"I'll see that Emma gets her tip." She stacked his plates and set the empty cup on top. She couldn't help asking, "Get a lot of mail, do you?"

"Telegrams mostly. Why?"

"Well, you said you have so many papers on your desk."

"If someone's wanted by the law you say he has a paper out on 'im."

"I see. You mean wanted posters."

He nodded.

"How much do those papers actually look like the criminals? I mean, can you actually recognize an outlaw from one of those drawings?"

"Depends mostly on the artist." He stood and pushed in his chair. "Pinkertons have the best artists."

They glanced at each other and she looked away.

"Have a good evening, Marshal."

He picked up his hat from the seat of a chair and held the brim a moment before settling it on his head with a nod. "Evenin', Miss Hollis."

He turned and strode out the door.

For the rest of the dinner shift, Sophie thought of little else than that stack of "papers" on the marshal's desk. She didn't even taste her chestnut pudding as she sat in the employees' dining room after her shift.

It was probable that her likeness was on one or more of those wanted posters. But she'd used so many disguises that even the most talented Pinkerton would have trouble capturing her true image, she assured herself. If there was a drawing, it was most likely a picture of a young woman with fair hair and a beauty spot. Or of a curly-haired redhead wearing wire-rimmed glasses.

None of her personas resembled the way she looked and dressed today.

Here, she couldn't disguise herself beyond her darkened hair. Mrs. Winters did periodic checks of their faces with a damp towel. No hussies allowed in the Harvey House.

Sophie added her dishes to a pile, thanked the kitchen workers and found the lad who carried wood and kept the stoves free of ashes. "Jimmy."

"Miss Hollis." He was stacking wood on a canvas sling.

"Did you run my errand for me?"

"Yes'm." He reached into the bag that hung on his hip.

She placed her hand on his arm to halt him while she took a moment to glance around. "Okay. Where are they?"

"Right here." He produced three cigars.

Sophie gave him four coins from her tip money and closed her fingers around the cigars with a smile. "Thank you."

"Anytime, miss."

She hid her stash in her skirt pocket and made her way up the back stairs to change clothing. She needed to get out and get some fresh air. Speculating was getting her nowhere.

It was unlikely that the marshal would connect any of the faces on those posters to her, but she couldn't afford to take any chances.

Willard DeWeise snored loudly from his cell at the back of the building. His dinner tray, licked clean, still sat on the corner of Clay's desk. Clay picked up a rib bone and whistled low.

Sam, his aged hound, made his ambling way to Clay and stuck his nose under his hand. "Here, fella. Can't ya smell it?"

Clay stuck the bone between Sam's yellowed teeth and scratched one scarred and floppy brown ear. Sam settled himself at Clay's feet with a grunt and licked the bone.

"Why don't you put that damned dog out of its misery?" Hershel Vidlak, the other marshal asked. "Thing cain't see, cain't smell, cain't take a piss lessen you walk him out and hold it for him."

"Why don't you shut your yap before I put you out of your misery?" Clay volleyed back with his usual lack of humor. It was dark, but the confined office was still sweltering. If the lawmen were cranky, he couldn't imagine what the rowdies in the saloons would be like.

He got up and grabbed his hat. "I'm gonna make rounds."

"I'm leavin', too," Hershel told him. "The missus made a strawberry pie this mornin'."

"See you tomorrow." Clay walked out behind Hershel and locked the door. They walked along opposite sides of the street, Clay checking the stores he passed.

Discordant music blared from the open doors of the Side-Track Saloon, yellow light spilling across the boardwalk. He pushed open the batwing doors, peanut shells and grit crunching beneath his boots.

"You workin', Marshal?" Tubs McElroy, the burly gravel-voiced bartender, wiped beer from the polished bar with an already soggy cloth and paused with his beefy hand on a glass mug.

Clay rested his boot on the brass rail and thumbed

his hat back on his head. "I'm callin' it a night. Set one up for me."

Tubs slanted a mug beneath the barrel spigot and foam ran over his sausagelike fingers onto the floor. He sat the brew on the bar with a whack.

Clay reached into his pocket for a quarter.

"Nope." Tubs held up a glistening palm. "Mr. Dotson don't let me take no payment from marshals or deputies. Havin' a lawman sittin' in stops a whole lot o' trouble from ever startin'."

Clay shrugged and sipped the lukewarm brew. He wasn't the sociable type. His presence might raise the eyebrows of the regulars, but a stranger to town, like the one he'd come to observe, wouldn't know this wasn't his usual routine.

There were many establishments nicer than the Side-Track for killing an evening if one had a mind to, but this was where the fellow registered at the Strong Hotel as Monte Morgan had chosen to spend the last few evenings.

Clay glanced into the grainy mirror behind the bar and observed the other men standing on both sides of him, the haze of blue-gray smoke that hung near the low ceiling a ghostly backdrop behind their heads. He turned enough to speak to the man on his right in a friendly fashion, one elbow on the bar, both eyes casually scouring the crowd.

A few stockmen and herders sat at one of the green felt poker tables, seriously attending to their game. Cowboys, gamblers and soiled doves filled most of the other tables.

"Heard a new family from Vermont bought the Bowman place," Clay said, just to come up with something to say.

The store owner beside him looked up in surprise. Everyone in Newton knew the marshal wasn't one for small talk. "Bought himself a whole rig over at the livery, he did," he replied.

From a platform at the rear of the building, a tall skinny man in faded trousers and a leather vest preached and read passages from his Bible. After several minutes he was replaced by one of the scantily-clad girls, who belted out an off-key rendition of "When The Roll Is Called Up Yonder."

"The daughter's easy to look at," he went on. "One of these cowboys'll snatch her up fast."

Clay nodded, feigning interest in the conversation. Monte Morgan sat with a bunch of well-dressed men who were taking turns listening to the singing and preaching while patting the bottoms of the girls who sat on their laps. Morgan was lean, but Clay sensed whipcord muscle beneath the dark suit, silk vest and string tie. The weapon at his hip was an ivory-handled .45, a six-shooter in an embossed holster. Pretty.

Morgan's confident smile and grandiose mannerisms gave him the larger-than-life quality ladies liked. That was apparent by the fawning and almost laughable way they maneuvered themselves, trying to be the one who got his attention. Maybe he tipped well.

Clay couldn't put his finger on why the man troubled him. Newton was the home of the Sante Fe roundhouse and hundreds of strangers passed through each week. It was impossible to watch or even check out each one of them. Morgan hadn't done anything to draw attention, hadn't so much as tossed a match off the board-walk. But something about him made Clay wary. Morgan didn't seem like just another rancher. Clay's gut instincts had paid off more than once, and he figured he should go through the papers to see if there were clues to this Morgan's past there.

Sophie strolled along Oak to Broadway where the darkened park beckoned. There were gas lamps along the street, but in the one square block between Broadway and Seventh, only the moon lit the dark brick walkways, hedges and flowers.

The park wasn't much farther than the boarding-house from the railroads tracks, but it was a good bit farther from the roundhouse where men worked and switched the tracks all night long. Both of Newton's public parks were in the First Ward, nestled in housing areas and away from businesses, saloons and billiard halls. It was the closest thing to being out of the city she could find, and she loved the impression of peace and privacy, no matter how false.

Taking a tin of matches from her skirt pocket, she settled on a stone bench still warm from the day's heat, lit a cigar and blew a smoke ring into the star-filled sky. Hours like these presented more freedom than she'd known in all of her twenty-three years. With liberating calmness, she attempted to clear her thoughts, lying back on the bench to study the night canopy overhead.

She thought of the coming weekend, of three days she could spend any way she chose. She could take a train to Wichita and shop. She could don a disguise and attend the opera right here in Newton. Her lips curled up at the idea. There was something wickedly gratifying about carrying out a pretense such as the last one she imagined. No one would be harmed in the process.

Those thoughts led to others of former guises and the reason she had a need for anonymity. The image of those wanted posters swam against the sky, the stars twinkling like the city marshal's badge. She'd feel so much better if she knew he wasn't going to shuffle through a stack of papers and wonder why a drawing of a certain female criminal looked familiar.

She eased the chain from the collar of her shirtwaist and squinted at the face of the dainty watch. Only an hour left until the doors of the dormitory were locked for curfew. Her fingers curled around the sleek leather case in her pocket and her mind raced. She'd secretly let herself back in on more than one occasion. She could do it again.

She hurried to the northwest corner of the park where she stubbed out her cigar and scuffed dirt over it with the toe of her shoe. One more block to the north and a little farther west, and she made out the wooden-framed jail. No light shone from the windows. Confident in her skills and her ability to talk her way out of any situation, she continued on.

After peering through the panes of glass into the darkened interior, it took only seconds to work her magic on the lock. The door swung open, and she closed it behind her quickly, acclimating herself to the dark. Snoring droned from a hallway at the rear of the building.

She drew the shades and lit the lamp on the largest desk, turning the wick down low.

A scratching sound and an oomph made her heart

leap, and she whirled, expecting to find someone who'd been waiting in the darkness. She readied herself to run.

A big old dog struggled to its feet from a pallet near the wall, and, with nails scratching the wood floor, padded over to where she stood poised.

Her whole body slumped with relief. She bent and rubbed the animal's head and soft floppy ears, and it turned its nose into her hand and gave a halfhearted lick.

The stack of wanted posters was in plain sight and nearly as thick as the marshal had described. A brass key ring was being used as a paperweight. She gave the dog one last pat and sat, subconsciously noting the leather seat of the chair had been worn to fit the contours of the man. She set the keys aside. In silence broken only by rustling paper, the hiss of the lamp, and the resonating snore from the depths of the building, she turned pages, scanning drawings and descriptions.

She'd learned that there was more than one marshal in Newton, and several deputies: so, if someone should catch her here, she would say another had let her in to wait.

From somewhere in the back, the prisoner gulped air and mumbled in his sleep, startling her. She paused to listen until the monotonous snore resumed. The dog went back to its pallet and lay down with a grunt.

Two names and drawings caught her attention and snagged her breath from her chest. Gabriella Dumont and Joseph Richardson the caption read. Garrett had been darkening his mustache the last time she'd seen him. He'd had his head shaved, and the baldness had completely changed his appearance.

She'd have been offended at the drawing of her if she

hadn't been so grateful for the artist's lack of talent. Plain eyes, plain nose, plain mouth, nondescript hair— the likeness could be any young woman.

But beneath the drawings and descriptions were the words *theft* and *extortion* and a specific list of petty crimes. One word in bold type leaped off the page and brought a sick lump to her throat; the allegation she'd most dreaded and feared: *murder.*

Sophie shuffled through the rest of the papers, found two more depicting her and folded the incriminating evidence into her pocket before straightening the pile and returning its order. She set the key ring exactly as it had been on top.

She extinguished the lamp and raised the dusty shades before stepping out the door. Hopefully anyone returning would think that the last person had forgotten to lock the door. She was halfway to the corner, when an odd whooshing sound stopped her. She spun on her heel.

Flames rose above the jailhouse from the back wall.

Chapter Three

Sophie's heart stopped, thinking of the prisoner who'd been sleeping in a cell, of the old dog inside. She glanced around, not seeing anyone nearby. Icy dread compressed her chest. Minutes ago she'd been glad the street was deserted; but now she wished for someone to appear so she wouldn't have to reveal her unexplainable presence there.

She never did anything impulsively, but instinct took over this time. Running back, she threw open the door and nudged the dog who still lay on its bundle of blankets. "Go outside! Get!"

She grabbed the keys. A hallway brought her to a row of cells lit through the barred window by the nearest streetlight on Main. Thick acrid smoke filled the entire rear portion of the building, and flames licked at the outside corner. A man she could barely make out through the haze clung to the bars of the cell where he was trapped. He attempted to shout at her, but only coughed.

Sophie knelt to the cell door and wasted precious

seconds wiping tears from her burning eyes. She couldn't take a breath without her lungs feeling as though they would burst. The waves of heat were terrifying and the acrid smell of burning wood cloying.

"Get me outta here!" the man shouted.

"I'm trying!"

The ring slipped from her fingers and clanged on the floor. "Shit, shit, shit!"

"Lady, ple-e-ase!"

Sophie fumbled for the right key and slid it into the lock, twisting until the tumblers rolled and the door swung open, clanging against the next cell.

The choking prisoner stumbled past her.

"Is there anyone else?" she called after him.

He was gone.

The other doors were slightly ajar, indicating empty cells so she ran toward the front, pausing at a wheezing sound. *The dog.*

"Where are you, fella?" She stumbled across the room, smoke billowing from the rear now. Her lungs ached and her eyes burned. She couldn't draw a breath that didn't taste like ash.

"Anybody in here?" someone called from the open doorway.

"Yes!" She coughed. "I'm looking for the dog!"

"Get outta there, lady!"

Following the wheezing whine, she found the animal cowering under the desk. She had to get down on all fours and use every last ounce of strength to catch its front legs and drag the mutt toward her.

"Lady!"

The dog weighed as much as she did, and she was

out of breath, but she tugged with all her might, inching the trembling animal toward safety.

The man met her at the doorway, and helped her lift the dog. Together they stumbled away from the burning jail until she collapsed in the middle of the street with the dog across her lap.

Several men gathered around and stared.

"Did someone go for the fire department?" she asked, her voice a rasp.

"Harry went," was the reply. One by one they turned to watch the fire.

She coughed until her chest ached. Sophie moved the dog aside and used the hem of her skirt to wipe her running eyes.

When she could squint, she glanced around. The prisoner was nowhere to be seen. Sophie collapsed backward in the dust. Of all the luck.

What seemed like an eternity was only minutes as she waited. Finally the firemen turned out with their horse-drawn wagon holding barrels of water.

Marshal Vidlak and another deputy arrived and helped Sophie out of the street and over to a patch of dry grass. "You're one o' them girls from the Arcade, ain't you?"

Sophie glanced at the man and nodded.

The younger deputy had gone back for the dog and laid him beside where Sophie sat. The poor animal sounded as though it couldn't catch a breath.

"I'm surprised that damned dog made it out," the marshal said. "Cain't walk further'n two feet at a stretch."

"I pulled him out," Sophie said.

"The hell you say."

"Sam!" came a concerned shout.

The dog's head jerked up.

"Sam!" Unmistakable, that voice.

"Over here, Clay," Marshal Vidlak returned.

Clay ran toward the gathering and hunkered down on one knee, looking from the dog to the girl with the soot-streaked face.

"Lady here saved your worthless mutt," Hershel said.

"You saved Sam?" Clay turned his attention to the rescuer. Her midnight-dark hair was loose and falling over one shoulder. Even though the black streaks on her face melded with the darkness, he recognized her. "Miss Hollis?"

She nodded, turned her head aside and coughed so hard, it sounded downright painful.

"You all right?"

"I'm fine," she replied with a hoarse voice.

Sam's breathing didn't sound so good, but he licked Clay's hand. Clay studied the smoke and ash rising from the nearly destroyed jail where the firemen were directing the water. He couldn't turn the thought of Willard DeWeise over in his mind without bile rising in his throat. He glanced at Hershel, and the two men shared an uneasy look.

"Hell of a way to die," Hershel said with a grimace.

Clay's gut knotted.

"If you're talking about your prisoner, he got out," Miss Hollis croaked.

Clay turned and stared down. "He *what?*"

"He got out," she repeated.

All three lawmen turned to listen.

"I—I was—" A racking cough halted her explanation. "I was in the park."

Her voice was so low and raspy, they knelt to hear.

"The park across from the First Ward School?" Clay asked.

She nodded. "From the corner there I saw the flames. I ran this way. As I got closer, I saw the man you arrested from the lunch counter that day running out the door." She pointed to the south. "He went that way."

Clay was relieved to hear the man hadn't turned to a cinder inside the jail, but the question of how he got out of a locked cell was damned puzzling.

"I heard the dog whining, so I just went in and helped him out."

Clay and Hershel exchanged another baffled look.

"How the Sam Hill did DeWeise get out of that cell?" Hershel asked aloud.

"Someone had to have unlocked it," Clay surmised. "One of the deputies."

They turned and looked at the building. If one of the lawmen was still inside there, he was dead now.

"Account for all the men *right now*," Clay ordered the young deputy.

"Yessir." John Doyle shot away from them.

Miss Hollis attempted to get to her feet, and Clay helped her up with one hand under her arm and one around her slim waist. Her hair smelled like smoke. Few people would have risked their life for a dog's. "Bet you were sorry you risked your neck once you saw the old mutt," he said.

She glanced up, but when their eyes met, she looked away. "No."

Another bout of coughing bent her at the waist.

"I'm takin' her to Doc Chaney's," he told Hershel. "You make sure John reports back so we know if anyone's missin'."

"No. I'll be fine," the young woman protested.

"Don't be foolish." He called to one of the bystanders, "That your wagon? Give us a lift over to the doc's, will ya?"

He assisted her into the back of the wagon, then settled the dog in. Clay jumped up beside them and nodded for the driver to move the horses forward. "Drive past Doc Chaney's place on Seventh. Most likely he's at home."

Most of the fire was out, but smoke poured into the night sky. The entire ride Clay watched it rise. He wouldn't have a moment's peace until all his men were accounted for.

Shortly after Clay turned the bell, the young doctor answered the door. "Evening, Marshal."

"Doc. Have one of the Harvey Girls out front. The jail's on fire. She pulled my dog out and now she's coughin' mostly. That's my main concern."

"Anything coming up when she coughs?"

"Not that I've seen."

"Is she burned?"

"Don't think so."

Caleb Chaney turned to the woman who walked up behind him. "The marshal says one of the Harvey Girls breathed in smoke, Ellie."

"Bring her into the kitchen," she said immediately. "Don't waste time taking her to the office."

Clay was grateful Miss Hollis would be taken care of quickly. "Thank you, ma'am."

Mrs. Chaney accompanied Clay to the wagon and assisted Miss Hollis up the walk and across the porch.

Inside it smelled like apples and cinnamon. He'd been treated a few times at the man's office—scrapes on a couple occasions and a bullet wound a year or so ago—but Clay had never been in the doctor's house before. Doctors earned a hell of a lot more than marshals, he surmised, taking note of the furnishings. Then he remembered Doc Chaney came from a well-to-do ranch family.

The doctor's wife pulled a rocker toward the kitchen table. "Sit here," she offered.

Sophie took a seat and the woman lit several oil lamps.

"Can I do anything else, Caleb?" she asked.

"I'm guessing these two could use some water," he suggested.

"I'm fine, ma'am," Clay told her. "It's Miss Hollis needs attention."

Sophie coughed.

Doc asked her to lean forward. "I'm gonna thump you on the back and see if there's anything that needs to come up," he told her.

Sophie nodded.

He used his flattened palm to hit her good and hard a couple of times. The awful sound and the resulting expelled breath gave Clay a lump in his chest. He understood the treatment was for her own good, but he sure didn't cotton to watching.

Ellie Chaney met his eyes with sympathetic understanding. He looked away and rubbed a hand down his face. He'd feel the same about anyone.

"See if you can drink now," the doctor told Sophie.

She drank a whole glass of water and wiped her chin with the back of her hand.

Mrs. Chaney soaked a cloth and wrung it out. "Let me wash her up a bit now."

The young doc backed away, giving his wife room to reach Sophie.

"I think she's fine," Caleb told Clay. "Doesn't seem as though her lungs were affected."

"She can go home then?"

"Isn't the dormitory locked by this hour?" Mrs. Chaney asked.

Sophie nodded. The whites of her eyes were reddened. "Past curfew."

"She can stay here," the woman suggested. "I'll take the baby into our room and Miss Hollis can sleep on the cot in the nursery."

"That won't be necessary," Sophie protested.

"What else would you be doing?" the woman asked. "You're locked out of the dormitory, so you'll stay here. Caleb and the marshal will explain to Mr. Webb in the morning. I'll find something for you to wear."

After a moment, Sophie said, "That's very kind of you."

"What do I owe you for your time, Doc?" Clay asked.

"I will pay my own bill." Sophie's emphatic objection started another bout of coughing.

"You wouldn't have had need of the doc if you hadn't gone into the jail for *my* dog, Sophie."

"I made the choice. I'll pay my own bill."

He studied the fractious woman, stubborn and proud

as all get-out. Even with remaining black smudges on her chin and forehead and her dark hair a disarray of tangles, she was something to look at.

"Let's not worry about that tonight," Dr. Chaney interrupted. "Everyone needs some rest."

"Make yourselves useful and heat some water," Ellie directed the men. "Sophie needs a bath before I take her upstairs and get her settled."

Clay helped pump water and heat it on the stove, then he and the doctor walked out to the front porch.

Caleb raised his face to the sky. "There's still smoke in the air."

"Better go see what's left of the jail. Got some fig-urin' out to do, I reckon."

"Don't worry about Miss Hollis," Caleb told him. "She's going to be just fine."

Clay took a coin from his pocket. "Will a dollar cover it?"

Dr. Chaney closed his fingers around the coin with a grin. "I have a feeling she's going to be madder'n a hornet when she finds out you paid."

"She'll just have to get her mind right about that," Clay replied. He glanced out at the wagon still on the street. "Know anything about animals?"

"Know a little about horses."

"Dogs?"

"Your dog out there?"

Clay nodded.

Caleb followed him down the walkway and through the arbor trellis laden with fragrant roses to the wagon bed.

Sam raised his head with a soft whine.

Caleb petted the animal, then turned him over and put an ear to his chest. "He was probably low enough to escape most of the smoke, unless he was directly in the fire."

Clay shook his head. "I don't think so."

"He's getting up there in years, isn't he?"

Clay nodded. "Can't see or hear much anymore. Doesn't move farther than a few feet on his own."

Caleb scratched behind the dog's ear. "His old bones probably hurt something fierce."

"I know there isn't a miracle for the old boy." Clay leaned a hip against the tail gate. "Just don't have the heart to put 'im down."

"An injection would do it. It wouldn't hurt him."

Clay absorbed the words. "You could do it?"

The doctor nodded.

"I'll be thinkin' on it, Doc. Thanks."

The driver was still waiting on the seat. "She gonna be okay?"

"She'll be fine," Clay called and offered the doc his hand. "Thanks again." He climbed onto the wagon seat. As the driver pulled forward, Clay glanced back at the big white two-story house.

It was tough to imagine someone running into the burning jail for the sake of a dog. The impression he had of Sophie was one of a capable women. A woman sure of herself.

She claimed she'd seen the fire from the park and come to have a look. Alone in the park, an unprotected young woman on the streets of Newton at night—she was either fearless or foolish. It was his job to care which.

* * *

Ellie Chaney picked up a sleeping infant from the crib. "I'll be right back as soon as I lie him down in my room."

Sophie nodded. All she wanted was to sleep and with any luck escape the burning pain in her chest and throat. This kind stranger had helped her bathe and wash her hair, but the stench of smoke remained.

Ellie returned a few minutes later with a cotton night rail. "In the morning I'll find something for you to wear home."

"How did you know Mr. Webb's name?"

"I used to work at the Arcade," she replied. "Until I broke my arm. Caleb hired me to take care of his son, Nate, until I was better, and one thing led to another. Now here I am, crazy in love and married to him."

"How old is your baby?"

She turned back the covers on the narrow bed with a smile. "Seven months. His name is David." She paused a moment, then fluffed up a pillow. "I wasn't sure I wanted a baby. Caleb had his own child when I married him, and we're raising my two younger brothers. I had kind of a history, you could say."

"I understand history." Sophie had never said anything quite as revealing to anyone, and surprised herself by doing so. It must be because she was so tired and her chest burned so badly. She couldn't resist asking, "What made you change your mind?"

She'd never believed she would make a good mother, so it was better that she spare a child the suffering.

"Caleb changed my mind. I didn't know any good men before I met him. It took a while but I learned to trust him. And I learned to trust myself. Our life was good. Our marriage would have been fine just the way it was. But choosing to have a child together formed a deeper trust."

Sophie studied the other woman, wondering what kind of history she spoke of, wondering if Ellie Chaney had a past that could even compare to Sophie's. If she knew the people Sophie had known, she would have thought twice about bringing another child into the world. "Well, you seem very happy."

"We are. Caleb is the kindest, most gentle man I've ever known."

"You're very fortunate."

Ellie turned the wick on the lamp low. "I would never ask questions," she told Sophie. "I know there are some things that can't be shared. But if you ever need a friend or someone to talk to, I want you to remember I'm here."

Had Ellie somehow seen right through her? Sophie's throat tightened, adding to her discomfort. Her eyes had done nothing but burn and streak tears since she'd escaped that jailhouse. The high level of tension from the evening had obviously weakened her defenses. She wasn't an emotional person. She was stronger than this. "Thank you."

The woman wished her a good night and closed the door on her way out. Silence wrapped around Sophie. She imagined the handsome doctor and his pretty wife in their bedroom with their baby lying between them. They were kind and compassionate, unfamiliar qualities where she'd come from. Their generosity unsettled her thinking, shook her world. Were they normal? Was this what other people were like? She compared them to Amanda and Emma and the families they'd spoken of.

How many good people like these had been victims of Sophie's deceit in the past? She couldn't bear to think of it.

She glanced at the window, where the parted curtain revealed a slim portion of night sky. Newton was filled with dozens of neighborhoods and rows of houses just like this one—well, not all quite as nice, but similar homes where families dwelled.

Sophie squeezed her eyes shut and remembered a time many years ago, a time before her father had sold their home and bought a covered wagon, a time when she'd had older brothers—when her mother had tucked her in at night. The long forgotten memory of a rose-papered room and a small simple bed wavered at the edge of her mind. With that memory drifted the scent of lilacs on a summer night. Her mother's perfume or fragrant bushes outside the window? She struggled to make the elusive memory clear, but it wavered and vanished.

All that was good and safe had changed along the westward trail when a Sioux war party had attacked their wagon train, and killed her father and her brothers. She and her mother had been taken captive. The chief had taken Sophie, adopted her and treated her well. Her mother had been given to a brave and had conformed to her life as a captive. She had advised Sophie to do the same. *"You're a brave girl, Sophie,"* her mother had whispered. *"Do whatever you must to stay alive."* Sophie had been following that advice all the years since.

They'd been in the Sioux camp five winters when her

mother caught the typhus and died. In mourning her mother's death, pain over the loss of her father and brothers surfaced, pain she'd avoided facing before. Acute loneliness had become her constant companion. To comfort her, the old chief had given Sophie her mother's possessions, among them her mother's gold wedding ring. Tek Garrett had taken the ring for safe-keeping, that loss becoming the one regret she had in running away from him. She hadn't dared tried to find it and suspected he kept it on him.

Sophie barely remembered family, scarcely remembered feeling loved. Her memories were distorted by time and anger. Getting up, she padded to the open window, drew aside the gingham curtain and peered into the night. The doctor's house was one of the tallest in the neighborhood and afforded an expansive view of the neighboring rooftops.

The sky to the north was still hazy with smoke. Had the marshal bought her story? How crazy would it make him, wondering how that prisoner had been freed? The keys still hung in the lock, and the iron doors would be standing there when the marshals looked the place over tomorrow.

Damned sloppy job of making herself invisible.

Chapter Four

The next morning Ellie brought Sophie a pitcher of water and clothing. "You're taller than I am, so I looked for the longest skirt I could find. Fortunately you'll only be wearing it until you get to your dormitory."

"It's fine, thank you. Can I help you with anything this morning?"

"Just come down to breakfast. Everything will be ready in a few minutes."

A short time later, dressed in Ellie's fresh-smelling clothing and with her hair braided over one shoulder, Sophie found her way to the kitchen by listening to the chatter and following her nose.

The chairs around the table were nearly filled, and Ellie was carrying full plates from the stove. The enticing smells of sausage and coffee made her stomach rumble.

Ellie greeted her with a wide smile. "*There* you are."

"Good morning, Miss Hollis," the doctor said, standing.

The young men followed his lead and stood until she was seated.

Ellie rested her hand on a tall slender young man's shoulder. "Sophie, this is my brother Benjamin."

"How do, miss." He was probably about seventeen, tall with bright blue eyes and fair hair.

"Benjamin."

"And my youngest brother, Flynn," Ellie added.

Flynn was dark complected, with brown eyes and a bashful, dimpled smile. "I'm having a birthday soon. I'm gonna be eleven!"

"Well, happy birthday," Sophie told him.

"This little man is Nate." The toddler hid a bashful smile in Ellie's white apron. "And that's David."

The baby Ellie had carried from the room the night before was awake and sitting in a wooden high chair. He paused in drawing one stubby finger through a puddle of oatmeal on the scarred tray to give her a toothless smile.

"You have a lovely family."

The doctor and his wife shared a smile.

Ellie handed her husband a plate of eggs; he helped himself to a couple and passed it. "After school Benjamin works with my husband. He's going to go to medical school."

"That's an admirable goal," Sophie told him.

"I been thinkin', Ellie," Benjamin said.

"What about?" She set a stack of pancakes on the table and Flynn immediately stabbed two.

"Guests first, little brother," she scolded him.

"Oh. Sorry."

"I been thinkin' about studying to be a veterinarian," Benjamin went on. "Instead of medical school."

His sister paused with a tray of sausage.

"It's an animal doctor."

Ellie smiled and handed him the tray. "I know what a veterinarian is, Ben. I think you'll be good at whatever you set your mind to." She touched his hair in a loving gesture, and his lean cheeks tinged pink.

He leaned away. "C'mon, Ellie."

"I'm sure Miss Hollis isn't shocked. She probably has brothers and sisters of her own. Don't you, Miss Hollis?"

Sophie set down the fork she'd picked up, keeping her expression placid. "Of course I do. I have a whole family back in Pennsylvania."

"What's in Pennsylvania?" Flynn asked.

"Boys a lot like you," she replied with a practiced smile.

The rasp of a cranked doorbell sounded.

"I'll get it!" Flynn shouted and jumped up to run for the front hall.

He returned moments later with Marshal Connor.

Clay toyed with the brim of the hat he held. "Mornin'."

"Good morning, Marshal." Ellie rose to grab a cup. "Join us for breakfast."

"Oh, no thank you, ma'am. Just came for Miss Hollis."

The impact of those particular words zigzagged an alarm inside Sophie's skull. *He'd come for her?* Had he learned something? Sophie studied the lawman standing in the Chaneys' kitchen. One moment she'd been swept into the family atmosphere and the next, familiar tension crept into her muscles.

"She's having her breakfast," Ellie said easily. "Have you already eaten?"

He glanced at the table, his attention clearly on the food now. Sophie relaxed a degree. He'd come to escort her to the Arcade, not to jail.

The doctor got up and scooted Flynn's chair and the baby to make more room, then reached for Clay's hat. "Make yourself comfortable."

"Looks good," he agreed and took a seat.

Ellie fried a few more eggs and poured him coffee.

"All the men are accounted for," he told them.

"That's good news," Caleb said.

"That it is." The marshal took a sip of his coffee. "But it sure leaves me wonderin' how that prisoner got away. Keys were left in the cell door."

"Do you have any idea how the fire started?" Ellie asked.

"No, ma'am. If the man had an accomplice, it would make sense that someone broke in and let him out. Someone might've started a fire thinkin' there was a marshal inside and that the fire would distract him. But anyone halfway smart would've watched the jail and known where all my men were. Still, can't quite picture DeWeise with a partner though. He didn't seem the type. Just a freeloader, travelin' from one place to the next."

Sophie had never heard him string so many words together all at once. "Is it common practice to leave the jail unattended when there's a prisoner locked inside?" she asked.

Marshal Connor appeared uncomfortable at her question. He used his napkin. "No, miss. That's a mistake I take the blame for."

"You had no way of knowing what would happen," Ellie assured him.

"Makes no difference," he replied. "A lawman has to be prepared."

Ellie changed the subject by asking Sophie if she knew Goldie Krenshaw.

"Yes, of course. Her room is down the hall from mine."

"I used to be her roommate," Ellie said. "We're still good friends."

Once they'd finished breakfast, Clay picked up his hat. "Thank you kindly for everything, Mizz Chaney. Doc."

Sophie stood and picked up her plate.

Ellie stopped her. "You run along now."

"Thank you for your generosity. It was a pleasure meeting you and your family."

Ellie touched her arm. "I'm sorry about the circumstances, but I'm glad we met."

"Be waitin' out front," the marshal said.

Sophie glanced at his broad back in the leather vest and followed slowly. Her skirt was an inch or so too short, revealing her boot tops and stockings, and she felt awkward.

"Your clothing is in here." Ellie handed her a bundle. "I'm afraid it smells like smoke."

"Not a worry," Sophie assured her. "Our laundry is done for us, as you know. I'll instruct them to throw it away if it smells too bad."

Dr. Chaney was standing near the front door when they reached it.

She thanked him again. "I'll bring your payment around tomorrow."

"No need. The marshal paid."

She raised her gaze to his.

He shrugged. "Told him you wouldn't be happy."

He opened the door and she preceded him out to where the marshal waited.

Sophie glanced from the horse and buggy to the stone-faced man. "I could have walked."

"I'm sure you could've, but I brought a rig so you wouldn't have to."

Secretly glad she wouldn't have to parade down the busy streets of Newton with her boot tops and stockings on display, she let him assist her to the springed seat.

The Chaneys waved from the porch of their home as the buggy drew away.

"Nice folks," the marshal said.

He had told her he would make things right with Mrs. Winters and the manager, so Sophie was going to have to let him do that.

"Breathin' easier today?"

She nodded.

Horses and vehicles lined the street they turned onto. The wood platforms and bricked area in front of the Arcade were crowded with passengers waiting to get back onto the two trains that stood on the tracks, smoke bellowing from the stacks on the black steam engines.

"Looks like we'll have to leave the buggy here and walk," Clay said. He stopped and helped her down.

The train crews had eaten and were the first allowed back into the cars. Passengers crowded in close behind them.

Clay took Sophie's hand and blazed a path through the tight gathering. "Looks like you just missed a big rush."

"Undoubtedly there's plenty of cleanup before the next arrival," she replied.

He said something else, but loud voices distracted her. In a language Sophie understood perfectly, two braves were arguing with a man in a black jacket and a bowler. She identified the man right off as a fakir, a man who picked pockets and sold worthless tickets and land deeds to unsuspecting travelers.

The plains Indians were drawing attention from the crowd.

"That man...the one there." She pointed him out to Clay. "He doesn't look like a passenger, does he?"

"Which one?"

"The one with the hat who's arguing with those Sioux."

Clay maneuvered them closer. The Indians were talking among themselves now. Clay shrugged. "There does seem to be an argument."

Shit, shit, shit, Sophie thought. Why wasn't he picking up on what was going on? Convinced he'd catch on in a minute, she bit her tongue. The Indians were digging into their pouches now, and Sophie couldn't waste another minute. "He's one of those men who sell fake vouchers to the passengers."

Clay shouldered his way through the crowd to confront the man she spoke of. He spotted Clay, slapped his hand on his bowler, and turned to flee. Clay waded through the crowd, but the man had disappeared, impossible to find.

Before he returned Sophie quickly explained to the dark-skinned brave who wore a flannel shirt with fringed deerskin pants that they shouldn't trade their money for papers. There wasn't a word in their language for lie. "No food vouchers. You buy food with your coins."

"Did you give him any money?" Clay asked, coming up to them.

The man replied, but Clay only frowned. Another Indian beside him added something as well.

"No money was exchanged," Sophie told Clay. "You chased him off before he got their money." She pointed to the pieces of paper in their hands. "No good," she said with a hand gesture and took the papers. "The marshal will take these."

The Indians spoke among themselves and Sophie drew Clay away.

"How did you know what was going on?" he asked.

"I've seen that man out here before." She hadn't of course, but she knew his kind.

A woman placed her hand on Sophie's arm. "Kathryn? Kathryn Fuller?"

Sophie recognized her immediately as someone with whom she'd had dealings in another city. *Shit, shit, shit!* Her pulse increased at the surprise, even as she shrugged off the woman's touch. "I'm afraid you've mistaken me for someone else."

"But I was *certain.* You look just like the woman. Your hair is different…and your eyes now that I look more closely. Look, Robert, isn't she the spitting image of Mrs. Fuller?"

The tall thin man at her side peered at Sophie through gold-rimmed spectacles. Sophie heart hammered. Would he recognize her, whip a poster from his pocket, scream "aha!" and ruin her new life? She concentrated on appearing bored and inconvenienced.

"There is perhaps a vague similarity."

Relief flooded over Sophie. Perspiration had formed under her clothing.

"Come dear, our train will be leaving shortly."

"Excuse us now." Clay took Sophie's arm and led her away.

That had been another close call. Sophie was like a cat with nine lives, but the stress was wearing and those lives were quickly getting used up. When she showed up in the busy dining hall with the marshal, all attention diverted to them. Mrs. Winters quickly whisked them away from the prying eyes of customers and employees. Minutes later they stood in Harrison Webb's office, the small wood-paneled room smelling of lemon wax.

"A night away without a pass is cause for immediate suspension, Miss Hollis." Mrs. Winters wore her haughtiest look. "It's inappropriate behavior for one of Mr. Harvey's employees. Especially if you are in some sort of trouble with the law."

"Hold your horses." Clay stopped her cold, then turned to Harrison. "How're you doing?"

"Not complaining," the man replied with a nod.

"Excuse me?" Mrs. Winters stiffened. "We have an errant girl here."

"You heard tell of the fire at the jail last night?" Clay went on.

"I did," Harrison replied.

"What does that have to do with my employee?" Mrs. Winters asked.

Clay gave them an explanation of the previous night's events. "Miss Hollis ran into the burnin' building in search of lives." His deep voice and solemn inflections made the story even more dramatic. He told of Sophie's role in saving old Sam's life and her consequent night at the doctor's home.

"Thank you for looking after Miss Hollis," Mr. Webb said. "And for coming in like this to explain."

"Miss Hollis risked her neck. There could've been an injured deputy in there for all she knew. Or prisoners."

"Er. Wasn't there a prisoner?" the hotel manager asked. He knew all about DeWeise.

"Got away during the excitement," Clay answered.

Mr. Webb grimaced. "Mr. Harvey won't be happy about that."

Clay turned his hat by the brim as he spoke. "None of us are real happy about that."

"Heard the jailhouse is burned clear to the ground."

"We're settin' up temporary quarters in a building across the street from where we were. Liveryman used the old bars to put together a couple o' cages. They'll do for cells while a new building is built."

With a nod, the marshal excused himself and Mrs. Winters marched away, clearly displeased.

Sophie was left facing the manager. "I don't know whether what you did was brave or foolish, Sophie," he said.

"I couldn't not do it."

He nodded, his face a study of concern. "I must insist you keep a far less public profile from now on. None of us can afford for you to bring this much negative attention to yourself. Harvey Girls have a strict standard to uphold. Your record must be impeccable."

"I understand, sir."

"Are you up to performing your duties today?"

"Yes, sir."

"Very well." He gave her a stern look. "See that you stay in Mrs. Winters's good graces."

That had always been her intent, she thought, leaving his office.

The bundle Ellie had sent was still in the hallway where Sophie had left it. She carried it up the back stairs and emptied the pockets of her smelly skirt. Adding her clothing to the nearest laundry bag in the hall, she took time to include a note.

Back in her room, she dressed in a clean pressed uniform, dabbed lilac water on her wrists and throat and arranged her hair. She paused with the folded papers in her palm. She needed to destroy these posters. Hiding them wasn't good enough.

It was easy to slip down to the overheated bustling kitchen, slide aside a stove lid, and drop the papers into the fire. Pleased with herself, she stepped back. The whole task had taken a turn down a dirt road last night, but she'd accomplished what she'd set out to do. Now no one was going to run across those drawings and connect her to her past.

She could truly breathe easy again.

After a long blistering meeting with the city and county officers and an exchange of telegrams with the county seat, Clay met with George Lent, a mason, and a carpenter named Frank Prouty to create a list of supplies. He then sent a wire to Topeka ordering brick.

Al Greene pushed a stack of telegrams across the counter toward him. "All these came this afternoon. I knew you'd be back so I didn't send a runner."

Clay thanked him and took the messages.

Standing in the shade of the roof over the boardwalk, he thumbed though the papers. He read a couple of follow-up notes regarding the construction of the new jailhouse followed by replies to his queries to neighboring counties and states.

None of the lawmen had information about anyone meeting Morgan's description. So far the news didn't flesh out his instincts. He stuffed the messages into his pocket and reached to unloop his horse's reins from the hitching rail. He still had a full day of getting a temporary office put together ahead, and he had yet to visit the gunsmith and the hardware store.

Mounting, he headed toward north Main. The same group of plains Indians he'd seen earlier were loading supplies into the back of a wagon with the help of one of the mercantile owner's hired men.

Clay nodded to the men and tipped his hat to the women. The females greeted him with smiles. "No paper," one of the women said to him.

"No paper," he agreed, with a grin.

Odd how Sophie had spotted that con going on right there on the platform with so many people crowded together. But then Newton was the place for it, the railroad hub, and everyone who came through by rail passed that station. The people who worked at the Arcade probably saw more than anyone else.

He found himself wondering if he'd have a chance to visit the dining hall with all he had going on. Eating there had become much more appealing of late.

Chapter Five

That night in their room, Amanda had a hundred questions.

"I just did it," Sophie replied for the third time. "I didn't think about it."

"What were you doing in the park so late?"

Sophie wished she was there right now, lying on a warm stone bench, peering into the limitless heavens. "I go there to think sometimes."

"You're so brave. I'd be too afraid to be out alone at night."

"And you'd be smart to be afraid," she assured her quickly. "There are dangers out there that you're unprepared for."

"What about you? Are you prepared for them? Could you protect yourself?"

Sophie glanced at the girl sitting on the other bed. "I know how to take care of myself, Amanda. Have you heard from your father?"

"Not directly. I had a letter from my mother's sister

though—my aunt June. She said father's doing well. My cousin Winnie is going to have her baby any day. I wish I could be there when he's born."

"You can go visit as soon as you hear."

"Winnie is so fortunate to have found a wonderful man to love her. She's so happy. I want someone to love me like that."

Sophie turned back her covers and lowered the wick on the lamp. "I know, but just think about how good you have it here and be patient."

"I've been patient. I thought coming here would open up new opportunities, but so far the only young men who've invited me out have asked half the other girls as well. It's as humiliating as being back at home."

"What do you mean?"

"My stepmother always treated me like I wasn't as good as her children."

Sophie understood wanting to be accepted. She'd been resented by the Sioux children because she was white and the chief had treated her as their equal. "She was probably jealous because your father loved your mother."

"Probably. But here I am with competition again."

"There is quite a buffet of young ladies at the Arcade," Sophie mused aloud. "I suppose it's difficult for the gentlemen to have so many choices. Rather like a boy with a penny standing before the candy counter at the mercantile."

Amanda laughed, but then her expression dimmed. "Suppose I'm not the most appealing gumdrop in the jar?"

Sophie heard the wistfulness in her voice and ached

for that naiveté she'd never known. She climbed into bed. "I rather think you're a delectable twist of licorice. Not everyone likes licorice, but those who do find its appeal irresistible."

"Do you really think so, Sophie?"

"I do."

"I'm a licorice whip." Amanda grinned and appeared to think a moment. "What are you?"

Sophie snuggled into her covers and closed her eyes. "I am a lemon drop."

The following day Sophie watched for the marshal to arrive for lunch. By one-thirty, he hadn't come, so she took her meal break and walked the sun-baked streets of Newton to Eighth Street. The blackened shell of the old jail sat alone on the south side of the street. The smell of smoke still hung in the humid summer air.

Two men were moving what looked like a large cabinet of some sort into a building across the street. When she recognized one of them as the marshal, she walked closer and watched as they maneuvered the wooden piece through the doorway. After much grunting and a couple of curses, they disappeared inside the building.

"Marshal Connor," she called from the open doorway.

His shirt was damp, and a trickle of perspiration meandered down his cheek. He took a kerchief from his pocket and mopped his face and neck. "Miss Hollis. Come on in."

Inside was as hot as the outside. The musty smell was stifling. There was a desk hobbled together out of an old door and a couple of chairs that had seen better days.

A paint-chipped table held odds and ends of dented cups and a few supply tins.

"If that's it, I'll be headin' out," the other man said. He tipped his hat and left the building.

The old dog lay on a blanket, but raised its head to sniff the air. It didn't look toward Sophie.

"How is he?" she asked.

"Seems fine. How are you?"

"What is that?" she asked, nodding toward the big cupboard against the interior wall.

"New gun cabinet," he answered. "This is our temporary jail."

She noted the freestanding cages that had been rigged together. There wasn't a piece of paper in sight. It had struck her round about dawn that her escapade had been for naught since everything in the jail had been burned up without any help from her. Wasn't that just her luck?

"I brought you this." Reaching into her pocket, she produced a coin and held it out.

Clay saw the dollar, and knew she meant for him to have it. His first instinct was to refuse to accept it, but something in her expression warned him to reach for it.

She dropped the coin into his palm. "We're straight now."

"Hardly."

"What do you mean?"

"You saved Sam from burning to death."

"Yes, well you stood up for me that day. Over the broken plates I mean. You saved my job."

"That was my fault anyway, so it's not the same."

"Just say we're even."

Beneath the brim of her beribboned straw hat her eyes were dark and deep, filled with feminine mysteries. Her delicate beauty belied the strength she exhibited and the wide stubborn streak he'd had cause to come up against. For some reason it was important to her that she not be beholden to him. Right then he understood and respected her even more. "We're even."

She glanced around the nearly empty room. "All right then."

He didn't want her to go. "Let me know if I can do anything for you."

"I don't need anything."

"I'm sure you don't."

She turned on her heel and headed back into the bright sunlight. Once again Clay felt the heat. Eventually the subtle scent of lilacs dissipated and all that remained was the austere room, and the disturbing memory of Sophie.

The rest of the week passed uneventfully. Glad for that, Sophie took her three-day leave as planned. Bag packed, she showed her pass to the ticket agent and boarded a train headed for Wichita, though everyone believed she was going to meet an aunt in Kansas City. She'd heard recommendations for a moderately priced, clean and safe hotel, so she checked in and spent two days shopping and two evenings at the theater.

On her last night in a hotel room similar to the many others she'd lived in over the years, she sat near the window watching the street below and relishing her freedom by puffing on a two-dollar cigar.

Her reflection in the pane of glass showed an attrac-

tive young woman, a woman who received attention and
invitations from men. She considered Amanda, a lovely
girl with honey-colored hair and a bright smile, a whole-
some and attractive young lady, and wondered how it
could be that no one had taken a fancy to her yet. Was
she too eager? Too available or unassertive? Perhaps
when Sophie returned she might mention the appeal of
mystery. Amanda deserved the husband and family she
desired. It wouldn't be long. Soon she would be married and have moved on to a new life.

An image of the Chaneys' kitchen in Newton wavered in Sophie's thoughts, and she remembered the
family seated around that table. The vast differences in
her life from everyone else's struck her anew. The fact
that she never returned interest in men set her apart
from other women. What about five years from now,
should her luck hold that long and her identity remain
a secret? Ten years. Where did she see herself?

But she wasn't looking for the same things, she assured herself. She had a different plan. She was setting
aside money to start her own business. But somehow
she needed to speed up the process.

Eventually no one would tell her what she could do
or what she could wear or how to act. She would be…
The reflection in the glass revealed smoke curling
around her head into the room behind her. The empty
room.

Was this how she intended to live her life from now
on? Independent, but unattached? Free, but…

Dare she recognize the thought?

Lonely.

An all-consuming ache welled inside her chest and

played havoc with her plans and her beliefs. She had nearly a year remaining on her contract. If she didn't have enough money saved by then she could sign a new one. As long as she played things safe, her strategy was secure.

She would be set for the future. There was nothing wrong with that.

A spinster. She was making plans to be a spinster.

Independent, she corrected. In charge of her own life. Her destiny was something she wasn't willing to let go of.

But she didn't have to be lonely, did she? The other girls accepted invitations to dinner, attended local dances. They blended in more that way, she realized, fit themselves into the community.

She could do that.

Sophie made a decision. She wasn't going to be lonely. The next time an acceptable man offered her an invitation, she was taking it.

"Would you attend the dance at the Social Hall with me this Saturday, Miss Hollis?"

Louis Tripp owned a photography studio and ate in the dining hall three evenings a week. On several occasions he'd offered invitations, but she'd declined each time.

Sophie swallowed and remembered her vow before she spoke. He was boyishly handsome with a lean face and a cap of fair curly hair. His clothing was well-cut and pressed, and he displayed courtesy and good manners. Definitely an acceptable sort. "I'd be pleased to attend the dance with you, Mr. Tripp."

Her answer caught him off guard, and his glance shot from her to his dinner plate and back again. "You will? I mean great. I mean, what a pleasure! I'll pick you up at seven."

"I'll look forward to it."

He grinned, showing straight teeth and laugh lines at the corners of his eyes. "I can't believe you said yes." Immediately, he looked embarrassed to have spoken that aloud.

"Would you like another glass of milk?"

"I would! Thank you, Miss Hollis."

"You may call me Sophie."

"You're the prettiest girl here, Sophie. And I the luckiest man."

"You're the most persistent for sure."

He chuckled and she moved away.

"He ordered the veal," Amanda said as Sophie poured milk at the counter. "The marshal."

"I don't care."

"Black-eyed peas and mashed potatoes on the side."

"Why is the marshal's dinner of concern to me?" she asked.

"Come on, Sophie. Are you denying you have a yen for him?"

"Here's a tidbit for you. I accepted an invitation to Saturday's dance."

Amanda's wide pale eyes sparkled. "From who?"

"Louis Tripp."

She squealed, and Sophie shushed her. "He's so tall and handsome! Sophie, you never let on he was your type."

"I don't have a type. It's just a dance, not a wedding."

"I don't believe you don't want a husband. Every woman wants a husband."

"How about a jailer? Do they all want one of those?"

Amanda slanted a questioning look at her, and Sophie knew she'd gone too far. She picked up the tray holding the glass of milk and walked away.

At precisely seven on Saturday evening, Louis was waiting for her in the same courting room where a dozen other men stood, hats in hand, hair slicked into place, like a row of shooting targets at a carnival.

When he saw Sophie, his face lit up. "You look beautiful—but you always look beautiful—what I meant to say is you *are* beautiful."

"Thank you. You look quite nice yourself."

His ears turned pink. "Shall we go? I have a buggy outside."

"Will you help me with my shawl?" She held out the delicate lace and fringe scrap of fabric, and he slipped it over her shoulders.

He extended an elbow, and she took it.

He had indeed rented a buggy, complete with gas side lamps, which were as yet unlit since the sun hadn't set.

"Have you been to the Social Hall on many occasions?" he asked.

"A few times when the girls had birthdays. Once when there was a wedding reception."

"Do the girls marry often?"

She grinned. "As often as they can."

He chuckled. "That didn't come out right."

They were among the first to arrive, and the musicians were warming up on the platform. "I guess we're a little early," he said. "I was in a bit of a rush."

"That's okay. Would you mind if we went for a walk?"

"Not at all. Where to?"

"I'm fond of the park."

"Want to take the buggy?"

She shook her head.

They strolled along Eighth Street until they reached the trellis that marked the entrance to the park. Climbing yellow roses created a fragrant bower to pass through.

"I don't walk to this park as often. It's farther from the dormitory." She offered him a smile. "This is nice."

Bachelor buttons along the brick path drooped from the day's heat.

"So you like to walk," Louis said.

She nodded.

"What else, Sophie? Tell me more about you."

"I'm just a boring Pennsylvania farm girl. Tell me about you."

He told her how he'd become interested in photography as a young man. "One of the most regaled photographers of our century is coming to Newton in two weeks' time."

"Is that so?"

"Yes. A. J. Russell has been commissioned by the railroad, surely you've heard."

She shook her head.

"His shots of the newly expanded west are making history. The railroad has given him his own coach, and he sets up his equipment on a flatcar so he can shoot from the train. He's assigned to photograph Mr. Harvey's hotels and restaurants. All the employees will be photographed, too. Just think of it. You'll be immortalized by a famous photographer. I plan to meet Mr. Russell while he's here."

Sophie's brain stumbled over the "employees will be photographed" part, and she started planning how she would avoid participating. There were less prominent places she could have found work, but none of them paid as well as this job.

Her escort continued his earnest tale of how he had worked to buy his storefront and equipment, and she turned her attention back to what he was saying. "Someday I want a house and a family," he added.

All those girls at the Arcade wanted exactly the same thing and yet he'd picked her. "Louis."

"Yeah."

"Just so you know. I'm not her. I'm not the wife you're looking for."

His expression didn't fall. "You could be."

"No. I couldn't. And I wouldn't feel right letting you think otherwise. This is as honest as I get. I'm tired of all the questions as to why I don't accept invitations. The reason is because I'm not looking for a husband like most of the other girls. If you're shopping for that wife, you need to look back there." She gestured over her shoulder. "If you want to spend time together without thinking of it as something romantic or a prelude to more, I'm your girl."

His gaze scanned her face, perhaps searching for some weakness, something to give him hope. Finally, he nodded and glanced away.

"There's nothing wrong with you," she hurried to add. "You're handsome and smart. And a really good catch—for someone else."

"That's a grand comfort."

With nothing more to say, she shrugged.

"Well." Louis stopped beside a tree and used his thumb to pick away a loose chunk of bark. "You surely didn't give me much of a chance."

She didn't respond.

"But you didn't let me make a fool of myself either, so I'm thankful for that."

She could have done it easily. Played him all the way to the end—wherever that would have been. She was trying to change her life, end the deception, but it was impossible. Every day was a deception. As honest as she'd been with Louis about their relationship, everything else about her was a lie.

A shameless, glittering lie.

The Social Hall was one enormous room with a polished wood floor and open rafters. A platform stretched across one corner, and men of diverse ages and sizes played instruments with varying degrees of talent.

Benches had been built the entire lengths of the south and west walls, and the east wall held tables for food and drinks. The décor changed with events and decorators, and tonight the remnants of July Fourth remained, with red, white and blue streamers sagging from the overhead beams and paper stars dangling in the breeze.

Louis was attentive and charming as well as an excellent dancer. Sophie felt admiring eyes on them as they traversed the floor in time to the music. She'd been instructed by the best dance tutors in New York and Philadelphia, and Louis was obviously no stranger to the steps.

Out of breath, they paused and Louis went to pour punch.

"Sophie, you are positively magnificent," Emma gushed from beside her.

Amanda and one of the other girls joined them. "Mr. Tripp is handsome and incredibly agile on his feet," Amanda added.

"Will you teach us?" Emma asked. "To dance like that?"

"Oh, yes, please say you will," Rosie MacPhee begged.

"Yes, all right," Sophie agreed.

A figured loomed over Sophie's shoulder and the marshal's soul-deep voice was unmistakable. "Glad to see you're sufferin' no ill effects from your brush with death, Miss Hollis."

"Please, Marshal," she replied. "You make it sound far more dangerous than it actually was."

"Is it true that Sophie ran into the fire, Marshal?" Emma asked. "She doesn't want to tell us about it."

"It's true," he replied. "I'm afraid old Sam wouldn't have made it without her help."

"She's very brave." Admiration was clear in Amanda's voice.

"And an accomplished dancer." The marshal indicated the dance floor with a nod.

"She's going to teach us," Rosie told him.

The marshal raised one brow speculatively. "Pennsylvania farmers must hold some fancy barn dances."

"Pennsylvania farmers possess all kinds of skills," she replied.

The music changed, and a few dancers left the floor while others took their places.

"And you, Marshal," Sophie said with a long glance. "Are you here to dance?"

Chapter Six

At that moment Louis returned with Sophie's cup of punch. His expression dimmed when he saw the man standing beside her. "Marshal Connor."

Clay seemed to size him up with one dark glance. "Mr. Tripp."

Sophie sipped the sweet fruity liquid.

Marshal Connor glanced from Sophie to Emma. "Would you care to dance, Miss Spearman?"

Emma took his arm immediately. "I'd love to."

They moved into the crowd, and she looked back over her shoulder with a wide smile.

"I wouldn't mind sitting for a few minutes." Sophie glanced meaningfully at Rosie and gave Louis a hard stare. "Perhaps you'd like to dance with someone else while I rest."

"Oh." Louis understood her intent. "Will you dance with me, Miss MacPhee?"

Rosie blushed and accompanied him to the dance floor.

Amanda and Sophie chose seats along the wooden benches that lined the wall.

"I still haven't heard word of my cousin's baby," Amanda told her.

"You've saved your passes?"

"Oh, yes." After a moment, Amanda leaned close. "I met someone the other day."

"Who?"

"A man, silly."

Sophie turned to study her. "Yes?"

Amanda was absolutely glowing. "He's very handsome and charming. Kind, too, with impeccable manners. He asked me to have dinner with him at the hotel."

"Did you accept?"

She nodded. "He thinks I'm smart and pretty."

"You are smart and pretty," Sophie told her.

"It's nice to have a man say it."

"Yes, I suppose it is." She patted Amanda's hand. "You will have to tell me all about it."

"I will." A moment passed. "I don't think my father would approve, however."

"Why not?"

"He's a few years older than I am."

Sophie didn't want to sound discouraging. "That probably means he's established," she said. "He already has a profession and some of the worldly things he wants, and now he's looking for more in the way of a special person so he can share those things."

"I knew you'd understand." Amanda gave her shoulders a squeeze.

Sophie caught a glimpse of the marshal with Emma. The girl smiled as though he'd caught a star for her. Another couple blocked them out, and Louis and Rosie waltzed into their view.

"Mr. Tripp is a nice man," Amanda commented.

"That he is. He says a famous photographer will be here soon. A man taking pictures to document the Harvey Houses."

"I would never have had the chance for a job like this if not for the Harvey Houses," Amanda said. "A job where a woman is treated well and respected is a true phenomenon. Not to mention pay equal to a man. Why, I make as much as any of my step-brothers. How about you?"

Sophie agreed with a nod. "I'm saving for my own business."

"I admire you and your family," Amanda told her. "I'm sure if my father didn't need the money, I could be saving up, too."

"What you're doing is admirable," Sophie said.

Amanda shrugged. "Most of the girls send their earnings home. It's a lot of money when you're struggling to keep a family fed."

"Your father's fortunate to have you." Sophie gave her an assuring nod and turned to watch the dancers.

A wailing sound caught their attention over the music, and Sophie realized the wind had picked up. Within minutes rain pelted the roof overhead. The sound always reminded her of a night long ago and a man she prayed never to see again. It took all her fortitude to swing her thoughts to the present. She possessed an abundance of fortitude.

"Do you think it's a tornado?" Emma asked as the marshal escorted her to the benches.

"No, I don't think so," he answered.

She wore a worried expression. "I heard all about tornados."

"Thanks for the dance. I have rounds to make, so I'll be movin' along. Good night. Miss Pettyjohn. Miss Hollis."

"Marshal." Sophie tried not to watch him go.

Louis returned Rosie just as thunder rumbled overhead. Emma shrieked and scuttled closer to the other females for comfort.

They stood to form a protective circle around her and Amanda patted her back. "It's all right. Are you afraid of storms?"

"Maybe a little."

"It's just rain," Sophie told her. "Nothing to be afraid of tonight."

Clay paused beside the door and turned back to observe the townspeople gathered in the Social Hall. The four waitresses from the Arcade huddled together on the opposite side of the room. As usual, they were among the most well-dressed women. He didn't know much about fashion, but he knew the girls made enough to dress well and spend their fair share in Newton. The shopkeepers and dressmakers loved them.

Funny how much he resented that nice Tripp fellow just for escorting Sophie. It was nothing to him who either one of them kept company with. Was it? This nagging feeling was too much like jealousy for comfort.

And he didn't like the way the wind had come up. Most likely the ruffians would be trapped in town overnight if they didn't ride out soon: he should probably move on to make rounds of the saloons.

Rain pelted his hat and shoulders as he made his way to the temporary office. He shook water from his hat and studied the brass ring of keys on a nail for the hundredth time, still trying to determine how Willard DeWeise had escaped the cell and a gruesome death that night, and how that fire started. He had a tough time letting the puzzle go.

Thunder shook the windows and rain clanged on the stovepipe. The reek of damp ashes emanated from the stove.

Boots struck the boardwalk and John Doyle stuck his head through the doorway long enough to shout an alarm. "Marshal, there's trouble over at the Red Ace!"

Clay grabbed a rifle from the case, jammed his wet hat on his head and locked the door before running back out into the downpour. All of their slickers had been lost, and he hadn't thought to purchase a new one yet.

An hour later he had three drunks in the two make-shift cells and a fire lit in the stove. He took off his shirt, wrung it out and hung it on a nail.

After getting out his cleaning materials and rags, he cleaned and oiled all three of his guns.

Sam dragged himself from his spot by the heat with a grunt and stood at Clay's feet.

"You gotta go out *now?* Don't that just figure." Clay didn't bother with the shirt, he just grabbed his hat and walked the dog out beside the building. Old Sam could barely make it back, and Clay had to boost his rump up the last step and over the sill.

He found a length of toweling that didn't smell like oil, dried his hair and chest first, then dried the dog best he could. By now Sam was shivering from the cold rain.

"There you go, boy. Lay by the fire and you'll warm up." After rubbing the mutt's damp ear, Clay stood. He'd had mixed feelings ever since the night of the fire. Feelings that made him feel like a blackened soul. Of course he wouldn't have wanted Sam to die a frightened and painful death, but maybe just being overcome by smoke wouldn't have been such a bad way to go.

Cowardly, that's what his thinkin' was. Mean and cowardly. Clay knew what was best for his old friend. Knew what had to be done. He'd been putting it off for nearly a year while Sam got weaker and lost more of his senses. He would take Sam by the doc's place first chance he got.

"I'm a big coward, boy," he told the dog. "You wouldn't have made me suffer if it was the other way around."

"Let me the hell out of here!" Gil Tucker shouted. "These apes stink!"

"You'll get out in the mornin' after you've slept it off," Clay called back.

"Who the hell kin sleep in this place?"

"I didn't tell ya to get drunk and shoot up the saloon," he answered. "Now you're just gonna hafta make the best of it."

The man cursed and flopped on the bedroll he'd been given. "Hell of a place for a man."

Clay stretched out on one of the bunks at the front of the room. The city marshals had decided among them that there would be someone present at all times whenever a prisoner was being held. Clay had told Hershel to go on home to his wife. Clay didn't have anyone waiting for him, after all.

Lightning brightened the interior in sporadic bursts, followed by darkness and a clap of thunder. Come to think of it he wouldn't mind someone waiting for him when he got back to his place. Wouldn't mind it at all.

"Oh Sophie, he's a perfect gentleman. He knows about art and literature and music. He's been to Spain and to London, and has even met the president. He's been to exciting places and done so many things." Amanda leaned across the cutting table and squeezed Sophie's arm. "And I think he's rich. *Really* rich."

They were in the spacious sewing room of the dormitory early Sunday afternoon, and Sophie cut a salmon-colored sleeve around a pattern piece for Amanda's new brocade dress for fall. "What does he do?"

Amanda took straight pins from her mouth to reply. "Some sort of investments for cattlemen. He's planning a trip to Switzerland, can you imagine?"

Sophie merely raised her brows with a nod.

"He's staying at the Strong Hotel. That's where we had dinner. He ordered champagne! Have you ever tasted champagne? It was bubbly."

"It sounds as though he went all out to impress you," Sophie replied.

"I *was* impressed," Amanda assured her. "But Sophie, he likes me. He thinks I'm funny and interesting. Isn't that the most outrageous thinking?" She bubbled with laughter. "Why, he's the one who's absolutely fascinating. And handsome. Not to mention polite. Did I say that already?" She pressed a hand to her breast. "He's almost too good to be true."

Exactly what Sophie had been thinking. "You be very, very sure of his intentions before you accept more invitations," she warned, wanting to say more, but regretting she sounded like a paranoid mother.

"He's a nice man, Sophie."

"He *seems* like a nice man. You don't know a man's true character right up front. Not everyone is what they seem at first."

"Sometimes you say things like you know bad people firsthand," Amanda told her.

Sophie laid down the scissors and picked up the sleeve she'd cut. "What do you mean?"

"I just get a feeling that there are things you don't say."

"All I am saying is be careful. Don't jump into anything or make any commitments until you're one hundred percent sure."

"I'm not a child, Sophie. I won't. I just want to be happy."

Sophie held her tongue. Amanda was as fresh and innocent as a child, which often touched Sophie, but more often terrified her. She almost felt like a parent. Life lessons had given her a steely maturity she'd never asked for. "You deserve to be happy."

"Thank you for helping me," Amanda said quietly.

Sophie looked up.

"Not just with the dress, but for caring about me."

Sophie didn't know how to answer. She hadn't been close to anyone since she was a child. She simply nodded. "I'll be working on my own creation after this is finished," she told Amanda. "I have the fabric and trim

ordered. I saw it in a catalog at Miss Brimly's hat shop.
I even ordered white gloves, and extra satin trim to
make them match."

"I'll help you," Amanda promised.

Olivia paused in the doorway and spotted them.
"Sophie! Is it true you're giving dance lessons this
very afternoon?"

"It's true."

"Is there room for me in your class? How much is a
lesson?"

Sophie blinked in surprise. "Of course there's room for
you. And…" She'd never given a thought to charging for
lessons. The whole thing had come about so unexpectedly.

"Your first lesson is free, isn't that so?" Amanda
caught on to the concept quickly and was giving Sophie
a chance to think on it some more.

"Oh!" Olivia clasped her hands together. "That's
wonderful. I'll be there. In the courting room?"

Sophie nodded.

After Olivia had gone, Amanda grinned. "This is a
golden opportunity for you to add to your savings.
Dance lessons are costly, and most of these girls have
never had the opportunity."

"I'm not a professional," Sophie objected.

"It doesn't matter. You have an ability and can offer
a service that will benefit others."

"I suppose you're right."

"Of course I'm right. Surely you see how the girls
admire you and wish to have a measure of your same
composure and style. You're a fine example, Sophie."

Amanda's generous words pierced Sophie's conscience anew. If she was their example, they were all in a

lot of trouble. Sophie could become anyone she wanted or contrive an elaborate scheme, but she truly didn't know the first thing about really being a young lady of quality. Or a friend for that matter.

Pinning a sleeve together, she came to a conclusion. She could *pretend* to be a dance teacher, though, and she could be darned good at it.

News of Sunday afternoon's lesson had made the rounds at the dormitory, and eight girls showed up. The courting room was tastefully furnished with tufted Roman divans and an assortment of chairs. Velvet draped windows overlooked the front street. Sophie rolled up the floral print rugs, wound up the Victrola, and paired the young ladies.

"You are in charge," she told them. "Remember that at all times. You are women of destiny, your own destiny. Your job is to become the woman of his desires. You must deliberately fashion your image and create the situation you can command. Men will feel more powerful and more desirable because they're in your company."

The girls looked at each other and back at Sophie like dogs with new bones.

"Think of it, ladies! Think of the women that men admire most. Men are fascinated by someone who is not easily flustered or embarrassed. They're intrigued by confidence. You are strong and clever. You are resourceful and charming. Size up the person you're going to impress and give him what he wants. Show him the woman he's looking for."

"Is that why all the men pay attention to you, Sophie?" Rosie asked. "You're the woman they want?"

"They *think* I'm the woman they want," she replied straightforwardly. "There's something very attractive about a much-sought-after partner, isn't there? There's mystery and appeal in the one who is confident and, yes perhaps even aloof. Show me aloof."

Expressions changed one by one as her row of pupils practiced.

Sophie stepped up to Freeda Barnhart and bowed from the waist. "May I have this dance?"

Freeda immediately stepped forward.

Sophie urged her back into her place and took a spot at the end of the line. "Now ask me."

Freeda slipped forward with a shy grin. "May I have this dance, Miss Hollis?"

Sophie deliberately touched her gaze on Olivia standing beside her before slowly bringing it to Freeda. She studied her with seeming disinterest for a moment, then extended her hand.

"Did you see the difference?" she asked of the gathering. "I'm doing this man a favor by accepting his invitation. He's not in charge. Do you recognize my control over the situation?"

Chatter buried her next words.

"Let me try!" Emma begged.

Sophie gestured for Emma to take her place in line. Slowly, Sophie strolled along the row as though taking measure of each. When she reached Emma, she asked, "Will you do me the honor of dancing with me, Miss Spearman?"

Emma raised one brow in an amused question before glancing at the girl beside her. As though deciding, she gave a slight nod. "Why yes, thank you."

The girls all burst out with exclamations and excited laughter.

"I thought we were going to dance," one of them called through the noise.

"Oh, we're going to dance," Sophie returned. "But not until each of you possesses the correct demeanor. Not until each one of you knows she is a gift to the man who will be her partner.

"You are young ladies from good families who are respected for your discipline and sense of adventure. Anyone can come west on a wagon train, but only a real lady can become a Harvey Girl. Your title and position carry prestige."

One by one the girls straightened their postures. "Sophie's right," Emma said. "We're always the most popular at the dances. And for good reason."

The Victrola had wound down, so Sophie cranked it up again. Now was the time to show them how to dance in graceful steps, how to hold their heads erect, to use their hands for effect and stand with their spines straight. By evening she watched as they paired up and waltzed one another around on the carpet.

Since meeting these girls there were so many lessons she now wished she'd never learned. Sometimes she sat back and envied their lack of sophistication and their youthful naiveté. They'd led such carefree uncomplicated lives that she felt like a spoiled apple in the bin. Some of her knowledge was too valuable to keep to herself, however. The way they interacted with men appalled her. If she could prevent any of them from losing their self-respect, she would.

Maybe she did have a service to offer that would actually benefit these girls. Depending on how well this first lesson went and how they applied what they learned, she could consider charging for sharing her skills. It could be one more way to add to her savings and earn her way to freedom.

Just the word encouraged her: *freedom.*

That week Sophie attended the Saturday-night dance with the rest of the waitresses, watching as her protégés applied their lessons. By ones and twos the women were asked to dance. Sophie recognized the ranges of response they'd practiced, everything from coy hesitation to aloof confidence in their expressions. Emma even looked over her shoulder to wink at Sophie as she accompanied her partner onto the dance floor.

Only Sophie remained standing at the side as the others danced. What must it be like to be carefree and anticipate a promising future? They had the right to make choices for themselves, and she wanted them to make the best decisions. She was so caught up in watching their graceful movements and the rapt faces of their partners that she was caught off guard by the man who stepped up beside her.

"Miss Hollis." That voice was unmistakable, as was the accompanying shiver along her spine.

"Marshal."

"Nice evening."

"It is. How's Sam?"

"Had a little more spunk than usual this week. It was good to see." He studied the dancers. "Care to take a spin around the floor?"

She wasn't acting when she brought her gaze to his

face and studied his expression. Her girls would have applauded her hesitation, but she was merely sorting her thoughts. It was becoming more and more difficult to breathe when he stood near, and she was a master at composure, physical as well as mental. He made her feel things she had trouble stifling. He was the last person she should let affect her, but also the last person anyone on her trail would expect her to associate with.

With a flutter in her belly as though she was preparing to jump off a cliff, she extended her hand.

Chapter Seven

He took her hand. His fingers were long and hard and hers felt tiny in his. The flutter in her belly turned into a quaking and wreaked havoc with her senses.

He led her into the crowd and faced her squarely. Sophie rested one hand on his shoulder, and he took the other in his solid grip. She didn't want to lose herself. He was the one person in this town who made her feel vulnerable, and she didn't like it.

"Mr. Tripp didn't escort you tonight."

"No."

"Did you discourage him?"

She studied the marshal's intense blue eyes, sensing no hostility. "Perhaps."

"Shame."

"For whom?"

"For him."

She glanced into the throng of dancers with half a smile. "He doesn't seem to be suffering any ill effects."

His gaze followed hers. Louis was dancing with

Rosie, his expression one of fascination while she gazed over his shoulder with an indifferent smile.

"You may be right," the marshal agreed.

Sophie nodded. "I am."

"I take it the dance lessons have been going well?" She brought her attention to his face.

"The girls mentioned you were giving lessons."

"Quite well," she answered.

"I was wondering if you'd like to take a ride tomorrow afternoon."

His invitation surprised her. "Horses?"

"Do you ride? I can rent a rig if you don't."

Sophie thought the idea over with battling degrees of longing and hesitation. Getting away from the city and seeing more of Cottonwood Valley than the train tracks would be a treat. She pictured peaceful landscapes and imagined an afternoon with less pretense to keep up. Agreeing to a tryst with this man didn't set well however. As one of the city marshals, he was among the last people she should be dallying with.

She'd been toying with a notion, but recently it made more and more sense. Why avoid him? How much more unlikely was it that a fugitive would be right under the law's nose all along? She was an expert at playing to people's perceptions. She could be the person he wanted to see.

"I've always wanted to ride again," she told him, imagining what a girl with her supposed history would say. "It's been years. I'm afraid I don't have appropriate attire, however."

"How about we take the rig out tomorrow and then

next week—after you've had time to find clothes—you can ride?"

"I would enjoy the opportunity to see some of the countryside, Marshal."

"Think you could call me Clay?"

They were so close she could feel the heat from his body. The scent of bay rum made her pulse throb in uncomfortable places. *Clay*. She nodded. The musicians wound down, and the dancers milled about, exchanging partners, going for refreshments.

Clay didn't release her hand. She liked the feel of their entwined fingers entirely too much. "Do you have lunch plans?" he asked.

"No. I usually eat with the girls in the staff hall."

"I could come early and we could have lunch out of doors together."

She thought a minute. She didn't want to sit in the dining hall with an audience. "I'll purchase a picnic lunch. We can eat somewhere pretty."

The fiddle player began a lively tune, and the piano man joined in. Pairs of dancers swirled around them.

"I have time for another dance before I make rounds," he told her.

This time Sophie's smile was genuine. Being with this man was a different experience than she'd ever known. He was a pleasant partner, agile for being so tall and broad, and his arms were hard and muscled.

Sophie spared a glance up at his face. She liked him. Enjoyed his company. Found herself interested in what he had to say, in what he thought. And it had nothing to do with keeping an eye on him or protecting her interests. That realization was new and surprising. She

liked the scents and feelings she associated with him.
That he was kind and respectful added to the mystery
of the attraction and to her emerging pleasure. She'd
never known a man who didn't push his will on a
woman.

Still she purposed not to become too lax in her guard.
She might be in the last place anyone would expect her
to be—in the marshal's arms—but life had a way of
turning the tables at any moment.

Sophie had to be prepared.

She secured her hat against the dry Kansas wind
with a gloved hand and studied the landscape from the
seat of the buggy. She'd traveled aplenty by train and
stagecoach, always with a purpose, always with caution
for what lay behind. She'd never deliberately set out for
an afternoon of unhampered leisure.

"Not as pretty as Pennsylvania, I'd guess," Clay said
from beside her.

Sophie tried to remember what little she knew of the
countryside in Pennsylvania. Philadelphia was no farm
community, and that's where she'd spent time. "It's not
as flat there, and it's greener."

"What does your pa grow?"

"Hay. For the horses and cows."

"What about a cash crop?"

"Wheat." They grew wheat everywhere, didn't they?
She studied the flight of a noisy jay that swooped across
their path.

"You lived on a farm, so you're pretty good with a
horse."

Well, that sounded right, didn't it? "I rode as a child,

but it's been a long time, and we didn't use saddles. I've forgotten how."

Clay headed the horses toward a slope where the grass was vibrant green and cottonwoods grew along a riverbank. Gurgling water spilled over rocks farther up the bank, but at this spot the water was clear and calm. "It's cooler here. I'll stake the horses where they can drink and crop grass if you want to get the blanket and the basket."

Sophie'd seen many a Hudson Bay blanket like the one Clay had placed in the back of the wagon. The Sioux traded beads and moccasins for them, and she'd slept beneath one for most of her childhood. Something about its familiar simplicity was comforting. Avoiding exposed roots, she spread the blanket under the knobby branches of a tree, removed her hat and gloves and unwrapped fried chicken.

Clay set his hat on the corner of the blanket and eased himself down to reach for one of the jars of lemonade.

They ate in comfortable silence, commenting only on the food or the sound of the river. A chattering squirrel inspected their feast from a safe distance, scampering off after Clay tossed it a crust of bread.

He scooted back against the trunk of the tree. Overhead shiny leaves rustled in the breeze. "Did your mama teach you to cook?"

She shrugged. "She's a wonderful cook, but I'm afraid I never acquired the knack. What about you? Tell me about your family."

"Not a very excitin' story." He plucked a clover leaf and twirled it between long blunt fingers. "My father lost nearly everything we owned gambling. Eventually he just ran off or got himself killed, we never knew which."

Sophie had expected a pleasant tale of home life and family, so she didn't know what to say.

"My mother cooked and cleaned for the ladies in Florence. I worked at the mill 'til I was old enough to be on my own. A few years ago she got married again and moved east."

"I'm sorry," was all she could manage.

"Nothin' for you to be sorry about."

"It sounds as though you had a difficult childhood. Did you have brothers or sisters?"

He shook his head. "My mother made sure I went to school. I had clothes and enough food, and she's a kind generous woman. She deserved to find a good husband."

"What about…?"

"What?" he asked.

"Have you ever been married?"

He studied something in the distance, giving Sophie a chance to observe how blue his eyes were in the bright daylight. "I herded cattle up from Texas for a few years, learned to use a gun. Did some sheriffin' from time to time."

He hadn't answered her question, but she had no room to pry, so she held her curiosity in check.

"There was a woman once."

Sophie pretended interest in the flow of the river over the rocks, but her attention was riveted on his words.

"Settled here with her pa. He was a newspaperman. I called on her. We made plans to marry."

Reaching for his hat, he used it to swat away a bee. As though deep in thought, he ran his fingers through his dark hair. She prepared herself for a tragic explanation of his fiancée being struck down by a carriage in the street or pierced by the stray bullet of a bank robber.

"Cowboy passed through one spring. Young, he was. Full o' piss'n vinegar." He grimaced. "Sorry."

Sophie waved away his apology. "What happened?"

"She took a shine to 'im. Packed everything she owned plus her pa's valuables and left a note."

"What did it say?"

"Said she was sorry to disappoint him, but that she had to live her life the way she wanted." He flicked the clover away. "Guess she wanted that cowboy."

He picked a blade of grass and shook his head. "Soon after I took this job and came here."

"So you think all women are untrustworthy now?"

He grinned. "That would be unwarranted, wouldn't it?"

"I suppose." The relentless prairie wind caught Sophie's hat where it lay on the edge of the blanket and swept it into the air. She jumped up to chase after it, and Clay followed.

The lightweight straw hat tumbled end over end until it reached the bank, where it sailed out into the slow-moving water.

Sophie stood with her fists on her hips. "Shit!"

"How much do you like that hat?" Clay asked, shading his eyes with a hand. His own hat was lying safely on the blanket behind them. Amusement turned up one side of his mouth.

She realized she'd just sworn in front of him again. "It was the first thing I bought with my pay from the Arcade," she told him honestly. She owned several nice hats, but that one symbolized her freedom of choice.

Quickly Clay bent over and removed his boots. He unbuckled his gun belt, laid down the holsters and loped along the bank to get ahead of the hat as it was carried by the current. Without hesitation he waded out into the water.

With a mixture of disbelief and appreciation she watched as he plunged in.

"Ouch! Damn!" he muttered, apparently discovering the rocks beneath his feet. Fortunately the hat was bobbing along only a few feet from the shoreline. He was in water up to his thighs by the time he reached it.

He gingerly climbed back to dry ground, made his way to Sophie and extended the prize he'd recovered. "I don't usually take a swim with my clothes on."

She accepted the hat with a lump in her throat. His kindness was still new and surprising. She was used to greed and didn't know how to react to this man's unselfishness—she'd never felt anything like this before because she never allowed herself to feel. Apathy was how she protected herself.

He picked up his boots, socks and guns.

"Thank you," she managed and followed him back to the blanket.

He sat and motioned for her to join him. Below the darkened denim of his wet trouser legs she couldn't help noticing his long feet, his toes dusted with dark hair. He curled them into the grass. "Feels pretty good."

Sophie settled a couple feet of away and plucked

soggy silk daisies from her hat. She laid a rock on the brim so it wouldn't blow away. "I can replace the flowers."

He was wiggling his toes. "Try it. Take off your shoes and stockings and put your feet in the grass."

She wanted to. She'd gone barefoot all her summers with the Sioux, and the daily discomfort of shoes had been a big adjustment. Choosing, she unlaced her boots and removed them.

"Be a gentleman and look aside," she told Clay, and then unrolled her stockings and folded them away. The cool shady grass felt delightful under her toes.

Clay grabbed his hat and shot toward the stream. He returned with it brimming and trickled the water over her bare white feet.

She had the prettiest toes Clay had ever seen, though he hadn't really looked closely at a lot of toes. He imagined the rest of her skin was as white, as soft-looking…calves…thighs…

Dangerous thinking.

When she smiled like she was doing right now, her pretenses seemed to slip aside, and that sweet vulnerability twisted a knot in his belly. She was more beautiful than any woman he'd known, curvy and dark-eyed, with full perfectly shaped lips and hair that begged a man to sink his fingers into its silky tresses.

He didn't stop to think, he just followed his instincts and dropped to his knees beside her. She glanced up in surprise, and her lips parted, though no sound came out. Wide-eyed, she studied him in return, her gaze falling to his mouth.

Irresistible. Clay leaned forward and pressed his lips

against hers. She tasted like the lemonade they'd shared, sweet and tangy. She made a sound of surprise or pleasure and raised her fingers to his jaw.

At her touch, Clay lowered himself over her, pressing her back against the blanket without separating their joined lips. He was astonished by the sweetness and rightness of this first taste of her, by the way his mouth fit perfectly over hers.

He didn't want to end the bliss he'd only just discovered, but he wanted to look at her, assure himself she was flesh and blood and not a fantasy, so he eased away. Her eyes were deep dark pools of wonder, her lips damp from their kiss.

He threaded his fingers into her hair. "It's as soft as I imagined."

She skimmed her fingertips over his jaw until one reached his lower lip, where she drew a line. "I never imagined."

Clay felt a little disoriented, as though he was in a dream. He was strangely hungry, though he'd just eaten. Drunken, though his only drink had been lemonade. He was dizzy from wanting her. He knew every moment since he'd met her had been leading to this one, and he was afraid this flash of pure joy would disappear before he could capture it. "Don't wake me up."

Their lips met again, a bond of warm sensations. Teasing, yet complete. Enticing and absolute. Everything he needed. Nothing compared to what he wanted. He wanted her, Sophie Hollis. Pennsylvania farm girl away from home for the first time.

Clay eased kisses across her chin to her neck, where he tasted her skin, felt her pulse against his lips and inhaled lilacs and woman. With resolve, he sat back and pulled her up with him.

Sophie straightened her hair without meeting his eyes.

"Didn't mean to scare you," he said.

She shook her head. "You didn't."

"Meant no disrespect."

"None taken."

"Can we still meet again next week?"

She looked up then and their gazes locked. "Yes."

Sophie polished the last of the silver and washed her hands, hoping Mrs. Winters didn't come looking for her for at least another hour. The week had been blistering hot, and as she worked she kept thinking of that riverbank with the shade trees. Maybe this Sunday she would dangle her feet in the water. Maybe Clay would kiss her again.

She knew better than to get involved, than to lead him on—especially a lawman! But she'd never known there could be pleasure in a man's kiss. The new discovery kept her awake nights. Kept her thinking of little else.

She was losing her control, and she needed to be more guarded.

She returned the silver to its wooden trays and got herself a drink of water. Maybe she should slow down a little, stretch out the tasks. Dawdling didn't suit her, however, and she'd just as soon be busy.

"Miss Hollis!"

Sophie turned at Mrs. Winters's voice to be sure she hadn't conjured it up. "I'm finished with the silver."

"I'd like you to run and buy sugar. We shouldn't have run out, but there was none on the train yesterday.

I'd go myself, but my foot's bothering me something fierce."

"I'd be glad to," Sophie replied.

"You remember where?"

"Iverson's on Seventh."

"That's right. Charge it to our account. Can you carry twenty pounds?"

Sophie nodded and hurried out the door, pleased for the opportunity to get out of the hotel and walk. The day would be a scorcher later, but for now a breeze stirred her hair and rustled her skirts. The sun was pleasantly warm on her face.

Rigs and wagons of all types passed her on the dusty streets. Shop owners waved from their doorways and the few women she met on the boardwalk greeted her courteously. As always, she marveled at how the uniform lent her respect. Mrs. Iverson hurried to take her order and left to fill a bag with sugar.

Enjoying the change of scenery, Sophie wandered about the cool confines of the mercantile, absently looking over the supplies, paying scant attention to the other customers.

"Well, well. I wondered when our paths would cross again."

At the sound of that voice her world turned inward.

The hair on the back of Sophie's neck stood on end.

Dread and recognition tumbling in her stomach, she turned to face the man behind her. The man she'd hoped never to see again. Tormenting thoughts of him had shadowed every moment of her life for the past two years. Yes, life certainly did have a way of turning the tables.

"Tek," she whispered in stilted horror.

Chapter Eight

Sophie refused to show the fear numbing her scalp and propelling her heartbeat.

"Mr. Morgan," he corrected.

It would have taken her a moment to recognize him had she not heard his voice. The man she remembered usually wore a thick mustache, so the shape of his mouth was unfamiliar. His hair was darker and longer, but his eyes were unmistakable: steel gray and chilling in their intensity. "How did you find me?"

His relentless cool gaze assessed her clothing, but she refused to wince at the caustic smile that creased his otherwise handsome cheek.

"A Harvey Girl. That's rich." He laughed aloud, attracting the attention of other patrons. "Positively rich."

"Hush," she warned, glancing to the side and questioning the miserable luck of him finding her. With all of Kansas to search, with the entire West to cover for that matter, he'd uncovered her refuge. Sophie didn't even know a curse word fitting enough for this situation.

"Is everything all right, miss?" A fatherly looking rancher in dungarees and a faded work shirt ambled toward them, appearing genuinely concerned. "Do you know this man?"

Sophie stiffened, angry at having attention drawn to her in the company of this man. How could Garrett be so stupid as to attract the notice of the other patrons? "Thank you for asking, sir. No, I don't know him. He was inquiring about the food at the Arcade. I've assured him that the best fare in the West is available along the Santa Fe."

The ranch hand nodded. "That's so."

"Well, then I'll jest mosey on over there and get me some vittles," Garrett deliberately drawled in an insulting imitation of Midwestern speech.

The man's eyes narrowed, but his voice still held its friendly quality, as though unsure if Garrett was mocking him.

"You do that." With a nod to Sophie, he said, "Miss," and retreated to the back counter where he kept a protective eye on the two of them.

Garrett's gaze narrowed on her. "You're a gem," he said with that superior, gall-provoking smile lurking at the edge of his naked mouth. "My most apt and ingenious pupil. I can't wait to hear how you passed the requirements for employment." One eyebrow rose suggestively. "Mr. Harvey make an *arrangement* with you?"

Anger welled inside her chest, but Sophie held herself in rigid check.

"What *are* those lucky customers finding on the menu these days? Two bits for a cup of coffee and a quick grope under that dowdy skirt?"

Hating him, Sophie turned her head. If his attire was any indication of how he'd fared since their last encounter, he'd come up smelling like the proverbial rose, as usual. He wore deep-green trousers with matching vest and a loose white shirt rolled back at the cuffs in deference to the temperature.

"I want the money." His tone was deadly.

"I don't have it," she snapped.

He grabbed her wrist. "Oh, you have it."

She jerked away. "I said I don't."

"Sugar's ready, Miss Hollis!" Mrs. Iverson called.

Sophie looked Tek Garret square in the eye. "Leave me the hell alone. You don't own me anymore."

Gathering her skirts, she moved past him, thanked the woman, and hurried from the store. She paused on the shaded boardwalk to catch her breath and wait for the furious beating of her heart to abate and her knees to stop shaking.

She'd prayed never to see that loathsome face again. Never to hear his repugnant voice or stand on the same ground he'd tread. There was no one she hated as much. No one who had as much power to destroy her.

Newton had just become a lot more dangerous. Her life hung in serious peril.

Should she run? Garrett's appearance had proved that pointless. He would find her again. In his eyes, she was his most valuable commodity.

She would have to make her stand here.

"Sophie! What's wrong?"

Sophie flung the heavy bag of sugar on the long

table that ran down the center of the kitchen. "What do you mean?"

Amanda stared at her. "Why, your face is beet-red and your hair has flown a dozen different directions. You look as though you've been running from a wild animal."

Sophie touched her hair self-consciously. "It's unbearably hot and I ran an errand uptown." She glanced around the room to see if others were watching. Fortunately the cooks were occupied. She grabbed a pail of water. "I'll freshen up."

She felt Amanda's curious gaze as she ran up the stairs. A wild animal couldn't have been any more frightening or dangerous than the man she'd just encountered. She dashed to their room, shut herself safely inside and leaned against the door.

All her plans were at stake. Her safety was in peril. Her worst fears were nearly realized. The man who had controlled every facet of her life had found her once again. The man who'd bought and paid for her body and soul, who had made certain she was malleable and indebted before shaping her into the person he wanted, had returned.

How she despised Tek Garrett.

Sophie undressed and washed, wishing she could shed her past and wash away the corruption of her character as easily. She put on a fresh uniform, then brushed and arranged her hair before composing herself to carry on with her day. She had a job to do. She needed this position. Garrett could hardly waltz into the Arcade and point her out as a criminal. He'd been the one who'd pulled the trigger and killed that man in Denver. If he informed on her, he would implicate himself. She had that small fact in her favor. But knowing him, he would find a way at her sooner or later.

He wanted the money. He got what he wanted.

There had been several thousand dollars on the table the night Garrett lost control and shot one of their marks. In the ensuing confusion, Sophie had seen her golden opportunity. A chance to escape Garrett—and a chance to do so with a bankroll.

She'd grabbed the cash and run for her life.

It had been effortless for her to disguise herself and travel. She'd been doing it for years. She'd become even better at it than her teacher. That probably had infuriated him as much as her taking the money. As much as the fact that she'd had the courage. As much as the fact that she'd eluded him for so long.

A weak, spineless internal voice taunted her, saying that it was pointless to continue. He'd find a way. He always did. She wasn't as strong or as smart or as evil as he. *Give up. You can't win.*

Another part of her, the desperate, instinctively self-preserving part proclaimed that if she couldn't succeed, she was better off dead. But she wasn't dead yet, and while she was still kicking and able, she was going to fight. She wouldn't be sucked back into his clutches. She was a new person. She was Sophie Hollis, the person she *wanted* to be. And nobody was going to take that from her.

Clay stopped the wagon in front of Doc Chaney's. The doctor had opened this office a little over a year ago, giving him more room on a ground floor. His first place had been over Eva Kirkpatrick's dress shop.

There was no writing on the blackboard that hung beside the front door, and Clay took that to mean the doctor was in. He jumped down from the wagon. In the back, Sam raised his head. "Stay."

Trusting and obedient to the end, the dog lay his chin back down between his front paws. Clay had drummed up the gumption to come this far; he wasn't losing his grit now. He steeled himself to carry out this inevitable task.

Caleb Chaney was washing instruments in a basin of steaming water when Clay entered.

"Afternoon, Marshal. What can I do for you?"

"I brought old Sam. I figured it'd be the kind thing to give 'im that shot you spoke of." Clay took a deep breath to steady his voice. "He's ready."

Caleb stopped what he was doing. "I can do that for you," he replied. "Do you want to leave him?"

Clay shook his head. "No. I'll stay, take him and bury him after."

"All right then. Whenever you're ready."

Clay had done a good many unpleasant things in his life. Carrying Sam from the wagon to the doc's office was one of the most difficult. He felt like a traitor. A traitor with a sick ache in his belly. He stroked Sam's ears and looked into those trusting eyes for the last time.

Less than an hour later, Clay stood with his hand on the handle of a shovel, sweat blurring his vision. He wiped a kerchief across his eyes and tied it around his neck, glad to be alone and unobserved. A grown man shouldn't get so choked up over a mutt.

Leaving a worn blanket wrapped around the dog's body, he lowered Sam into the hole he'd dug and scraped in dirt. This mutt had been his closest companion for a good many years. Wouldn't seem right not having the old boy by his side.

When there was nothing left to do, he laid down the tool and stood back. The hardest part had been turning him over to Dr. Chaney and then watching as his old friend slipped into eternal sleep.

Clay surveyed the spot he'd picked, a woodsy area a fair distance from the house on the three acres he owned at the edge of town. In his younger days Sam had run wild and free on this land, chasing rabbits and digging for gophers. Many an unfortunate critter had fallen prey to the energetic canine.

Sam had been Clay's housemate on snowy winter nights, his companion on lazy summer afternoons. Clay felt foolish for getting all sentimental, but saying goodbye to a friend wasn't easy.

"You were a good dog," he said, needing to finalize the deed, but feeling inadequate. "I hope there are rabbits wherever you are now." Clay wiped his nose on the kerchief and carried the shovel to the back of the wagon.

Sophie closed herself in her room that evening, but Amanda brought Emma in to ask advice about shoes they'd seen in a catalog.

"Visit the shoemaker," she advised them. "You'll get a more comfortable fit and better quality." Going to her bureau, she slipped a cigar and match tin into her skirt pocket, then turned to them. "I'm going for a walk."

"Be careful," Amanda told her.

Sophie hurried down the stairs and along the boardwalk toward the First Ward. Glancing around, she assured herself she wasn't being followed. It was still light enough to be able to detect if Garrett was on her trail.

She hated looking over her shoulder. She hated the person and the life he'd molded her into. She wanted an uncomplicated existence like the girls with whom she shared jobs and living space had. She resented being cheated out of a normal childhood and silently railed against the way her formative years had shaped her.

She was Sophie Hollis now, she told herself, but the reminder didn't sound altogether convincing this time. Sophie was the person she wanted to be. The real her was a small scared girl who'd lost her family, a young woman who'd become a captive and a possession. Whenever she tried to remember her real family, other memories and a vault of lies distorted the truth. She had played so many parts, it was hard to remember who she really was. She'd been so many places she could scarcely remember them all.

With the money she'd snatched that fateful night, she'd made it her mission to find as many people as she could whom they had scammed and to pay them back. Garrett would kill her when he found out. But while she was still alive, she was going to do the best she could.

As she passed opposite the billiard hall, a sound alerted her to a rider coming up behind her. She spun around. Atop the horse was a broad-shouldered man wearing a familiar hat.

"Evenin', Sophie."

"Clay," she said in relief.

"Where you headed?"

"The park."

He slid from the saddle and fell into step beside her, leading his horse by the reins.

She fingered the cigar in her pocket wistfully.

"How's Sam?" she asked finally.

Clay took a minute to answer, and at his hesitation she looked at him. "Buried 'im today," he said.

"What happened?" she asked, halting in surprise.

He paused beside her. "I asked Doc to take care of it with an injection. Sam just went to sleep and didn't wake up."

"I'm so sorry," she answered, feeling inadequate.

"He could hardly get around anymore." Clay resumed walking, prompting her to join him. "It was time," he assured her.

At the nuance of emotion in his voice, Sophie studied his expression. She doubted anyone else would have picked up on that tiny crack in his composure he'd almost succeeded in hiding. "That's good then."

He thumbed his hat back on his head and she could see his eyes more plainly. "It was tough bringin' myself to do it."

"You're a kind man."

"'Bout average I expect."

She studied his profile against the streaks of orange in the sky to the west. "I hardly think so."

"Why do you say that?"

"Most men are solely concerned with themselves. Making money any way they can. Finding women to do their bidding."

He studied her a moment. "You say that like you've known a lot of selfish men."

She shrugged. "Enough."

"Is your father like that?"

She hadn't had a father for years, but she tried to imagine what Sophie Hollis's father would be like. "No, my father is kind to my mother and concerned for the welfare of his family."

"Who were all these bad examples you've known then?"

She gestured with an uplifted palm. "I overhear conversations in the dining hall. I read the newspaper."

"I see."

"You buried Sam somewhere?"

"My place."

She'd never heard him mention his home before. "I don't even know where you live."

"Northeast a ways."

"You have a house?"

"Didn't want to live right in town, even though it would've been easier most of the time. I wanted to be able to get away and didn't want neighbors spyin' on my every move."

"What's it like? Your house?"

"Just a house. Nothin' fancy."

Residents sitting on the porch of Mrs. Ned's Boarding House on Broadway waved to them as they crossed the street to the park. Clay tipped his hat, and Sophie wondered if there would be speculation concerning the two of them now that they'd been seen together more than once.

Clay tethered his horse to one of the cast-iron rings set into the ground at the park entrance.

"You're coming with me?" she asked.

"Is that all right?"

"Sure." It couldn't hurt to have the law by her side if Garrett decided to show up. For a crazy second she considered telling Clay about Garrett, but then she would have to explain everything, and she imagined the look on Clay's face if he learned what she'd done before she'd come here.

They strolled deep into the park to one of the stone benches, and Sophie perched on the edge. "This is where I usually sit."

He took the opposite end.

"What thoughts are in your head tonight?" he asked.

"Just silly girl things." She fingered the cigar in her pocket.

"I have trouble believin' that."

"Why?"

"You're not given to the same silliness as the other girls, that's why."

"You find them *all* silly?" she asked.

"Find 'em all obvious."

"Meaning?"

"Just that they've got their caps set on findin' husbands. I get the feeling it's something else that you're looking for."

"And you think you know me?"

He tilted his head. With a self-deprecating grin, he replied, "I don't know what women think on. I'm sure it's a lot different than what men think about." He glanced around. "What is it you like about this place?"

"It's private."

"It's right in the middle of town," he disagreed.

"You've never lived in a dormitory with twenty women. *This* is private."

"Does it wear on you bein' around the others day and night?"

She nodded. "Not that they aren't lovely girls. I just don't share much in common with them."

"I can see that." He took off his hat and ran his fingers through his dark hair. "You're different from them. I don't mean that in a bad way, Sophie. They seem… younger."

He was right. They were innocent girls fresh from the bosoms of their families, just as Sophie'd thought a hundred times. She was a magpie in a cage full of canaries.

"Not that you're on the shelf or anything," he added quickly.

She touched her pocket. "No offense taken."

"What did you do before you came to Newton?" Clay asked.

"I told you I lived on a farm with my family."

"Where you didn't learn to cook."

"Right."

"And you didn't ride after you were small."

"That's right."

"What *did* you do? With your days? Can you sew?"

"I can sew. And I was tutored."

He glanced at her. "No wonder you're so smart. Why a tutor? Why didn't you go to school?"

If she was smart, she wouldn't be trapped in this lie. "My mother was ill, and my father wanted me nearby in case she needed me."

"You said before she did all the cookin'. She did that even though she was sick?"

"Uh-huh."

"Who takes care of her now that you're not there?"

"She's better now." It was getting more and more difficult to keep her story consistent. She'd never had to sustain a lie for so long and to so many people. She was used to the short con. She changed the subject. "You said your mother sent you to school."

"She did."

They glanced at each other. Sophie wasn't eager to continue an exploration into her fabricated past, so she persisted. "So this place of yours…what's it like?"

"Just a small house on a few acres of land. I bought it from a family who fell on some bad luck and moved on. I could show it to you—Sunday if you'd like."

"I would like that."

A few minutes passed before he spoke again. "Are you lookin' for a husband?"

"I'm not."

His deep voice was intimate when he asked, "What *do* you want, Sophie?"

Chapter Nine

Sophie paused, uncertain how much to reveal about herself.

"I want to be able to take care of myself. I want my own business and to make decisions for myself."

"Did some man do this to you? Make you not want marriage?"

"Why would you think that?"

"You sound like you know a different way is all."

She didn't reply.

"You're not afraid of me."

"No."

"But you don't trust me."

She looked at him in the twilight. "I think I do. And because of that it's me I don't trust."

"Are you afraid of what you might feel if you let yourself?"

She looked away without answering, studied the half moon shining down from the darkening heavens.

"Just how did you discourage Mr. Tripp anyway?" he asked.

"I told him I wasn't the wife he was looking for, but that there were plenty of other eager prospects."

"So he moved along to one of them."

"Seems he has."

"And you're not jealous?"

"Goodness no."

"You haven't discouraged me."

"Do I need to?"

"You askin' if I'm going to pursue you if you don't?"

"I'm not asking anything. You're the one with all the questions."

"Sorry. Just my nature I reckon."

"It's what makes you good at your job."

The night stretched silently between them until he asked, "Where do you want this to go, Sophie?"

She shook her head. She didn't know and she couldn't say. All she knew amidst the confusion that was her life was that Clay had become part of her existence in a way she'd never anticipated any man could. That fact terrified and soothed her at the same time. If she was smart she'd call a stop to this right now. She wouldn't let things get any more complicated than they were.

She'd had small selfish thoughts of using him for protection, of staying near so Garrett wouldn't be tempted to seek her out or continue his threats. But she couldn't do that. She'd be no better than the person she'd been before. Than the person Garrett had taught her to be.

A realization came to Sophie at that moment. A realization she wasn't sure she could afford to recognize since she needed to be safe.

She wanted to change.

She'd been lying and deceiving people for so long that it had become second nature. She'd come to think of deceit as normal. But it wasn't.

Clay wouldn't lie if someone had a gun to his head. He had more character than a dozen of her or a hundred of Garrett put together.

But how could she change now? How could she tell the truth regarding anything without condemning herself to prison? She couldn't. Not yet. Maybe not ever.

She would be assuming identities and pretending for the rest of her life.

Or she'd be in jail.

Not much of a choice.

An uncharacteristic sense of hopelessness swept over her. She blinked back the sting of tears.

But he'd seen. "Sophie? What is it?"

How could a person be so kind? She'd never known tenderness or kindness, and the touch of his hand on hers made her want to let down her defenses and sob.

But she didn't. She was stronger than that. She was a survivor. She'd been through a lot worse than this and she wouldn't crumble now.

"What makes you so sad?"

She shook her head.

"Can I help?"

Only if he could find Tek Garrett and shoot him in the heart without any questions asked. She shook her head again, stood and studied the now dark sky. In the distance the jangle of an off-key piano blended with laughter and a far off train whistle, but she felt safely cocooned where she was.

Clay remained seated but took her hand and raised it to his lips. His warm breath and a soft kiss sent a tingle up her arm, and her breasts tightened unexpectedly.

Sophie brought her other hand to her breasts in surprise and closed her eyes to the night, giving herself over to the sensations he created within her.

"Your fingers smell like...tobacco."

She attempted to pull her hand away, but he grinned and held on. Clay kissed each of her fingertips, then turned her hand over and pressed his lips against her palm.

She turned toward him then, her heart racing and her head a jumble of confusion. "What is this insistent *yearning* you make me feel?" she asked. "What causes this flurry of anticipation and expectancy? Why is it I can't turn away or run or do what I know is best?"

Releasing her hand, Clay got to his feet where he towered over her and bracketed her face between his hard palms.

"I don't have fancy answers for you, Sophie. My life has always been simple. Black and white. I take life as it comes, and I just know I feel good when I'm with you. And I think about you when we're not together. It's not complicated for me."

A good man. An honest straightforward man. He was as different from her as the moon was from the sun. She shouldn't let this go one moment longer, because thinking of the two of them together was hopeless.

She shouldn't let the way his touch warmed her twist her thinking or allow the beauty of having him favor her with kindness cloud her judgment.

She was weaker than she'd ever imagined. All that

resolve about being strong was a joke. But she wanted to have a piece of goodness more than she could say. More than anything she wanted to savor something clean and decent and know what it was like.

Kiss me, she cried silently. *Kiss me and let me feel the beauty just for this one night.*

Sophie grasped his upper arms as though she might spin away if she didn't hold on. Beneath his sleeves, his skin was warm and solid, the muscles toned. As though her touch was a signal, he leaned to capture her lips in a kiss that made her heart skitter in her chest. The sounds of the night and the heat faded away, and all she knew was the rightness of having this man desire her.

In the back of her mind she knew she was sneaking something that didn't truly belong to her, something that belonged to the woman he believed her to be, but she was greedy and selfish, and she didn't want to lose a moment of the heady experience.

Clay released her hand to wrap his arms around her and draw her close. She relished the feel of his hard body, the strength of his embrace. She wrapped an arm around his neck and met his kiss with all the longing she'd kept dammed up inside.

When his tongue touched her lower lip, she understood the invitation and welcomed the deepening kiss and the heat of his mouth.

Sophie was no stranger to a man's desire. She wasn't ignorant of what happened between men and women. But Clay had introduced her to *feelings.* He was introducing her to respect as well, and she knew that if she pulled away right at this moment he would honor her wishes. He wouldn't use coercion or force to get what he wanted.

Some insidious little voice inside her prompted her to test him. If a mean streak surfaced it would be easy to write him off and walk away. She eased her mouth from his...looked into his face in the moonlight.

He stroked her spine with a thumb, but his hold on her was loose, his posture and expression undemanding. His breath fluttered against her chin. Testing him, she'd robbed herself of something she hadn't known she needed with all her being.

"I want to kiss you," she said.

"That's what we've been doin'."

"No." She cupped his jaw. "I want to kiss *you.*"

"You won't have to tie me up, darlin'."

The tender endearment spurred her nearer. She pressed her hand to his chest, urging him to sit once again. His eyes didn't leave hers.

She sat beside him, but that wasn't close enough, so she eased herself onto his lap. As though he couldn't resist touching her, he threaded his fingers into the hair at her neck.

She ran a finger over his jaw, traced the shape of his wonderful mouth, used her thumb to part his lips. He touched his tongue to the pad of her thumb and she felt the damp heat all the way to the core of her will.

Sophie framed his jaw with one hand and kissed him square on the lips. He closed his eyes and seemed to hold his breath.

She ended the kiss and nuzzled her nose along his cheek to his ear. His hand tightened in her hair, but he held the rest of his body in check.

"What game are you playin', Sophie?" he asked.

"No game," she replied near his ear. "Just a little test."

"Am I passin'?"

She kissed him again, parting her lips over his and savoring the indulgent pleasure before pausing to answer, "With flying colors, Marshal."

She shouldn't be enjoying kissing him so much. She shouldn't be using him. He had no idea how powerfully seductive his gentle compliance was to a woman who'd never before had a choice.

He had no idea she wasn't innocent. For all he knew she was tasting seduction for the first time. He trusted her to be who she said she was.

What would Sophie Hollis do?

With a last delicious kiss, she pushed herself up from his lap and smoothed her skirts. "I'm embarrassed I did that."

"Why?"

She looked away.

His voice was low and uneven when he asked, "You think it's shameful to kiss a man?"

"No. No, I'm…embarrassed at the feelings."

"Nothin' wrong with honest feelings, Sophie."

She couldn't even look at him after those words. "I'd better get back before I get locked out."

He stood and quickly fell into step beside her. "We're still on for Sunday?"

She walked ahead. "We're still on."

Even as confused as she was, she wouldn't miss the next time for anything.

Midweek Mr. Webb closed the dining hall and instructed all employees to change into fresh uniforms and report back within fifteen minutes.

Sophie joined the curious Harvey Girls who climbed the stairs to their rooms and returned in crisp clothing. Murmurs of speculation trickled through the gathering.

A whistle announced the arrival of a train that hadn't been on their lunch schedule, which indicated something unusual, like the train that sometimes brought Fred Harvey for an unannounced visit. This time neither Mrs. Winters or Mr. Webb were barking orders or sending waitresses scurrying, however. And the restaurant had never been closed before. Even the kitchen help had been summoned.

Minutes later a commotion drew them outside. Sophie and Emma standing together on the platform spotted half a dozen men carrying cases and arranging them between the tracks and the building.

Another crew was roping off the perimeter of the platform as well as the front of the hotel and placing men in positions to keep the onlookers out.

A man who seemed to be in charge of things stepped forward and called out. "We have forty minutes before the next train arrives," he called. "Form lines in front of the building, in order of duties, with kitchen help in the back, dining hall workers in the front and the managers on each side. I would like the chef front left, please."

Recognition dawned on Sophie too late. She could have escaped when they'd been ordered to change, but now it would be obvious if she left. This was the renowned photographer Louis had told her about. She took a place among the waitresses, moving back several rows by saying, "I'm tall, you stand here."

There were at least sixty people gathered. Who would recognize her in clothing like everyone else, within a sea of faces? Who would even see the picture? When the photographer was ready, she could edge her face behind the person ahead of her. This wasn't a problem she couldn't handle gracefully and without drawing attention.

The sun was hot and the workers grumbled at having to stand in the heat. Sophie endured the perspiration trickling down her back under her starched dress, and scanned the crowd that had gathered. She spotted Louis Tripp making his way to the front of the crowd and talking with one of the posted guards. She knew how badly he wanted to come forward and meet A. J. Russell.

The guard hurried to say something to the man setting up the camera, and he motioned for Louis to come closer.

"I believe I have time to use the necessity," Sophie said and inched her way to the end of the line and toward the side of the building.

"Miss Hollis!"

She stopped in her tracks and faced Mrs. Winters. "Ma'am."

"Where do you think you're going?"

"To use the outhouse, ma'am."

"Not until you've been excused you won't. You had time to take care of that when you were changing."

"Yes, ma'am."

This time she edged her way back another row. Mr. Russell called instructions to his helpers and to the subjects who were getting restless.

He ducked his head and shoulders beneath a black cloth and counted backward from five.

As he reached one, Sophie leaned inconspicuously to the right, just enough for her face to be obscured behind Constance Jenkins's hair.

"Don't move! One more," he called.

Sophie had a sudden itch and raised her hand in front of her face to scratch her forehead. She was happy Louis was able to meet the man he admired and had never been so glad to go back to work.

"Monte's coming for me in a few minutes," Amanda said, aquiver with excitement. "You'll meet him tonight."

"I'm looking forward to it."

"My dancing is much improved, thanks to you. He'll be impressed."

Sophie gave her a humble nod. She'd been wondering all day if the marshal would show up at the Social Hall like he usually did during the course of a Saturday evening.

Amanda checked her blond curls in the mirror one last time and picked up her white gloves before hurrying out of their room.

Sophie enjoyed the calm and quiet for a few minutes, feeling no need to rush. There were always carriages waiting out front of the Arcade on Saturday evening, and it was easy to catch a ride with a group or a couple.

Amanda had helped her button the lemon-colored cotton lawn dress she'd recently finished, and now she donned her soft kid leather slippers. She arranged her hair with a matching ribbon wound through the curls that hung down her back. Choosing her own clothing and accessories lent a sense of power she'd craved. Anyone else would take it for granted, but she didn't. She gazed at her white ruffle and lace bodice and satin cuffs in the mirror with pleasure.

It felt good to be Sophie Hollis. It felt good to inter-act with others and develop friendships. Most of the guilt was stashed away where it couldn't gnaw at her. She couldn't let herself think that every relationship she had was based on a lie or she'd loose this euphoric feeling. She was going to see Clay tonight, and tomor-row they were going to go riding.

Satisfied with her appearance, she tugged on her satin-trimmed gloves and floated down the stairs. Louis had brought a buggy for Rosie. He cast Sophie a hesi-tant smile, and she nodded her approval. He grinned and offered her and Olivia a ride.

Charles Barlow greeted Sophie and Olivia as soon as they entered the already noisy building.

"Miss Hollis," the rancher said, smiling as though delighted to see her. "Will you join me for this dance?"

Not intending coyness, Sophie glanced at Olivia, then back. "Thank you, Mr. Barlow." She offered him her gloved hand.

"Charlie," he corrected.

"Charlie."

"Nice to see you have a Saturday night off," he said as they waltzed.

"Y-yes." Only then did Sophie remember telling him she worked most Saturday nights.

"Next time you're not on the schedule, why don't you send word so we can attend the opera?"

"I do enjoy the opera."

A cowboy in a new shirt and dungarees and with his hair and mustache pomaded asked her to dance next. After an hour she was hoping for a chance to sit out a few dances.

She hadn't seen Clay yet. She'd been watching, subtly, of course. She excused herself from the dance floor and was headed toward the benches when he strolled up beside her in the crowd.

"Ready for some punch?" His voice was like maple frosting on a sponge cake. Deliciously dark and sweet.

"I'm ready."

"Seems you have a camp of followers."

"The girls, you mean?"

He laughed, and she liked the low-pitched sound. "The men."

She glanced around. "Oh? Just a couple."

"All ready for tomorrow?"

"I have a riding skirt and proper gloves."

He glanced at the gloves she'd trimmed with satin bias and seed pearls. "I'll rent a horse for you. The liveryman will choose a well-mannered one."

"What color?"

"Color." His gaze rose to her eyes. "The horse?"

She nodded. "I wondered what color you'd get for me."

Amusement inched up the corners of his mouth. "What color would you like?"

"Does the liveryman own a paint?"

"I'll check."

"Thank you."

"My pleasure."

She looked up into his intense blue eyes. Catering to her whim gave him pleasure? "Truly?"

"Yes."

"Sophie! There you are! I've been searching all over for you." Out of breath, Amanda touched Sophie's arm. "Here's the person I wanted you to meet."

Sophie turned, only to find herself looking directly into Tek Garrett's cleanly shaven face, his expression one of barely constrained glee.

Chapter Ten

Her head swam.

"Sophie, this is Monte Morgan. Monte, this is my friend, Sophie."

"I've heard a lot about you," he said, gallantly bending at the waist in greeting.

She girded her composure. "And I of you."

"Monte, this is Marshal Connor. Marshal, Mr. Morgan."

The two men sized each other up. Neither extended a hand.

Finally Clay reached out. "Morgan."

Garrett grasped his hand. "Marshal."

Sophie's head spun with the shock of seeing Garrett in a place she'd felt safe. Seeing him shake hands with the marshal. He was Amanda's newfound beau!

Seething anger rose up and heated her face. Her heart was racing. She resisted clenching her fists. She was a professional at creating an image, and the image she was portraying was one of cool calmness and mild interest.

It wouldn't do to panic. Fear was an inhibitor, not a facilitator.

She looked at Amanda, flushed with the dew of infatuation, gazing up at Tek Garrett as though her knight in shining armor had galloped in on a white steed. Sophie wanted to yank Amanda away from him and take her far from this place and far from the man who had only evil in his heart and manipulation on his mind.

He knew exactly what to say and do to make Amanda think she wanted him, needed him. He could make her believe she couldn't live without him. Amanda wanted to be loved so badly she was an easy acquisition. She was too sweet and too vulnerable, a pliable and needy soul Garrett could use to his own advantage for as long as it suited him.

A feeling of guilt nagged at her conscience. Was she doing the same thing to Clay?

"Amanda is so light on her feet," Garrett said to Sophie. His hand at the small of Amanda's back made Sophie's skin crawl. She wanted to crush his heart. "I could dance with her all night."

Amanda beamed.

"Join me for another dance," he urged.

They swept back onto the dance floor.

The gall of the man! He knew Sophie wouldn't run away and leave Amanda in his clutches. He also knew Sophie wouldn't tell Amanda who he was. He would use any means possible, including Amanda, his new trump card, to coerce Sophie into turning over the money he still believed was in her possession. He obviously wouldn't believe she no longer had it.

"I'll bring punch if you want to sit a spell," Clay said from beside her.

Feeling unsteady, she took a seat along the benches.

Moments later he returned with two cups and sat beside her.

Thanking him, she accepted hers and sipped the cool, sweet liquid.

The fiddle player presented a solo in the middle of the song, and the sound of people's feet on the wood floor was loud.

Sophie strained to spot Amanda and Garrett. She found them and kept her attention riveted. His heart was as black as she remembered. She wanted to cut it out.

"Somethin' botherin' you, Sophie?"

Realizing her intent stare might be too revealing, she glanced at Clay. A frown creased his forehead as he turned to watch the crowd. Sophie paid attention and recognized he was watching the same couple. "No. Anything bothering you?"

"Just a feelin' I get about that fella. I've been watchin' him since he got to town."

A dismayed shiver crept down her spine. *Since he got to town?*

Her stomach dipped with nervous dread. Clay's perceptions were accurate. What if he'd gotten close to *her* because he perceived something artificial in her?

She was getting crazy now, she assured herself. There wasn't a deceptive bone in the man's body. If he suspected her he'd be forthright about it. He hadn't bothered pretending to be cordial to Garrett, after all. She focused her thinking on the new information. "How long has that been?"

"A few weeks."

Weeks! Garrett had been biding his time before revealing himself. Smart. A good con man always took stock of his mark. "What kind of feeling do you have?"

Clay pursed his lips a moment before answering. "Just a gut reaction to the man. Can't explain it. I'm usually not wrong."

Sophie's scalp tingled with anxiety. "A feeling like what?"

"Like I should keep an eye on 'im. Like I should check all the papers for his picture...and if I had any papers left I would."

The good news and the bad news. "They all burned?"

"Yup. Sent telegrams to other counties and nearby states askin' if they'd had dealin's with anyone meetin' his description."

A little quake of alarm rolled up Sophie's spine.

"Nothing has turned up," he added.

Relieved, she turned to study the crowd again. "He's too old for Amanda."

Clay raised a brow.

"Well. He is."

"Plenty o' Harvey Girls have married widowed ranchers. Man's not over the hill till he has a long white beard."

"You're defending him."

"I'm stickin' up for mankind."

She should have been able to laugh, but nothing about Garrett was funny. He was dangerous. She knew it, and she'd done her best to avoid him. But Amanda didn't have an inkling that she was playing with fire. If something didn't happen to save her, she'd be caught up in Garrett's blaze of deception. She was being set up because of Sophie. Because Sophie'd led him here. Because Sophie had handed him the perfect tool to use against her.

"I'm not feeling well," she told Clay. "I need to step outside for a moment."

"I'll come with you." He set their cups aside before leading her to the side door.

Clay led her away from the cacophony of talk, laughter and instruments. As the door closed behind them, the sound was muted. Sophie walked a few feet away from the building.

Clay followed. "You gonna be all right? I could take you home."

"No. No, I want to stay. I can't leave Amanda."

"Okay."

She touched her fingers to her temple. "It's probably just the heat."

Clay stepped close and brushed her hand aside to gently massage her temples with his fingertips. She let her eyes drift shut and sighed, and the sound shot straight to his loins. Sophie's scent and nearness drove him mad. He'd begun spending too many of his minutes away from her thinking on the meager minutes they were together. "You can't feel poorly. We have plans for tomorrow."

"I am looking forward to riding," she said.

"Hall's a mite crowded and stuffy tonight."

"Yes." She rested her hand on his shirtfront as comfortable as you please, and her touch was gratifying.

"Worried about your friend?" he asked, and let his hands drop to her shoulders.

She nodded. She could tell him right now. Just blurt out the truth and be done with it. He'd arrest Garrett and Amanda would be safe. He would arrest her, too, though. And he'd lose respect for her—a respect she didn't deserve anyway—and he'd never look at her with admiration or longing again. She'd spend the rest of her life in jail sorting regrets.

"I could take a ride to Florence," he said. "Look through their papers. I've been thinkin' on it anyway."

The thought panicked her. "There's no crime to being older than her now, is there?" she asked. "I'm just being a worrywart."

"Thinkin' of those selfish men again," he teased.

"And you always know what I'm thinking. You have anything lurking in *your* past?" she asked, keeping her tone light.

"Like an extra ten years?"

"Very funny."

"I told you all about me. Not much else to know."

"You're an open book, are you?"

"Would I be more appealin' if I had secrets?"

She didn't answer. Everyone had secrets.

"That must be a yes."

"It's a definite no. I'm just being ladylike and not saying what I really think."

"Sparin' my feelings?"

"Your ego."

He chuckled, then thought a minute. "Never laughed much before I knew you."

Clay wanted to wrap her in his arms and not let go. He liked the way she felt against him, loved her lilac scent and her soft skin. Kissing her was a pleasure he could get used to. Having feelings for her wasn't something he'd anticipated, but the feelings, and the desire, were there all the same. Now that he'd admitted to himself that he wanted her, he had to know how she felt about him.

She returned his kisses with tender passion. Sometimes she looked at him in such a way that made his stomach weak. In the park she'd seemed to be fulfilling a desire by initiating their kisses. He'd be glad to fulfill her desires any old time. He wouldn't fool himself by denying he was falling fast and hard for this woman who was still such a riddle.

"Never known anyone like you, Sophie. You seem wise, yet you're young and unsure 'bout a lot of things. Other things you have your mind made right up."

"Are you going to kiss me or talk me to death? I have a curfew, you know."

Her question prompted another laugh. He could definitely get used to this women askin' for his kisses.

He pulled her close, and if her sighs were any indication, both their desires were fulfilled with an eager melding of their lips. Sophie clutched the fabric of his shirt and held him close.

A loud gunshot startled them both. He released her, immediately pushed her behind him and drew his .45.

Shouts and the sound of a scuffle came from the front of the building. "Stay here!"

He dashed toward the noise. Two men were grappling in the street, their hands on each other's throats. Clay ran closer and spotted a gun several feet away both men were trying to reach. He grabbed the pistol and fired his .45 into the air.

Behind Clay the door to the Social Hall had opened and people were spilling out to see what was going on.

"On your feet, both of you," he ordered.

One of the young men took a last swing at the other, scrambling to stand as Clay jerked him back by the collar. "What the hell's going on here?"

"Son of a bitch not only wore my shirt, he danced with my girl."

Clay recognized them as hands from a nearby ranch. James Duffy wiped blood from his mouth with his sleeve.

"Which one of you fired the gun?"

"That was Lumpy. Damned fool. He coulda shot my foot off," James said.

"You two are gonna settle this peaceful-like or I'm gonna have to take you to the jail. You wouldn't like it there, so you might as well make peace."

A young redhead in a frilly blue dress slipped in and sidled up to Duffy. "Are you all right? Lumpy didn't mean any harm. He was only bein' friendly."

"Too friendly from where I was standin'."

The two men eyed each other warily, and after talking quietly the couple announced they were leaving.

"You can get your gun at the jail tomorrow," Clay told Lumpy.

Lumpy brushed the dust from his clothing with his hat and headed back inside the hall, probably to set his sights on someone else's girl.

Men and women chattered among themselves as they crowded through the doorway and reentered the well-lit building.

Clay hung back, watching to make sure the cowboy and his girl were gone. Sophie met up with him.

"Sorry you saw that," he told her. "Behavior more fittin' a saloon."

"Their behavior doesn't reflect on you," she replied.

They faced each other. He slid his .45 back into its holster and tucked Lumpy's pistol into his waistband.

"I have work to do," he told her with regret.

"I suppose you have important marshal duties even on Saturday night."

"Always somethin'. Only Owen and me are unmarried men. I don't cotton much to the saloons, so it's never mattered. I've always stopped by the Social Hall to greet a few people and that's been good enough." He glanced at the light spilling from the noisy building. "Maybe it's time to change that."

"Change your work schedule?" Sophie asked.

"Only if you think you'd want to spend some Saturday evenin's together. Don't wanna be pushy."

"You're not pushy, Clay."

But she didn't say she *liked* the idea. The other day he'd been considering how unfulfilling their time together always seemed. She didn't seem averse to his attention or his company, though she always held something back. "Well, guess I'll be movin' on. Evenin'."

"Good evening."

At the corner he looked back. She'd gone inside. There was so much left unspoken between them. They talked, but he never felt as though they communicated.

Tomorrow he'd see her again. Another chance to learn more about her. Clay shook his head at his boyish enthusiasm. He wouldn't get his hopes up, but he wanted to know everything about Sophie Hollis.

* * *

With her jaw set in exasperation, Sophie observed Garrett the rest of the evening. She didn't have to wonder what he was up to. She knew he was up to no good. Period.

When he returned Amanda to the benches and came toward Sophie, it was all she could do to not flinch.

"Would you honor me with a dance, Miss Hollis?" Garret's tone sounded innocent as could be.

Sophie turned her surprised glance on her friend, and Amanda nodded with a smile. "Go ahead, Sophie."

"I'm tired," she objected.

"Oh, go on," Emma said and gave her a little push from behind.

She followed, but didn't take the hand he offered. She faced him on the dance floor, his eyes boring into hers, that smirk at the corner of his narrow lips telling her he knew how much control he could still wield over her with a mere look. It was like watching a snake that could strike any moment, and she didn't dare look away. Insidious memories cut away the present, blotted out the music and the people until she was fourteen years old again. She couldn't breathe, couldn't move, and her head felt light.

You would be cooking scrawny rabbits over a fire and suckling a squalling brat. If I hadn't fostered you, you'd be living with a mangy trapper who beat you over every small offense.

His gaze was like a touch that made her skin crawl. *You should be grateful you've been spared all that. Grateful you're not down on Tucker Street, selling your-*

self to every drunk who comes through the doors with two bits.

I haven't taught you everything yet. There is more... much, much more....

Chapter Eleven

It became apparent that others were starting to look at her odd reaction to the man. She reminded herself that all that darkness was in the past. She was her own person now. She made her own choices. So, Sophie steeled herself and took his hand, allowed him to rest his touch on her back and quelled a shudder.

He'd touched her too much in her lifetime.

"You belong to me," he said in that superior tone she recognized with the parts of her she'd tried to bury. "I own you, body and soul. Did you think you could get away?"

"I have."

"Don't be foolish, Gabriella. I made you who you are. You're a perfect extension of me."

"I want nothing to do with you."

"A display of bravado might impress someone else, but this is me you're talking to, remember? I fed you, clothed you, taught you everything you know. You are indebted to me with your life."

Sophie had never wanted to hurt anyone, but if she

had a weapon she feared she could kill this man without a second thought. Her body was rigid with loathing.

"And—you have something that belongs to me."

"I told you I don't have it."

His grip on her hand became painful. *"Where is the money?"*

She wanted to wince and pull away, but she'd be damned if she'd let him see the pain. "It's gone."

"Gone where? You haven't bought an estate or fled to Europe. You have nothing to show to account for that much money."

"I paid it back."

His step faltered. "You what?"

"I found as many of the people we'd conned as I could and I paid them back. Not nearly all the money, of course, and not all the people, but a nice little dent on the debt."

He stopped his movements in the middle of the dance floor, his grip crushing her hand. He'd always controlled her with subtle threats and manipulation, his true temperament hidden for the most part. This burst of fury revealed his true nature, and she took a gratifying measure of delight from being the one to peel away his malicious composure. Couples on either side cast them curious glances.

"You stupid, stupid little bitch," he hissed, pulling her against him and leading her back into the steps of the dance. "What did you hope to gain from a move like that?"

"A small part of my self-respect," she replied.

"And what did it get you? Nothing but my ire. You will pay for this. One way or another, you will pay."

"I owe you nothing. You don't control me anymore."

"What do you think you're going to do?" he asked, leaning away and smearing a look of contempt over her. "You might have a few people fooled, but you're still the same person. No other man is going to want you or marry you after the things you've done with me. You can't give *those* sins away like you did my money, now can you?"

Dirty and used was how he always made her feel. "Leave me alone. Leave Amanda alone. Go away or I'll turn myself in to implicate you."

He barked a laugh. "You wouldn't. You'd want to die before being locked in a cell for the rest of your life. Before letting your marshal know whose bed you've occupied."

Sophie cringed at those words.

"You are a whore," he said matter-of-factly, his voice low enough for only her ears. "Bought and paid for at quite an excessive price, but a whore all the same."

She pulled away, shame and anger scorching her cheeks, pounding in her chest. She stared at the face she hated, the man she detested with every fiber of her being.

He took her arm and led her toward the side of the room. "Come to your senses, Gabriella. There's still time to make amends and ingratiate yourself into my good graces before anyone gets hurt."

"If you hurt Amanda, I will kill you."

"Come now, I don't hurt women, as you well know. I treat women well. Spoil them, actually. That's what's wrong with you." Then his tone changed. "Marshals are another matter altogether. Lawmen are killed in shoot-ings everyday. A small coin buys a big gun in a town like this."

Panic threatened to take control of her, but she tamped it down and tugged from his hold. "I know too much about you. You'd never get away with it."

"You're right about knowing too much," he answered. "And don't forget it. I'm giving you the benefit of the doubt right now. You're still an asset. Trust me, Gabriella. You don't want to become a liability."

He turned and threaded his way through the crowd.

His threat had done what he'd intended. She had so many words in her head she could barely hear her heart anymore. Sophie dropped onto a bench and covered her ears with both hands.

You're a whore, a whore, a whore.

You don't want to become a liability.

You're a whore.

No other man is going to want you or marry you after the things you've done. You're still the same person…a whore.

"Are you all right, Sophie?" Emma touched her shoulder.

Her insides were shaking and she felt as if she had to throw up. Sophie raised her head and forced a smile. "I'm fine. Fine."

Emma studied her curiously.

"Really. I was just thinking."

She stayed where she was, her thoughts a turmoil, her supper turning over in her stomach. She spotted Rosie with Robbie. Across the room, Louis Tripp was watching the couple as well. Sophie looked for Amanda and found her on the outskirts of the dance floor with Garrett. Sophie wasn't taking her eyes off them for an instant.

At a little before eleven Amanda came to her. "Monte is taking me home now."

"You're going straight to the boardinghouse."

"Yes, of course."

"I'll ride along with you. I'm ready to leave."

Garrett's expression was unreadable when she showed up with Amanda. He was either pleased that she was falling into his setup by coming along to protect her friend or he was angry that he wouldn't be alone with Amanda. Or both, she figured. There was no way she was leaving Amanda alone with him.

The young woman chattered all the way to the Arcade, effectively covering up the quivering animosity between Sophie and Garrett, and Sophie was relieved Amanda didn't notice anything.

Why should she? She was trusting and goodhearted. She'd never anticipate someone deliberately using her.

Sophie felt Garrett's eyes on her while he helped Amanda down. Sophie had jumped out of the opposite side of the carriage and now stood waiting.

"Thank you for your company this evening," he said to Amanda. Seeing his hands on Amanda made Sophie shudder. She wanted to run over and kick him where it would hurt his grandchildren. "You're a wonderful dancer and a delightful companion," he added.

"Thank you," Amanda replied breathlessly.

"A pleasure to see you, Miss Hollis."

Sophie took her elbow and steered Amanda toward the front door of the dormitory.

"Ouch!" Amanda pulled away. "What's your hurry?"

Sophie determinedly led her inside.

"Did you notice how he paid attention to me all evening?" Amanda asked. "Dancing with him was, oh it was divine. I'm so grateful for your lessons. He likes me, and he's complimentary. He couldn't be more of a gentleman."

Once inside, Sophie waved Amanda up the stairs. "I'll bring a pitcher of water."

Amanda gathered her skirts and cheerfully ascended the steps. She hummed and the sweet tune floated from the upstairs hallway. "Did you notice the looks we were receiving as we danced?" she called.

Several minutes later Sophie poured water into the basin they shared. The pitcher and bowl stood on a stand behind a folding screen. Amanda had removed her dress, shoes and stockings and padded behind the screen carrying her white cotton nightgown.

"Dixie Peterson was green with envy, could you tell?"

When Sophie spoke she tried to keep her tone casual. "Mr. Morgan's quite a bit older than you."

"Isn't maturity refreshing?" Amanda replied. "He's not stumbling over his feet or acting all awkward."

"However…he must be all of forty."

There was a long pause before Amanda said, "Sophie, you were the one who said an older man is established and knows what he wants. He's probably looking for a special person to share the things he's acquired? Sound familiar?"

Sophie distractedly checked her gloves for spots and tucked them into her bureau drawer. Garrett knew what he wanted all right, but he was looking for someone he could use to get it for him. "How much do you actually know about the man? I don't think you know enough."

"I've just been telling you." Amanda came from behind the screen tying a white satin bow at her neck. "He's dashing and polite and confident." She paused in listing perceived qualities and stared into their mirror for a long dreamy moment.

"I mean how much do you know about what he does and who he is?" Sophie prodded gently.

"I told you. He does investing for cattlemen. He's from the east somewhere."

"That's not much."

"Sophie! I know everything I need to know." Her tone had grown exasperated at Sophie's questioning.

No you don't! No, you don't. Sophie couldn't let her roommate fall into Garrett's clutches. She wouldn't. She removed her yellow dress and hung it in the armoire they shared. "You really don't know enough about the man—"

"Isn't that the purpose of courting?" Amanda asked. "To learn more about each other? He doesn't really know anything about me either."

He does. Oh, he does. He knows you're young and malleable and susceptible. Tears sprang to Sophie's eyes, the depth of keen and intense emotion a surprise after being barren of feelings for so many years. What was happening to her?

Grabbing her nightgown, she hurried behind the screen. She scooped her hair away from her face with a ribbon and washed, the water and the splashing covering her tears and the soft sobs she couldn't hold back.

She wasn't going to let Amanda be buffaloed into falling for Garrett. He would use Amanda to get to her without blinking an eye.

Perhaps Amanda would recognize his intent?

He didn't own Amanda, after all, Sophie tried to assure herself.

But what if Amanda learned too late? He could seduce her—or force himself on her. The sordid images in Sophie's head sickened her.

At the very least Amanda would have her heart broken and her reputation ruined.

After calming herself, Sophie dried her skin and undressed. "Please don't see him alone."

"Sophie, you're going riding with the marshal tomorrow. Alone."

"It's not the same."

"It is the same."

"No. Clay is the city marshal. Everyone knows he can be trusted. He is established in this town and has a good reputation. As a matter of fact he finds Mr. Morgan a trifle suspicious."

Dressed in her nightgown, Sophie came around the screen to find the other girl waiting for her, indignation in her expression.

"It's unfair of both of you to accuse a man you don't even know of being untrustworthy. Don't you think a good man could be attracted to me?"

"Of course I do, but…but…" Garrett was not a good man. She knew it. "I just care about you."

"Then show it by being happy for me."

Oh, how she wished she could. All Sophie could do was wrap her arms around her. Caught by surprise at the uncharacteristic display, Amanda held herself stiff for a moment before returning the affection. Sophie was experiencing new feelings all the time now.

This must be what it felt like to have a sister, Sophie thought. Amanda had undoubtedly hugged her family members hundreds of times, fought and made up, but Sophie had never shared that kind of affection or felt so protective.

Amanda turned down the wick and they climbed into their beds. So great was Sophie's concern for her roommate's safety, she wanted to cry again, but she reminded herself of her uncommon strength and vowed to protect her friend no matter what it took.

Sophie had purchased a ready-made split riding skirt at Miss Kirkpatrick's dress shop, and it had needed only minor alteration, which she'd done herself.

Sunday morning Amanda helped style her hair so it wouldn't escape her straw hat, which she'd adorned with fresh new flowers and a lavender grosgrain ribbon that trailed down her back.

Goldie Krenshaw burst in, exclaiming that the marshal had arrived.

Hat in hand, Clay waited in the courting room, half a dozen young women directing questions and fluttering their eyelashes at him. Relieved to see Sophie, he ran an appreciative gaze over her spring-colored lavender shirtwaist and serge riding skirt and offered a smile. "You look lovely, Miss Hollis. Ready for a ride?"

"I am, Marshal."

She took his arm and he led her out of doors where two saddled horses waited at the hitching post. One of them was a brown-speckled Appaloosa, taller than an Indian pony, but bearing familiar color and markings. Her smile was genuine. "He's beautiful!"

"She." He guided the horse close to the porch so she could climb easily to its back. "Hold on." He indicated the pommel of the saddle. "Your foot goes here, then pull your weight upward with your arms and use your foot for leverage. Once you're high enough, throw your leg over."

Effortlessly, she did just as he directed and beamed at him from atop her mount. Just as she reached for the animal's mane, Clay handed her the reins.

He mounted his horse, nudged it forward with his knees and instructed her to do the same. It all came back to her, though she couldn't remember ever riding with a saddle, and that took some getting used to. It was more comfortable than feeling every movement of the animal's hips as it stepped.

The morning was cooler than any day had been in weeks, the sun partially hidden by a layer of filmy clouds. Sophie drew in a breath and detected the fresh smell of the countryside. It was good to smell something besides burning coal or horses or food.

"It won't rain, will it?" she asked.

"Doesn't smell like rain."

She let the breeze blow her hat off. She'd wisely added a ribbon that caught around her neck and let the hat hang on her back. The gentle wind in her hair felt delightful.

Clay held the horses to a moderate gait, and she was grateful for the chance to get accustomed to the brisk bouncing. The clouds dissipated and the sun warmed her clear through. By the time they reached the same riverbank lined with cottonwood trees, Sophie was ready to slide to the ground. She did so without his assistance.

"Shoulda let me help you," Clay said.

She nodded. "I should have. My body didn't want to wait."

He chuckled and tethered the horses in the shade where they could crop grass.

"How far is your place from here?" she asked.

"Couple o' miles that way." He indicated a northwesterly direction.

"Are we going there today?"

"Still want to?"

She nodded.

"Then yes. I'll make us lunch. Nothin' fancy."

They took seats on the lush grass. She took off her hat and secured the brim with a stone. "You can cook?"

"I said nothin' fancy. I can slice ham and bread. You only have to wipe an apple on your sleeve before you eat it."

She enjoyed his easygoing manner, appreciated how comfortable it was to talk to him. No putting on airs. No forced politeness or artificial pretense.

Of course this was all a pretense, she corrected herself. Sophie Hollis was a pretense. How weary she was of that.

"I'm accustomed to doin' for myself," he said with a grin.

"Was your mother a good cook?" she asked.

He nodded. "Every boy's mama is a good cook."

"What was your favorite?"

He didn't even think about it. "Bread. Hot and crusty right from the oven." He set his hat aside. "What about you? You said your mama was a good cook."

Sophie tried hard to remember something her mother had made. She pictured her with her fair skin darkened from the sun, tanning hides and stringing dried deer meat. With her dark hair and eyes she'd blended in with the women of the tribe.

"Lemon-frosted tea cakes," she said finally. "With sweet tea."

Here she was lying again.

Lying to get a job. Lying to save face. Lying to save her neck. Lying to people who thought she was their friend. Lying to this man who stood for justice.

She'd fooled herself by thinking she wanted to change, but how would that ever be possible?

Just to hold conversation with the man she had to come up with stories. If she was going to change, she was going to have to start somewhere. Maybe she could start here with a small step. Maybe one less lie. She straightened her posture in preparation. "I haven't been completely truthful."

Chapter Twelve

Sophie felt sick at the confession she was about to make.

Clay's blue gaze rested on her face without obvious concern.

The breath Sophie drew shook. "I've led you to believe my mother is alive," she said. "But the truth is she's dead."

A crease formed between the brows he drew together. "Sorry. You could've just said so."

"I've never talked about her." That was one hundred percent the truth, and an exhilarating rush of relief pumped through her veins at this minimal unburdening.

"You don't have to now," he told her.

The cottonwood leaves rustled overhead. A bird chirped from a nearby tree and another answered.

"I just wanted to be like other people." Her explanation sounded lame even to her own ears. "So there you have it. My mother's dead, and I barely remember her."

Sophie bit her lip in self-disgust. She'd tacked another lie on to that one tiny harmless truth! She did re-member her mother. Now she was avoiding telling him the way she remembered her.

Clay studied her for a lengthy moment. "You didn't think you were like other people."

She knew she wasn't.

"You wanted to feel normal. Understandable. What else do you want?"

She gave him a puzzled look. "What else?"

"For your life?" he clarified. "You're not lookin' for a husband, so a family isn't on your list."

"I want...time and space to figure out what I want. I don't want anyone telling me my future." Another truth rose up plain as day. "I don't know who I am or what I want. But I want to learn those things more than anything." That and freedom from the man who meant to ei-ther own or destroy her again were her heart's desire. Sophie wanted to forget Garrett. She wanted him to dis-appear.

"Working at the Arcade is somethin' you wanted."

"Yes. I love the sense of accomplishment and pur-pose it gives me."

He nodded. "Admirable."

She enjoyed the sparkle in his blue eyes when they touched on her. "I've never had a friendship like ours before," she told him, another truth. "I've never been close to anyone. Comfortable like this."

"Same for me."

She had come to enjoy their time together. Talking like this was a rich satisfaction she appreciated with all her heart. Sophie studied the handsome line of his jaw, the sheen of his dark hair as the leaves above rustled and allowed little rays of sunshine to dapple his head and shoulders. "What about the girl you were going to marry? You never mentioned her name."

"Susan. It was years ago, but I can't remember wantin' to know all about her. Talked about herself all the time regardless."

"Was she pretty?"

"She was."

"What did she look like?"

"Small like. Hair the color of a wheat field in the sun."

"How poetic."

He grinned self-consciously.

"What else do you remember?"

He studied the green landscape as far as the river wound. "Remember feelin' like somebody dug out my heart with a rusty spoon." He rubbed his chest as though the ache was still vivid. "Couldn't catch my breath for a week."

Sophie's emotions surfaced again at his disturbing description of heartbreak. He was a brave man for not being ashamed of those feelings. Far braver than she.

She'd had to close off feelings in order to survive.

"I'm so sorry." She reached over and covered his hand on his chest with hers.

Clay took it and pressed her palm to the front of his shirt, keeping her closer. "Been feelin' that way again lately."

"You loved her that much?"

"Not because of her." His low-timbered voice made her insides quiver.

"What then?" She dreaded the answer. Couldn't wait to hear it.

He flattened his hand over hers and she could feel the accelerated beat of his heart. "Because I'm fallin' for another woman who wants somethin' else more than me."

His clear blue eyes held a sincerity that took her breath away. *Did she?* How was it conceivably possible to want something more than what he offered? All her years of conditioning had convinced her men were selfish and greedy. Garrett was typical of the men she'd known, the only kind of people she'd been exposed to.

She remembered Ellie Chaney's words about not having known a man she could trust before she met the doctor. From him Ellie had learned to trust.

Meeting her, meeting the diners at the Arcade, knowing the girls at the dormitory, and learning about Clay had shaken Sophie's perception of the world. A whole new view of people had been opened up to her, and she was still sorting it all out.

How much truth could she tell him without giving herself away and landing in jail? Without putting him in a position where he'd have to choose justice over her? She couldn't do that to him.

She was on her knees beside him now. "There are a lot of things you don't know about me." Just that much of an admission made her heart thump. "A lot of things I can't share."

"You will when you're ready."

"I never want to hurt you. Ever. That's the truth. And it's from my heart," she told him. "But things have happened that won't let me be the person you need me to be."

A muscle in Clay's jaw leaped. "Is this how you discouraged Mr. Tripp?"

That question hurt because he'd hit on part of the

truth. "I didn't care about him, Clay. I didn't want to waste his time— or mine."

"Are you wastin' my time?"

"I don't know, am I?"

"You're a risk I'm willin' to take, Sophie."

She wept inside, ached because a man as good and kind as this one cared enough about her to be willing to hurt that much all over again. She closed her eyes for a moment to experience the words he'd just spoken. To fully absorb the meaning.

"You could care that much for me?" she asked with her eyes still shut. "You see something in me worthy of your heart?"

Clay raised her hand and she felt warmth and moisture as he kissed her palm. "You already have my heart, Sophie. Don't you know that?"

She looked at him then. Threading her other hand into his hair she let herself feel the emotions he unleashed inside her. This good man loved her.

Loved her?

"What does it feel like?" she asked on a whisper. "Does love make you want to laugh and cry at the same time? Does it fill up a hole inside that you never knew was there before? Does it make you feel smart and pretty and all fluttery inside?"

"All except the pretty part," he answered, the corner of his mouth quirking up.

Her lips were nearly touching his, and now his eyes had drifted closed.

She covered his lips with hers, aching for closeness, yearning for a more intimate bond.

"Sophie," he said against her mouth.

"My real name is Sophia," she was impelled to tell him. "It's what my father named me."

"As beautiful as you." He kissed her, slanting his head and sending blood pumping through her veins in a rush. "Sophia."

How many years since she'd heard her own name aloud? Overwhelming gratification welled inside at her given name on his lips. He was speaking to *her,* the real Sophia. The urge to cry was strong and she masked it with a heartfelt embrace and by losing herself in his kiss.

All of Amanda's handiwork was gone in seconds when he delved into her hair and removed the pins so he could splay it over her shoulders and run his fingers through.

Sophie explored the contours of his chest and shoulders through the soft fabric, sliding her hand inside his collar to touch the warm skin of his neck.

He inched away, touched his hand to his top button and met her eyes.

She nodded and helped him unbutton it and strip the garment away, eager to have her hands on his skin. His chest was broad and muscular, silky dark hair curling around her fingers. She couldn't get enough of him and dared to test the sleek feel of his rib cage.

He drew her onto his lap, and she wrapped her arm around his neck. Their kisses grew more heated, his tongue teasing hers until her pulse pounded in her head. What was it he did to her? How was it she found herself returning his kisses and craving more? This was so new, so shocking and exciting, she could hardly absorb it.

He cupped her breast through her dress and groaned,

then suggestively skimmed the row of buttons with a fingertip.

Sophie's pleasure dimmed. The lies were undermining what she felt for this man. Clay had always been honest with her. If he knew all about her he wouldn't want her, wouldn't find her so worthy. If they gave in to this all-consuming fire, he would know he wasn't the first. She owed him that much honesty ahead of time.

He toyed with the top button, and she pulled away enough to look into his eyes.

"Didn't mean any disrespect," he said.

"Clay." She took his hands between hers and moved from his lap so she could think. "There's so much you don't know about me." Seeing Garrett had reminded her afresh of everything he'd stolen from her, her innocence, her chance to have a life with a wonderful person like this one.

"It doesn't matter," he answered.

She couldn't even enjoy this experience to the fullest because of the lies. "It matters to me, and it will matter to you."

"Tell me then."

The only way to enjoy this was to tell him. "I'm scared. You won't want me if you know."

"Try me."

She hated Garrett. Despised him for putting her in this position. Now it all came down to whether or not she trusted Clay. The irony in that fact didn't escape her. She wanted to experience the happiness she knew was waiting for her with this man. If she was going to go through with what she wanted, she had to clear this part of her conscience and be honest with him.

Amazingly, the sky hadn't fallen when she'd told the truth about her mother. It would still be overhead after he knew even more. And at least she would have been truly loved for the first time since she was too young to remember.

"Why don't you show me your place now?" she asked.

"Don't have to if you're not comfortable."

"I definitely want to."

He shrugged into his shirt and assisted her onto the horse.

"You're better at this than you let on," he said. "You sure it's been years?"

"Guess it all comes back," she replied and secured her hat before taking the reins and nudging the Appaloosa into motion.

Clay mounted and led the way. Riding gave her a giddy sense of freedom. She enjoyed the feeling of control.

They passed farmland and fields of bright yellow sunflowers waving in the breeze. They led the horses through a field, and the flowers brushed the hem of Sophie's skirt. It seemed as though they were in a fantasy world of vibrant color. Clay leaned over to pick her a sunflower and break off the stem. She tucked it in among the silk flowers on her hat.

"Ahead is my land," he told her. "It's just a few acres. But there's a stream and a wooded windbreak." The closer they got, the better she could make out the stable and another outbuilding as well as the square one-story house.

When they reached the dooryard she slid from the

horse's back and stretched. Her posterior had grown a little sore.

"I'll give the horses water," Clay said. "The necessity's out back there."

She didn't reply, but made a quick trip. Returning to watch him with the animals, she wondered how difficult his days and nights had been without Sam. Clay's attachment to his dog had touched her.

Her experience with the Sioux had shown her that men were hunters and warriors and that women and children were servants. She'd been an asset to Garrett, like a valuable horse, and he'd taught her how greed blinded men. She had never detected that trait in this man.

Clay's profession declared what kind man he was. He was honest and hardworking. Though kindhearted, there wasn't a weak bone in his body. He was strong and brave and human all at the same time. He had never treated her less than special. He showed true interest in her as a person of merit.

How could she *not* be falling in love with him?

He led her to the house where he ushered her through the back doorway into a large kitchen. The room held open shelving, a stove and a counter holding a basin and pump. He pumped water so they could wash their hands.

"I'll slice ham and cheese and bread. You set the table." He gestured to a shelf with a few plates and cups.

Seeing him in his home, learning how he lived seemed quite intimate. His hospitality spoke again of trust.

If she told him the truth about her past and it disgusted him, she would have to move on and get over him. Being disenchanted would spare him hurt later. Him withdrawing would take the decision away from her.

However, his change of opinion would break the heart she'd only today realized was alive and vulnerable. Honesty was a huge risk. But she owed him the truth.

Clay made sandwiches, but she only broke off pieces of meat and cheese. Her stomach was so nervous she didn't have much appetite.

He finished eating and explained how he'd made a few changes to the house since he'd bought it half a dozen years back. Getting up, he took cups from a shelf. "I only have water," he said. "I could make coffee."

"No, no, don't heat the house up by starting a fire."

He poured two glasses of water, then turned to a towel-draped pan. "The First Baptist ladies supply me with bread. The Methodists bake me a cake or pie every week." He drew off the towel. "Apple."

"Just a tiny slice for me."

The apples were tangy and the cinnamon not overdone. She finished her slice and watched him enjoy his.

Their eyes met as he finished chewing. "Want more?"

She shook her head.

He laid down his fork.

"I've noticed several churches in Newton. Amanda invites me to hers on occasion."

"Plenty of volunteers," he replied. "The Lutheran ladies clean the jailhouse, cells and all, and the Congregational women offer Bible readin' if there's a prisoner."

"I haven't heard you say anything about the new jail."

"Ordered brick this time. Unloaded a rail car into three wagons to get it all there without taxin' the teams. Foundation's done. Walls are almost up. Next week the roof goes on."

"I'll have to have a look."

He stood and gestured for her to follow. "I'll show you the rest of the house."

Someone had wisely built the dwelling beside a row of trees whose spreading branches provided shade in the afternoon.

Clay showed her a simply furnished room with a fireplace and two comfortable chairs. A shelf held several books and a collection of small animals carved from wood.

"Did you make those?"

He shook his head. "Belonged to my mother. Her father made 'em."

Sophie stepped closer to examine the tiny figures. "How lovely to hold a piece of your family's history."

"Don't you have somethin' that belonged to your ma or pa?"

"I had my mother's wedding ring."

"Had?"

"Someone took it from me."

His expression showed sympathy. "Family here before me had a passel o' kids," Clay told her. "That's why there are three bedrooms."

One wood-paneled room had bare bunks built into two walls. The other bedroom was empty. The third held a rope bed constructed from sanded and stained logs, a chest of drawers and two trunks. A table by the bed held a lamp.

Sophie studied the plain wool blankets on the bed. Everything about his home was so like him. Straightforward. Uncomplicated.

"I like your home, Clay."

"Simple," he said.

She nodded. "That's what I like the most."

Memories of elegant hotel rooms and fancy dining cars spun through her head. No expense had ever been spared in their accommodations when she'd traveled with Garrett. He'd insisted on the best, the most lavish. As quickly as the money was gone, there was more to be made. He always wanted more, even from her. Everybody owed him—especially her.

It was time for her to get past her anger and helplessness. Clay didn't deserve all the resentment burning inside her. She'd been holding herself in check for as long as she could remember.

She made up her mind once and for all to tell him the truth about her background. Maybe then she could let some of her past go and build the new life she wanted so badly.

"I have some things to tell you. About me," she began. Her knees felt so weak at the words she'd managed to get out, she sank onto the side of his bed.

Clay took off his holster and hung the gun belt on a hook beside the door. He got a wooden chair from the corner, sat it directly in front of her and seated himself.

It was hard to meet his eyes. Hard to face herself in their depths. She looked everywhere else in the room and then forced her gaze back to his. "I told you I hadn't been honest. And the reason is because I'm ashamed. Well, one of the reasons."

Without a word, he nodded.

"It's true my family was from Pennsylvania, but I was too young to remember much at all. I have early memories of my parents and brothers, but they're vague and jumbled up with so many other memories."

The blanket under her fingers was rough, and she grounded herself in its simplicity. "I was about five when we were part of a wagon train headed west. I'm not sure of our destination."

Clay's expression changed as though he expected bad news. "You sure you wanna talk about this?"

She'd come up with this much courage, she wasn't stopping now. "I have to."

He nodded.

"A party of Sioux attacked us. My father and my brothers were killed."

He held his mouth in a grim line as he listened.

"My mother and I were taken captive. We became part of the tribe. My mother was given to a brave and she took care of his children and cooked. It was all right because we saw each other often."

"And you?"

"The old chief took a liking to me and took me into his tent. I was regarded as a favored child. I learned from his wife and his grown daughters."

"That's how you understood what was going on with the Indians in front of the Arcade that day. You speak their language."

Sophie nodded. "I played out of doors, had plenty to eat. But the other children never accepted me because I was different and because I received preferential treatment."

"But you're such a lady. Your speech, your manners…the dance lessons. Where did you learn all that?"

"That was only a small part of the story. I'm not finished."

He leaned forward, elbows on knees.

"One winter an epidemic spread through the camp. My mother took ill and died. She had taught me all along to be brave and strong and to adapt. Since we hadn't shared the same tent, I pretended she was still there and I could see her whenever I wanted."

"You were brave," he said.

"Or unrealistic," she said with a shrug.

"You did what you had to."

"It got me through. I was about twelve when the chief died. It's hard to know exactly, because the days and the years were marked by hunting seasons and tribal celebrations. Even though we weren't sure of which day it was, my mother had reminded me of my birthday each spring. Once she was gone, I lost track.

"I was sad when the old chief died because he'd been kind to me. Once she was gone, I was afraid of what would happen. That same season I was taken to a trading post where the tribe traded furs and beads, and I was offered up for sale."

Clay's eyes revealed shock and then anger.

"A man bought me." She didn't know if she could go on. The rest of this tale was one of shame and degradation. But she'd made up her mind. Suddenly she was sure he would be disgusted and what they had would end before it went further. She didn't have a hope that he would accept her the way she was.

But Sophie hardened herself to continue.

Chapter Thirteen

She refused to analyze and fret over any more of Clay's silent reactions from here on out. "I was frightened," she said. "But he seemed kind enough. He bought me clothing. Hired tutors for my education, speech and deportment. He taught me to be a lady.

"We never stayed in one city long. I was always locked in the hotel room at night while he went about his…business."

By not mentioning his business, she was leaving herself a margin of safety. She cared too much for Clay to place him in the position of knowing her part in their crimes. She was telling him the part he needed to know now.

"He's the one who took my mother's ring."

His expression was indecipherable. Pausing in her story, she looked away from his face and held back her humiliation so she could think about her next words. "There came a time when I realized I was as much a prisoner with him as I had been with the Sioux. I had to get away. I packed a few things in a small bag and picked the lock while he was out one evening.

"It took all my courage to overcome years of submission and do this one thing. I got out and I ran."

"Good for you."

"I didn't even make it across town before he found me. He took me back." Sophie concentrated on breathing evenly. Here the story took another sordid turn, and she gripped the wool under her fingers. Now that the floodgates had been opened there was no holding this back. This was the part he needed to know.

An ache welled inside her chest at bringing this truth to the light and forming the words. She trembled inside. "That night our arrangement changed."

Her ears rang with what she was going to reveal. "After that...I—I didn't have my own room or a separate bed."

Clay swiped a hand down his face and dropped his gaze to look at the floor.

Her heart was beating so fast she worried it would burst. Was this the end of it, then? He couldn't bear to look at her?

"How old were you?" he asked, his deep voice troubled.

"About fourteen."

He looked up and met her eyes with dark emotion in the depths of his. "He forced himself on you?"

The memory of Garret's hands on her body still turned her cold inside. The way he took her in insensitive greed, all the while telling her she belonged to him, always boasting that he owned her and convincing her she was no more than a possession made the shame fresh. "I submitted. I stayed alive."

His gaze touched on her hair, and she felt his compassion like a warm wave of sensation. She held in the cry that threatened to spill from her throat.

"It was another six years before I got away," she finished.

Clay got up and walked to the window where he pulled aside the plain muslin curtain and stared out at the sunny afternoon.

Sophie's body trembled as she studied his rigid posture, trying to gauge his reaction.

He clenched and unclenched his fists. "What's his name? Where is he?"

"He's not worth it," she told him.

By keeping Garrett's identity a secret, she was preventing Clay from having to choose the law over her. By sharing only this much she could have now. Today. Just enough so that he knew she cared for him and was willingly choosing him. "I've never told anyone. I made up a family and a story because I was ashamed. I'm sorry, Clay. Sorry I wasn't strong enough. I tried so hard to keep to myself and keep my secret. Secrets are so consuming. And I'm tired of keeping things…from you."

"*Where* is he now?"

Forcing out a lie now would be a backward step in the progress she'd just made. "It's over," was all she said.

He turned to look at her, and she could feel the nervous vibration of his anger in the air between them.

"I understand if you're disgusted," she told him. "I know I'm not worthy of the kindness you've shown me."

"Stop."

"What?"

"Stop blamin' yourself for somethin' that wasn't your fault. You sayin' you don't know where he is?"

"I got away from him in Boulder. That was two years ago."

"Let me find 'im."

"No."

"He should pay."

"No."

Clay came to where she sat and encircled her wrists in a gentle grasp. "What he did was a crime. What if he's doin' it to someone else right now?"

Sophie's heart ached. *He is! He is!* Clay was right, Garrett deserved to pay. She would have to tell the rest eventually. She would have to protect Amanda, no matter how much she implicated herself. But not yet. Not like this. Not until she'd known a bare measure of goodness.

"No more," she whispered. "Not now."

The pain in his eyes was so fresh and deep she recognized he would take all the hurt from her if he could. If she would let him.

"What we have is the best thing I've ever had in my life," she told him with a trembling voice. "If I've lost that because of the truth…because of him…I don't know what I'll do."

He brought her hands to his lips and kissed the backs of her fingers. She recognized the sting of tears forming behind her eyes and closed them so he wouldn't see. This man's touch was her salvation, his love a flood that could wash her clean of all the ugliness. She needed him more than she needed her next breath. Was this what love felt like?

At that moment Garrett's threat rose in her mind, and she was afraid for Clay. Afraid to lose him. Afraid to tell him the rest. Her secret was a burden of guilt that hurt inside. Love shouldn't be as painful as hate, should it?

"I'm so sorry, Sophia. Sorry you had to learn the hard side of life. Especially the dark side of a man. You shouldn't have had to feel trapped and alone."

Clay recognized the shame she'd accepted as her own. All the times she'd avoided him, all the questions she'd sidestepped made sense now. Little inconsistencies in her stories were accounted for. That feeling he'd always had that there was so much she wasn't saying had been right on the mark.

Her insistence on making her own decisions was perfectly understandable. She'd been some man's property growin' up. Sophie needed choices.

He remembered the day she'd asked to kiss him. Just kiss him. And how she'd enjoyed it. She'd discovered the wonder in *choosing* to receive a man's affections. He'd asked her what she wanted and she'd said she wanted to decide things for herself. It was all clear now.

"When you're through decidin' what you want…I hope it's me."

"You've shown me true strength," she told him. Her lower lip trembled. "You taught me kindness. You allowed me to discover who I was."

Sophie cradled his cheek in her palm and studied his face, tenderness evident in her eyes. Clay had a lump of hurt in his belly for the child she'd been, for her suffering and loss.

"I'm not anything special," he denied.

"I can't agree with that," she told him. "I've had so few good things in my life, and I can't be sorry for wanting the best thing I ever knew. I'm not ashamed of wanting you."

"I'm willin' to wait for you. As long as it takes 'til you're ready."

"I'm not. I've waited long enough. I want to know why I get this feeling when you're near me. Why your kisses turn me to jelly. I need to know kindness. I need you."

Clay didn't require any further encouragement. Meeting her desires would be the best thing that ever happened to him. He kissed her, and the emotion he felt in her response assured him of her willingness.

"Remember where we were before?" she asked.

It took him a second to comprehend. "I do."

He reached to find pins in her hair and let down the tresses.

She raised her hands to the row of buttons at her collar. When she had them undone, she reached to her side to unfasten her riding skirt and stepped out of it. He helped her ease the shirtwaist from her shoulders and arms, then draped it over the end of the bed. She took the initiative to sit and remove her ankle-high boots and black stockings. She stood in her prim drawers and chemise, her bare toes white against the dark wood floor. The scent of lilacs enveloped him. So feminine. So sweet.

"I'll wash," he said.

She stepped against him and touched her nose to the fabric covering his chest. "I like you just the way you are."

Clay was awed by her lack of hesitation, her eagerness for his touch. Knowing all he knew now, he hesitated for fear of stepping over an invisible boundary that would frighten her or remind her of the treatment she'd endured.

Her nimble fingers made quick work of his shirt, and it landed on the worn wood floor with a soft tick of buttons. She kissed his chest and his neck, and his blood pounded.

Sophie raised her face, and he kissed her reverently, as tenderly as he knew how.

She untied the ribbons that threaded through eyelet lace to hold her chemise together in front. The dainty garment gaped open, revealing pretty rose-tipped breasts. He was glad for the daylight.

"Beautiful," he managed, his throat dry with desire. Every breath he took held the scent of lilacs. He wanted to know the warmth and silkiness of her skin so badly his fingers tingled.

She glided her palms over his shoulders and neck, and still he didn't touch her. Despite her eagerness, she seemed so small suddenly, so fragile and vulnerable. Desire pounded everywhere.

He raised his knuckles to her delicate cheek in wonder, stroking as though she were made of spun glass.

Sophie let the chemise drop to the floor. Her shoulders seemed so small, her body so slim.

He swallowed hard. Kissed her gently.

She let her head fall back so he could press his lips along the column of her neck. She released a breathless sigh, and he wanted to take her right then and there, but held himself in check. The shame in her voice when she'd told him what had happened had made him want to erase her past with new experiences. The thought of that nameless, faceless man forcing a helpless young girl to submit made him sick at heart.

She had always seemed so strong and confident, so sure of herself. What she'd revealed today gave him a glimpse of a completely different side. He marveled at her power to overcome and thrive.

She was so beautiful, her features incredibly delicate and feminine. A knot formed in his chest at the image of someone mistreating her. Using her body. *Breaking her spirit.*

She raised a hand to his neck and pulled herself up into the kiss, which pressed her naked breasts against his chest. At the titillating contact he sucked in a breath.

Clay took his mouth from hers to keep his senses. He kissed the shape of her ear.

Sophie eased away, and he let her go. She took a step back, her lovely breasts rising and falling. He devoured her with his eyes.

Hers held dark concern. "Are you…do you feel disgust for me?"

It took his brain a minute to catch up with her words. "What?"

"Do you find me…repulsive now that you know my story?"

She was exquisite. "Hell no."

"You're holding back. It feels different."

"I—I…" He jammed his fingers into his hair and tried to find words.

"I'll understand," she told him. "If your perception of me has changed and you don't feel the same."

"Shut up a minute." He stood staring at her, his chest heaving with what he felt and what he wanted to say. "I don't wanna push myself on you. You should have…choices."

The sharp defensiveness in her expression dissolved. "I made a choice to come here. I made the choice to tell you about my past so you wouldn't feel cheated afterward."

"I'm not cheated, Sophie," he assured her. "I'm honored."

"So am I, and this is my choice. *You* are my choice." She gestured with both palms toward him. "I need something that's mine. Something I want." Her fingers curled into her palms.

Her voice came out a whispered plea. "Don't hold back. Don't cheat me."

Chapter Fourteen

He reached her in one stride, picking her up and falling onto his bed with her beneath, his arms solid on either side of her. She grasped his bicep, touched his face and dropped her gaze to his mouth.

In a kiss hotter than the Kansas summer, his tongue probed the succulent recesses of her mouth. Palms on his chest, she splayed her fingers wide, her nails scraping his skin, and he understood. Understood that she needed this experience for herself.

It was his privilege that she'd selected him. He kissed both corners of her lips, her chin, the column of her neck and the hollows in her collarbone. He began a sensory discovery, inhaling her soft feminine scent as he pressed his lips along her silken flesh all the way down to her belly and back up to the pebbled tip of one breast.

He took her into his mouth and she trembled.

"I have shivers through my whole body…" she said on a sigh.

He captured her mouth in a kiss once more, then slid the tip of his tongue to her other breast.

It occurred to Clay that he still wore his boots and trousers, so reluctant had he been to miss one second with this woman now in his bed. He drew to the edge where he perched to remove them.

As though she was equally as unwilling to miss a moment together, Sophie raised to her knees behind him and pressed herself against his back. The crush of her soft, damp breasts set him on fire. She kissed his neck, touched her tongue to his ear and a shudder coursed through him.

Clay turned and urged her onto her back, finding the ribbon that tied her drawers and tugging them down her legs. With one knee on the mattress he leaned over her and pressed his face to her soft belly and cupped her hips. She threaded her fingers into his hair. She was in his head now, filling his senses, pumping through his veins.

Divesting himself of his trousers required releasing her, but he kicked them to the floor and stretched his body out half over hers, his burning skin sliding against her soft contours.

She cupped his cheek and offered a smile of sincere enjoyment. He tucked a tendril of dark hair away from her temple. Catching his hand, she pressed her lips into his palm. "I've never felt like this," she told him. "I never knew how right it could be."

He'd never known he was so lonely until now. Until she filled up all the missing places inside him with her sweet smile and inflaming kisses. Until she'd trusted him with her dark, paralyzing secret, trusted him to know what to do to blot out that part of her past.

Breathless now, a burning need pulsed low and heavy in his body. She acknowledged his arousal by rubbing against him.

With his face buried against her throat, Clay spoke encouragement with soft senseless words, stroking her limbs and testing her readiness. Sophie clutched him to her with surprisingly fierce strength. He rose over her and kissed her, his chest tight with emotion.

"Say my real name," she whispered.

"Sophia. Beautiful Sophia."

She stifled a sob by catching her lower lip with her teeth while her eyes pleaded with him to continue.

He lowered his weight, eased himself inside her and shuddered with the sheer pleasure of being one with this woman. Perfection. Completion. He never wanted this moment to end.

If he was interpreting her eager movements and rapturous sighs, Sophie wasn't ready to be patient. Determined to be everything she needed, he gritted his teeth against the intense pleasure. "Patience, Sophie."

"May I kiss you?"

"What a thing to ask." Realizing then that a lover's kiss was far from her experience, he lowered his head.

She touched her tongue to his lower lip, parted her lips and met him with a kiss so intense and deep, his heart threatened to stop. "You're going to kill me, woman."

"Did I do something wrong?"

"You do everything so right I can't breathe."

"And you want me."

"I—want you. Sophia. Beautiful Sophia."

Her body grew taut beneath his. Perspiration made

their straining bodies slick. Sophie held her breath and closed her eyes and her body convulsed around him. Clay took his own fulfillment more leisurely, but afterward she didn't release him.

"Don't move," she said.

"I'm not in any hurry," he answered, resting his weight on his elbows and kissing her moist neck, then her swollen lips.

She pushed damp hair from his forehead, then let her arms go slack so he could move. "Let's cool off."

"Sorry I got you sweaty."

"Horses sweat," she informed him. "I'm glowing."

With a grin Clay found his shirt at the end of the bed, dried her glistening torso before wiping his face and chest. He stretched out beside her, and the breeze from the open window wafted across their cooling bodies.

After several minutes of silent communion she sat up, bringing her knees up in front of her and wrapping her arms around them. Her dark hair was a mass of damp tangles. He admired the line of her slim back, the curve of her hips and the curvaceous side of her breast. He drew his finger up the bumpy ridges of her spine, then splayed his palm against her back, his tanned hand dark against her white skin.

She turned to him, her expression undecipherable.

Sophie studied Clay's relaxed features, the defined outline of those lips that gave her such pleasure, the breadth of his shoulders and chest…and marveled at his restrained strength. How any woman could have rejected this man she couldn't understand.

"You and Susan," she asked. "Did you ever…?"

"No."

Of course not. His fiancée had been a respectable young lady, and gentleman that he was, he hadn't compromised her reputation. "Who then?"

He peered at her through slitted eyelids. "You wanna know?"

She nodded.

"Dance hall girls mostly. A widow lady west of here I visit now and then."

She hadn't expected to feel jealousy, but here it was in all its unpleasant glory. She recognized it as a feeling of resentment and possessiveness. Was this what love felt like? "No wonder they're willing…with you, I mean."

"What're you talkin' about?"

"I didn't know it could be…special."

"It's usually just ordinary," he told her. "Not like that."

"No?"

He moved his head slowly from side to side. "No. It's not."

Sophie couldn't resist stretching out along his side, her cheek against his chest. This man had done something no other had been able to. He'd made her feel things. Things intense enough to frighten her.

"I bought you somethin'." She felt the rumble of his deep voice against her cheek.

"You did?" She raised her head to look at him. "A gift?"

He nodded.

"Where is it?"

He untwined their legs so he could perch on the bed's edge and reach for his trousers. He pulled them on and caught a clean shirt from a drawer to toss to her. She shrugged into it and rolled the sleeves back.

Clay padded out of the room, and Sophie tried to imagine what kind of gift he'd buy for her. She'd pretend to like it no matter what it was. Candy? Ribbons? No, she *would* love it.

He returned with a small wooden box. Sophie saw the paper label on top. Whatever he'd bought her was small enough to fit in a cigar box.

The mattress dipped as he handed it to her, joining her again.

"It's heavy," she said. She studied his expression a moment. His face gave nothing away.

Sophie opened the lid.

Her gaze rested upon row after row of slim, perfectly rolled cigars. The tantalizing aroma reached her, and she blinked.

She met his eyes.

The corner of his mouth inched up. He produced a tin and flint from his pocket and extended them.

"What's this?" she asked.

"They're your favorite," he answered.

Something in her heart swelled to exquisite fullness. "How would you know that?"

He grinned. "I'm the law, Miss Hollis. I have my ways."

"But how did you…?"

"You carry a cigar to the park when you take a walk."

Sophie wrapped her mind around his acceptance of her eccentricity. The feeling in her chest was so intense it was almost painful. She adored his gift because it wasn't a bribe. Nor was it something he wanted her to have. She loved him, this man who wanted only to give to her. "You truly don't mind?"

"I'll try one with you. That is if you don't mind sharin'."

She grinned and plucked out two cigars. Clay lit them both and they propped pillows against the headboard and watched smoke rings curl into the air toward the pine ceiling. Sophie felt young and happy for the first time she could remember.

"Mrs. Winters would have a fit of apoplexy," she commented with a contented sigh.

"Over the cigars or over you bein' naked in my bed?"

Sophie coughed and he pulled her forward to pat her back.

"Both," she answered.

"It'll be our secret," he said with a grin.

Several minutes passed and Sophie enjoyed the quiet and the sense of well-being.

"Sophie," he said finally.

"Hmmm?"

"When you're deciding what you want, maybe you'd give a thought to marryin' me."

She stared at him.

"I'm not proposin' or anything. I wouldn't lay that burden on you. I'm just sayin' I'd be more than willin' if you wanted. That's all."

Sophie's head rang with those words. If she didn't have an even bigger secret hanging over her life, she would love nothing more than to marry Clay. To spend the rest of her life basking in the warmth of his goodness.

"You know I have a Harvey contract," she said.

He held up a hand. "Don't make any excuses," he told her. "Don't say more. Just store the idea up here."

He tapped her head with a gentle finger.

She'd choose him over life if she had the option.

Even if his acceptance of her was all based on a lie, Clay had become her heart's most compelling desire.

But she couldn't make a decision like that. She didn't have the right. Nor did she have the right to love him. There was still another shoe waiting to drop; there was still Garrett to deal with.

The day's pleasure evaporated into the sultry air as thoughts of the man who meant to control her by any means possible returned. Something had to be done about him. And about Amanda before Sophie could think of herself again. This day had been purely selfish. Purely a greedy taste of what life might have been like.

Her love for Clay was another one of her secrets now. All along Sophie had been thinking of herself. Now she had more to think about. Being Sophie Hollis wasn't about pretending anymore. It was about caring. She had to protect Clay from himself. If he learned, he would have to make a choice. His feelings for her weren't good for that purpose.

"I'd better get back," she said finally.

"Like to bathe? I'll fill the tub and wait outside."

"You wouldn't mind?"

"Be pleased to." He got up and left the room. Minutes later she heard the scrape of the metal tub as he set it on the floor in the kitchen.

She padded out to watch as he poked kindling into the stove.

"It doesn't need to be warm," she told him. "Cool will feel good."

He pumped several more buckets full and brought her soap and toweling. He took a step back.

Sophie sensed his intent to leave the room. Once again he was seeking her pleasure and comfort. "You don't have to go unless you have something you'd rather attend to," she told him.

He grinned with the cigar held between his teeth and remained.

She draped his shirt over the back of a chair. Clay's appreciative gaze swept over her, and he took a long stride forward to take her hand as she stepped into the water.

Sophie settled down into the cool water and leaned her head against the tall back. Puffing on her cigar, she blew smoke rings into the air. "You certainly know how to treat a lady, Marshal."

Clay sat backward on a kitchen chair to watch. "Wanna go riding next Sunday, too?"

It was late afternoon by the time Clay brought Sophie back to the dormitory. She ate supper in the employees' dining hall, thoughtful and subdued while the others chattered. She kept going over her poor selection of options. The most appealing was to buy a gun and shoot Garrett in his black heart. Tempting. But she didn't have it in her. She was a lot of bad things, but a murderer wasn't one of them.

She could march down to the jail and tell Clay the truth right then and there, let him deal with Garrett and put himself in the position of arresting her alongside him. Not tempting.

She had nothing to hold over Garrett's head, nothing to scare him off. He held all the cards.

She could tell Amanda the truth and pray she'd listen and not turn her in.

She could pack her things and run. She wouldn't get far, but she could spare Amanda, because Garrett would follow. Clay wouldn't understand, though. She'd be another woman who didn't want him enough to stay, enough to choose him.

If her options were cards, she'd shuffle them and see which one came out on top. She wasn't playing a game of chance, however. More than her own life was at stake.

She couldn't forget that Garrett had threatened Clay's life. Now that she'd sealed a relationship with the marshal, Garrett would have all the more reason to want him out of the picture.

The most palatable of all the options was telling Amanda. As evening arrived and the girls settled into their various activities in the sewing and courting rooms, Sophie thought the idea through.

Finally deciding, Sophie called Amanda aside. "I need to talk to you."

Amanda followed her to their room. "You look so serious, Sophie. What is it?"

"I have to warn you about something, so there are things I need to tell you."

"Warn me? What's this about?"

"It's about Mr. Morgan."

Amanda bristled. "Are you going to lecture me again?"

Sophie took her arm. "I knew him before I came to Newton. I knew him for several years actually. We were together."

Amanda just stared at her in stunned disbelief. "What are you saying?"

"I told you that you don't know what kind of man he is, because I do. I know he's not who he seems. This is all an act. He wants to manipulate me, so he's using you to get to me."

Tears welled up in Amanda's eyes. "You are being cruel! Why don't you want me to be happy? You have all the admirers you need! Why are you trying to spoil this for me?"

"I'm not. Please believe me."

"You're saying Mr. Morgan doesn't care about me? That he really wants *you?*"

"Not in a good way," Sophie said. "To control. That's the kind of person he is. You have to listen."

"I can't believe this. I can't believe you're so selfish and—and—jealous that you'd stoop to something like this! It's hurtful, Sophie. Plain hurtful. And mean."

"I know how it seems," Sophie said, her throat tight with regret. "I'm so sorry. You got caught in the middle through no fault of your own. You're in this position because I came here and let down my guard enough to make friends. I know your feelings are hurt, but I can't let this go on. I can't let him use you. It would only be worse."

"You think he's using me because he loves you?"

"No. He only wants to hurt me," she answered. "To get what he wants."

"I don't even know who you are anymore." Amanda's voice quivered.

Sophie barely knew herself. Her life was a mess, and she was a big fraud. She'd put the people she cared for in danger. "Can you trust me when I say I know he's not good for you?"

"We can't be friends anymore." Amanda's lips pursed tight as though she was holding back more.

"I am your friend," Sophie pleaded. "Please, listen."

"I'm not listening. Ever again." Amanda turned and fled from their room.

Sophie bit back the sting of tears and collected her wits.

There was still one more alternative. One option she hadn't shuffled with the deck of ideas.

She could buckle to Garrett's manipulation.

Chapter Fifteen

Sophie studied her likeness in the mirror. It was her or Amanda now. And she wouldn't let it be Amanda. She dressed her hair and changed into her walking boots. Minutes later, she'd run down the back stairs and was headed for the Strong, the only other hotel as nice as the Arcade. It being a Sunday night, he probably hadn't gone to a gaming hall. All the wealthy men were home with their families.

She found him in the hotel dining room. Garrett looked up from his newspaper. He set a teacup in its saucer.

That self-important smile spread across his face. "Well, well, well. To what do I owe the pleasure of this unexpected visit?"

A waiter immediately swooped in to pull out a chair for Sophie. He brought her a rolled napkin, silverware and a water glass. "I'll come back for your order, miss."

"I'm not eating, thank you."

"What do you want?" she asked, as soon as the

waiter was out of earshot. "What will put a stop to this and make you go away?"

"You're not thinking clearly if you think you can get rid of me."

"What do you want from me? Besides the money, which I've told you is gone."

"I want you to recognize the error of your ways, my dear, and make your indiscretions up to me."

"How?"

He leaned back and laced his fingers on the tabletop. "I'll let you work it off. Once the entire amount has been amassed you can be free."

"Steal that much money?"

"Come now. Steal is such an insulting word. We relieve greedy people of the excess they're perfectly willing to hand over." He picked up his cup.

She couldn't do what he was demanding in Clay's town, under his nose. She couldn't not do it or she would endanger the man she loved. "Pay it all back?"

He took a leisurely sip. "Surely you don't think I'd settle for only a portion. Not after you took it *all?*"

"The money we took was always all yours," she told him. "I never got a share. I never chose how you spent it."

"I gave you everything you ever needed," he argued. "The finest clothing and jewelry."

"That *you* selected and *made* me wear. I never had what I needed or wanted. What I needed was freedom."

Anger flickered across his narrow features. "Does your lawman give you freedom? Tell me, did he set you free today?"

Shocked, Sophie asked, "What do you know about him?"

"I know everything about you. You *belong* to me, remember?"

"Leave him out of this. This is between you and me."

"You leave him out of it, Gabriella. For both your sakes. Take my instruction and don't stand too close. Word is out that I will pay well for the bullet that pierces his heart."

Sophie's heart chugged with horror at the information. The realization sunk in at last. If she was no longer of use to Garrett, she became a liability. She knew too much. He wouldn't think twice about killing her. To him she was and always would be an acquisition. "What do you want?"

"I'm working on a cattleman. You will be the clincher."

Sophie knew the routine. She disguised herself and lured the cattleman to a hotel room. Garrett showed up once they were both naked and took the man for all he was worth not to tell his wife and expose him to other public humiliation. The same schemes she'd run away from and hoped were in her past. Now he wanted her right back where she had been before. "And then what? Then you'll leave?"

"I'm being generous here. I have an investment in you. A big investment. I could always take it further. I could turn you into the highest priced whore this country's ever known."

Her stomach lurched at his pronouncement, at the superior way he spoke as though he still controlled her every move.

"But I haven't done that yet, have I?" His voice was as syrupy sweet as though he was proclaiming love.

"You must appreciate my generosity. If you know what's good for you, you will cooperate. A couple of takes like this one and I'll be set to move on."

Sophie knew better. She would never work enough off to get out of his clutches. He always wanted more, more, more. This would be no different. The degrading feeling that accompanied all those years settled on her shoulders like a weight.

However…going along would buy her time. Time to get Amanda away from him. Time to tip off Clay.

"And Amanda. If I do this, you'll leave her alone?"

"As long as you're my girl, I won't need her, now will I?"

Sophie summoned all her fortitude, accepted the weight of what she had to do and called upon her inner strength. "Very well then."

Garrett raised his cup with a self-satisfied smile. "I'll send word when and where to find him. I'll make sure he's had the required drinks. The rest is up to you. You know the signal. Turn the light off and on. Open the window."

She knew. She'd done it more times than she could count. For Garrett the beauty of all this was in the perfection of the con. He appreciated the art of a perfect scheme. She'd always been exceptional. She stood. "Don't hurt the marshal."

"His fate is entirely up to you now, my love."

Sophie turned and hurried away.

Amanda didn't speak to her that night, and Sophie couldn't blame her. She would most likely feel the same way in her place. She lay awake long after the sound of her roommate's soft breathing told her she was asleep.

Guilt had been a part of her for so long, she didn't know what a night felt like without it. Telling Clay partial truths had relieved her conscience about taking what she wanted with him. She'd fooled herself into believing she wanted to change and that she could actually take the steps to do so. But she was still a coward. Still being controlled by her own fears.

When was she truly going to stop playing a role and actually be the honest normal person she wanted to be? Neither Amanda or Clay knew how dangerous Tek Garrett was. Her life wasn't about pretending or trying anymore. The only true changes that had taken place were in her heart, and they were disturbing changes. Her life had become more about caring than about hiding or protecting herself.

She was sick and tired of lies. Sick and tired of running and of being afraid. It was time to face her fear head on and make the only choice that really counted. She was ready to make the ultimate decision and risk her freedom.

She was ready to tell the truth.

But she needed a plan. Clay would want to think the best of her if she blurted out the whole story right now. He would be tempted to reason and excuse, and she wouldn't put him in that position. He had no evidence that she or Garrett had done anything wrong. She had to provide that first.

Sophie's head reeled. Giving herself up was the only way to expose Garrett. This was her chance to do that, and she had to do everything right. As much as it tortured her to think of it, convincing others of the truth would be easier if she cut some of the bonds she'd formed. It would be easier for them all the way around once she was arrested and sent to jail.

There was a measure of irony in all this. She was planning how to make the *truth* convincing! Mind made up and her emotional guards reconstructed, she closed her eyes and willed herself to sleep.

As much as she had taken pride in her position at the Arcade, as fond as she was of Amanda and the other girls, by far the biggest loss of all was going to be Clay. She'd been selfish in letting that bond develop. In letting herself care. In letting him care. He didn't deserve what she'd done. Or what she was going to do. He deserved to love a good woman.

The next morning Sophie tugged a wrinkled apron from her laundry bag and pulled it on over her uniform. She hauled her valise from under the bed and used kohl around her eyes, rouge on her cheeks and lips and powdered her nose.

Amanda stared at her, but she didn't say a word. She hesitantly followed Sophie down the stairs. Olivia and Goldie noticed Sophie and followed at a safe distance.

Sophie checked the blackboard for morning duties. Her name was listed under silver polishing yet again. She erased it and rewrote her name on the list of girls waiting tables, then took a place on the floor.

It only took Mrs. Winters seven minutes to spot her and double check the board. She huffed into the dining hall, her cheeks bright pink. "Miss Hollis! What is the meaning of this?" She stopped in her tracks. "Is that— is that—what *is* that on your face? I want to see you in Mr. Webb's office right now."

Sophie followed.

Mrs. Winters hammered the door with a fist, then raked her agitated glare over Sophie's apron and back to the offending color on her face.

"Come in."

The woman gestured for Sophie to lead the way into the room. "Three deliberate offenses right before our eyes," she sputtered. "And certainly no accident this time. Just look at the impudent girl."

Mr. Webb rose from his chair and studied Sophie's appearance.

"And she changed her assignment on the duty board!"

"Do you have anything to say for yourself, Miss Hollis?" the manager asked in bewilderment.

"I've polished silver every Monday for the past month. Mrs. Winters gives me that assignment purely to irritate me, I'm convinced."

"Mrs. Winters may assign any duties she chooses. It's a privilege to work in a Harvey House."

"It's a drudge," she replied. "We're treated like schoolchildren. What's the harm in tasteful cosmetic enhancement?"

"You see, it *is* deliberate," Mrs. Winters confirmed. "She had one last chance."

"You'd been doing so well," Mr. Webb said, disappointment clearly audible in his tone. "I don't understand this change that's come over you. Your appearance and conduct are unacceptable, as you well know."

Sophie turned her concentration to a single daisy in a glass of water on his desk and waited.

Her skin prickled beneath her uniform.

"Then you are dismissed, Miss Hollis. You are no longer a Harvey Girl. You may pack your belongings and leave without pay."

"What about my contract?"

"You've broken the terms of your contract. You are fined your most recent earnings. You may spend one more night. After that you will not be allowed in the dormitory."

"I won't need another night. I'll be gone today."

"Turn in your uniforms and aprons," Mrs. Winters ordered.

Sophie untied her apron and whisked it over her head with a flourish before tossing it toward a startled and red-faced Mrs. Winters. "With pleasure."

She turned and swept from the room, her heart hammering.

That had been easy. Strange how her livelihood had been so fragile that it had dissolved in a matter of minutes. Working here had never been about the position or the esteem. It had been about integrity, about earning her own way and gaining respect. She was putting her true integrity to the test now.

Several girls were staring as she exited the hallway and made her way through the dining hall. She could have taken the back route through the kitchen, but this was better. This way they'd all know.

Emma hurried to walk beside her. "Sophie, what happened?"

"They let me go," she said.

With a stricken expression, Emma touched her arm. "What will you do?"

"I'll be fine. I know how to take care of myself."

"Will we see you?" Rosie asked, joining them. "Or will you have to go back home now?"

"I lied about that," Sophie told them. "I don't really have any family in Pennsylvania. I just made it up to get this job."

She felt Amanda's gaze from the other side of the room. There were no customers at this hour, and their voices carried. She glanced and found her roommate looking.

Amanda looked away.

"You mean—well, where is your family, then?" Olivia asked.

"I don't have one." She turned to Rosie. "If you see me it won't be like you're thinking. I'll be staying in Newton a while longer, but I won't be going to any dances." She was letting them all down. They'd befriended her and trusted her. They'd even looked up to her for advice. What a fake she was.

Amanda didn't follow her upstairs, and Sophie hadn't expected her to. She went straight to her room and packed everything she owned into two satchels and a trunk Jimmy brought up from storage. She tipped him, and paused. "Jimmy."

"Miss?"

"Did you and Marshal Connor have a talk recently?"

"Haven't seen the marshal 'cept in passin'."

"You didn't tell him about our arrangement?"

"My errands for you? No, miss. Gave you my word I wouldn't tell no one."

"Thank you, Jimmy. Can you get a wagon? I'd like you to move my things to a hotel this afternoon. I'm going to make the preparations right now."

"Sure. You're leavin' the Arcade?"

She nodded. "I've been dismissed."

"Sorry to hear that. Don't sound quite right."

"Oh, it's right. And I'll be fine."

He nodded and ducked from her room. He was only allowed on the floor under special circumstances, and his first task was finished.

Sophie put on her most comfortable shoes, her porcelain-blue dress with embroidered trim, then settled her straw hat on her head and left the Arcade.

The city directory at the post office listed fourteen hotels, and she knew some of those to be boardinghouses. She wrote the addresses on a piece of paper and tucked it into her reticule. All of the establishments were on Fifth, Sixth or Main Street, centrally located near the heart of town.

She selected three to look at, toured the rooms and facilities and decided on the Enterprise Hotel on North Main. She had enough money to pay for her room and anything else she might need for at least a month or more. If what she had planned all fell into place, she wouldn't make it near that long.

After returning to give Jimmy directions, she went back to her new room to wait for him. Within the hour he arrived and delivered her belongings. She paid him generously and he wished her well.

Sophie unpacked her clothing, hung it in the armoire and filled the bureau drawers. She had accumulated a lot of clothing during her time in Newton. She would miss access to the sewing machines. As if making new dresses mattered.

What was she thinking? She would miss a lot of

things, like her own clothing and her freedom. She'd miss a lot of people, too.

Her throat constricted with regret and grief.

Taking the wooden box Clay had given her from a bag, she placed it right out in the open on her bureau. She ran her hand over the paper label and the wood, opened the lid and let the pungent tobacco aroma drift to her.

As bad as things were, she reminded herself how liberating it was to shake off more shackles and have her own room without constricting rules. She could smoke all the cigars she wanted right here. She could likely sit in the dining room with a cigar if she didn't mind some raised eyebrows.

A small writing desk was positioned beside the window. She took paper and pen and perched there to list the people she would contact and their cities of residence. On another page she wrote out what she wanted each missive she sent to say, and then she put on her hat and hurried to the Western Union Telegraph Company beside the train depot.

The long-necked angular man who read her letter and the list of recipients tipped his head back to squint at her through the spectacles on the end of his nose. "One dollar each, fifteen cents extra for New York."

"I suppose one would send a letter if she had more time," she replied.

He continued to squint.

She plucked fifteen silver dollars from her reticule and made a neat stack on the dusty counter. Beside it she placed fifteen cents and challenged the man with a raised brow.

"Whatever you say, lady." He took the coins and her papers and folded himself onto a creaky chair behind the counter. Sophie listened to the frantic clicking as he sent the messages, one after the other.

She had remembered several names of people she had helped Garrett swindle. Her messages asked for descriptions of the con artists. She was sending the law in Denver a request for information about the couple wanted for killing the man in the gaming hall. She also asked them to send wanted posters on the next train, and to deliver the package directly to City Marshal Clay Connor.

This was it. A chance to make her most important choice. A choice to do the right thing. Now all she had to do was wait. And pray Garrett didn't send for her before she had the proof she needed.

Clay stopped by the Arcade twice without seeing Sophie. He'd normally eaten at the lunch counter, until he'd taken an interest in her and changed his routine to sit in the dining hall. It was rare that he didn't glimpse her during the noon hour. On Wednesday he deliberately came by midafternoon between trains.

"Have you seen Sophie?" he asked Emma Spearman.

An odd look came over her face and she glanced behind him, then to the side. "No. Um. I haven't."

Clay turned his gaze toward another waitress. "Maybe someone else knows where she is."

"She's not here."

He turned at Amanda Pettyjohn's voice. "Day off during the week?"

"She was dismissed on Monday morning."

And she hadn't contacted him? Concern rolled over him. She must be crushed. This job meant so much to her. "What happened?"

"She took a high and mighty attitude with the managers," the girl said, shifting a stack of tablecloths in her arms. "I don't know who she is anymore."

"What do you mean?"

Amanda gestured for him to follow her out of earshot. "She told me she knew Mr. Morgan before she came here. That he followed her. We argued. I don't understand why she said that. She was hoping to scare me away from him. She has you—she doesn't need any more beaus."

Clay digested that odd piece of information and shook his head without a reply.

"Then when she was leaving, she told us she never really had a family in Pennsylvania. That she made it all up to get this job."

She'd told him the same thing. Clay's head swam with all the conflicting stories. "Where is she now?"

"I have no idea. She said she'd be in Newton for a while."

Clay walked away from the Arcade wondering what to believe. Anger blotted out the confusion. He mounted his horse and started checking hotels.

He found her registered at the Enterprise, the sixth place he checked. He rapped his knuckles against the smooth cherrywood door and waited with a knot in his chest.

Chapter Sixteen

"Who is it?" Her voice on the other side of the wood barrier.

"Me."

A key turned in the lock and the door opened. The sight of her took his breath away. She wore a dark blue skirt. Her white ruffled blouse was sprigged with tiny blue flowers. She'd fashioned her hair in a loose upsweep he'd never seen her wear before, soft and flattering to her delicate features.

"Clay," she said simply.

She backed up to allow him room to enter, closing the door behind him.

He looked around, noticing womanish fripperies. The hinged wooden box on the bureau. The room held the scent of a recently smoked cigar. He looked at her. "What happened?"

"I was dismissed."

"For what?"

"An accumulation of things as you might guess. I've

been a pain in Mrs. Winters's backside since I first took the position." She didn't sound the least bit disturbed over losing her livelihood. "It's for the best."

"I could talk to Harrison. Straighten things out."

"No. I don't want that. I'm going to do just fine."

He wanted to touch her. The memory of their day together was fresh and vivid on his heart. She'd been so open.

She was still so achingly beautiful, but she seemed so different. There was a harder edge to her as though she'd closed up, pulled away. The transformation didn't sit well with him. "Amanda told me what you said to her."

Sophie met his gaze without flinching. "Which part?"

"That you knew Monte Morgan before comin' to Newton. That he followed you here. That true?"

She look him square in the eye. "I'm never going to lie to you again."

"Is it true?"

"Yes, it is."

"What—?" The things she'd revealed to him finally whirled into place. His blood thrummed in his veins. "My God. He's the *one*. He's the man who bought you and forced himself on you."

She moved in front of him in an instant, as though she feared he'd run from the room.

Images of the man's face and long-fingered hands made Clay sick. The man who'd mistreated Sophie had a name and a face now. "He's mine."

"No!" She grabbed his forearms and held on in a fierce grip. "Not like this. Not in a confrontation. Not in public. Not where he has a chance to get away if he suspects you know. Not while he still has the opportunity to kill you or me or Amanda."

"I'm not lettin' him get away with it."

"But you couldn't prove it. He'd lie. I know him. He'd make me out to be a whore. He would lay the blame on *me,* claim he rescued me, treated me like a daughter. He'd say I got us chased out of every town. People will believe him because he's convincing. Trust me, Clay. Not like this."

Trust her?

"There's more to this story. More to pin on him than his mistreatment of a young girl. I can prove it if you'll let me. We can see him hang for murder."

She had his full attention now. "Murder?"

"Everything I told you the other day is the truth. I will never lie to you again, I swear to that. But I still didn't tell you everything. There's more. A whole lot more. It's ugly, and it's going to implicate me right along with him."

"*Damn,* woman!" He took off his hat and threw it across the room.

"I'm so sorry, Clay. Sorry you had to be involved. Sorry Amanda got caught in the middle. I can make it right if you give me a chance."

Clay took several steps back and forth in the confines of the room. The window was open to the sun and the breeze, the curtain billowing against the sill. How could things look so normal when nothing was as it seemed? How could a woman be so beautiful and have such dark secrets?

His gut instinct had been to tear out of here and kill

Morgan with his bare hands. That would have been a critical mistake, and Sophie had been right to block him. He needed all the facts, and apparently Morgan wasn't going anywhere any time soon.

Without another word, he pulled out the spindly chair from the writing desk and perched on the seat.

Sophie clenched her hands together and paced at the end of the bed. "I told you before how he paid for my education. Everything always had to be the best. The best tutors, the best seamstresses, the finest hotels, the most extravagant meals. In his mind it's all owed him.

"His family lost their land and home during the war. He thinks his birthright was stolen from him. Everyone owes him for that. Especially me. I'm an investment."

Clay couldn't speak, and he wondered how she could. How she could talk of this without tearing her hair or clothing or railing against the unfairness of life. She was as calm and in control as she always seemed.

"When he felt I was ready, he began tutoring me in his craft. I was rewarded for succeeding and punished for failure. I learned quickly."

Clay didn't ask what that craft was, but the question was a giant in the room. He didn't have to wait.

"He's a con man. A good one. High class, nothing petty. I was coached to use people's greed against them. And no doubt about it, people *are* greedy and selfish. He was right about that. Those were the only people I interacted with. It became a game to create a cunning plan and value the beauty of it. Executing the scheme was treated as an art."

"I've seen his kind," Clay told her. "Maybe not con men as high class, but I know his type."

"I was a prisoner, Clay. I was a tool he bought to help him trick people. He trained me to be an extension of him. The more time that passed and the more cons we accomplished, the clearer it became to me. I was a possession. He used me to gain people's confidence so he could take their money.

"When I was young, he had a favorite scheme. I'd leave a violin with a business owner, saying I had an errand where I couldn't take it and tell him that I'd be back that afternoon. Garrett would then go into that establishment, see the violin and tell the owner it was valuable. Garrett offered him a huge amount of money. The man couldn't sell it to him, so Garrett would promise to come back in case I didn't return for it. When I did return the store owner would offer to buy the instrument from me for about half the supposed value. I'd sell him a worthless violin for two or three thousand dollars and we'd be on our way."

Clay shook his head. "Takin' advantage of the man's greed?"

"It's awful, I know. Those people had families at home. Sometimes I couldn't sleep at night thinking of the money we'd taken from their wives and children."

She stopped and seemed to study the grain of the polished wood floor. "I told you I tried to get away once."

"And he found you."

"Things were worse after that, and I was afraid to risk another change. The schemes involved just enough seduction to lure the men into the web. He held the power to make my life even more miserable. But I planned. And I waited. All I needed was the perfect opportunity. He never knew what I was thinking because

I'm—I *was* a master at deception. I was the perfect accomplice, exactly the person he'd trained me to be. A puppet."

Clay remembered her words. *I submitted. I survived.* He didn't want to believe what she was telling him, but why would she make up a story that implicated herself?

"We're wanted in at least six states," she told him. "I'm a fugitive."

He jerked his attention to her face. Her lovely serene face. She said it as though she was telling him the time of day. He'd never seen her shed a tear now that he thought of it. Not even when she'd told him he wouldn't be the first.

A flash of regret crossed her features just then however, and he prepared himself for the next admission. With a swish of silken petticoats she moved to the bureau and took out a slim leather case. She opened it to reveal a set of peculiar tools. "I picked the lock on your jail and stole the wanted papers with our pictures. I knew that DeWeise fellow was sleeping in the rear because I heard him snoring."

Clay got to his feet slowly. "Did you...set the fire?"

"No! I swear I didn't. I had those papers in my pocket and was already to the next block when I heard a sound and turned to discover the flames. I'd seen your dog. I knew DeWeise was in there, too. No one was coming, so I ran back and let the man out. The cell keys were right on top of the stack of papers. I grabbed them, unlocked it, and he took off. I had to find the dog and drag him out."

Clay rubbed his chin in thought. "The hell."

"I couldn't risk you or one of the others seeing those

papers, so I broke in and took them. But I swear the fire was not my doing."

She went back to the bureau, replaced the tool set and withdrew a stack of small papers. He recognized them as Western Union missives.

"These will prove what I've been telling you. They're telegrams from places where we're wanted. The descriptions differ somewhat because of the disguises, but I can show you those, too."

She knelt in front of a trunk set against one wall and opened the lid. He didn't know whether to read the telegrams or look at the pile of wigs and makeup and padded clothing she produced. His head was a jumble of unwanted information.

Finally he thumbed through the telegrams. They all had one thing in common, the approximate age and heights of two people, a man and woman who were wanted for various con schemes. Hair color, dress, mustaches, beauty marks were all obviously changeable.

There were recurring names mentioned as well. Most often Joseph Richardson and Gabriella Dumont. "You called him Garrett. His name's Joseph Richardson?"

"No more than mine is Gabriella Dumont. It's what he named me. It's what he calls me. We used other names, too. Plenty of them." She turned from the pile of costumes and got to her feet. "His name is Tek Garrett. Today's train is delivering a set of wanted posters to you at the jail. You'll find drawings that will identify us."

Not knowing what he was hoping to see, he studied her expression.

"Both of us."

He let that soak in.

"He can't suspect that I've told you—that you know. He's hired a gunman." She touched her lip, then brought her hand down to twine with the other in an uncharacteristic move. "To kill you," she finished.

For the first time a crack in her composure opened, and he sensed her fear. He supposed the thought of a hired gun terrified her, but Clay'd had a gun aimed at his heart before, and the news didn't shake him.

"He's contacted me and used Amanda in the threat. He believes I'm going along with his plan to pay back the money I took from him."

Clay sat back down. "Had a feelin' there was more."

"I told you I was waiting for an opportunity. It came one night in Denver. We were setting up some wealthy cattlemen for a scam. They'd been playing cards nights on end."

"Garrett does card game swindles?"

"Nothing that small. Playing cards with the marks is his way to get into their good graces. He puts on a display of having plenty of cash and works at just breaking even.

"This night we'd gone to a hotel dining room for a late supper. I was there to soften up the mark. One of the men kept irritating Garrett. He'd been an irritant in the plan ever since we'd been working the scheme. This night Garrett lost his temper and went a little crazy. He shot the man straight in the chest—killed him outright.

"The whole place broke out in confusion. Someone grabbed for Garrett, and I saw my chance. I snatched the satchel with the money and ran.

"He must have escaped shortly behind me, because

he wasn't caught. It was too risky for him to come looking for me though. I disguised myself as a young miner
and caught a ride out of town."

"You're wanted for the same shooting?"

She nodded.

"You'll have a trial. You'll get to tell your story."

"Who would believe me, Clay?"

He rested his elbows on his knees and held his head
in his hands to stare at the floor. He didn't even know
if he believed her anymore. She'd told so many lies.
How much had she played him already? For what gain?

"I'm not denying my part. And I did pay back some
of the money. I used nearly all that I took that night to
return to people we'd swindled. Family men mostly. I
was trying to clear my conscience. They didn't deserve
to lose what was theirs. I didn't deserve to have it.

"That's why he's so mad now. I don't have the
money. He said if I didn't work it off he'd hurt you…or
Amanda. I played along. He has a plan and he'll send
word when I'm to do my part."

She seemed so detached from what she was saying,
as though there wasn't anything of importance at stake.
He knew different. "What's his plan?"

"It's a cattleman he's had in his sights. He knows exactly how much the man is worth, where his cash is, his
weaknesses, and then he sends me in as the setup."

"What's your part?"

"I'll tell you, but I want you to go along with it,
Clay."

"Why?"

"I want to catch Garrett at it. I want him to know I
set him up. I want to see his face and know I had the

last word." She moved forward, almost reached for him, then drew her hands back. "I know you don't owe me anything. Not after the way I lied to you and pretended to be someone I'm not. You probably don't think you can trust me, but I'm not trying to get out of anything, I swear to you.

"I'll pay my time just like I deserve. You can watch me so that I don't try to leave. You can assign your deputies to watch me. I'm going to play along just like I'm his pawn again. As soon as I hear from him I'll get word to you. And when Garrett comes to exact his blackmail, you'll catch him red-handed.

"If I'm going to sit in a jail cell for years, I want to know that he had to face the fact that he didn't own me after all."

Finally a flicker of emotion crossed her features. Enough for him to know how important this was, enough to sense her desperation. Clay couldn't think about her locked in a jail cell. But even though her position in all this wasn't her fault, he was angry. Why his town? Why him?

"If I *was* to go along with this…how does it work?"

"I keep the gentleman company, skillfully reel him in."

Clay didn't like the idea at all. "Seduce him?"

"I invite him to my hotel room. Leave the door unlocked."

Not one damned bit.

"I get naked—"

"The hell you will."

"Okay, I'm *supposed* to get naked, and then I signal Garrett by turning the light off and on, then opening the window. Garrett barges in with a witness. The mark has to hide his indiscretion from his wife and family, so he pays through the nose. We take the cash and disappear."

Clay scratched his chin. "I suppose I could be right here waiting for him."

"Yes."

"Have a couple o' deputies in the next room."

"Yes."

"You would have all your clothes on."

"Yes."

It wasn't a bad plan at all. But he stared at her, feeling like he'd never even met her before. "This is crazy. Are you using me, too? Is this what Sunday was all about? Softening me up to help you?"

Her expression couldn't have shown more shock if he'd grabbed her by the neck and squeezed. She placed a hand on her breast as though it was caving in.

Without another word he crossed the room, picked up his hat and left.

Chapter Seventeen

Clay stabled his horse and strode the block and a half to the jail. Across the street the bricklayers had finished and hammers rang as carpenters worked on the roof.

It was perfectly believable that Sophie had been there the night of the fire. The blaze could have started in any number of ways. A spark from the stove, a cigarette tossed by a careless passerby. He'd even considered the possibility that DeWeise had a partner or friend who'd lit it as a distraction. That would have been a pretty risky thing to do. Stupid, considering DeWeise would have cooked in there if Sophie hadn't let him out.

It made more sense that someone had picked the lock to get in earlier, then turned around to free the man from a horrible death. Why would she lie about that?

Why not? Apparently she'd been lying about a lot of things for a good many years, and she'd lied through her teeth since she'd met him.

When he really applied his mind to the facts about

Sophie, they all came together to form a kind of warped logic, however. If she had come to Newton to start over, she would have been forced to make up a suitable background and create enough references to get her by. Then one lie led to another until she'd been buried under a mountain of them.

It was perfectly conceivable that she'd be ashamed of what had happened to her, of what Garrett had turned her into. The way she'd told him, the look on her face testified to her humiliation. If Clay had let himself believe all of it at once, he couldn't have let Garrett draw another breath. Clay might be a lawman but he was flesh and blood, human, fallible. Mad as hell.

She'd been right to stop him from acting on his gut reaction. Without proof of the man's identity or of his crimes Clay could have killed him and been arrested himself. He had to take a step back, as impossible as that seemed, and do his job. He couldn't shake the nagging doubt that this might be another of her well-substantiated lies.

After entering the stifling building, he left the door standing wide open. There was a large envelope lying on his desk. He read his name and ripped it open to unfold a stack of posters.

He studied ink drawings which had been duplicated on a printing press. The names were the same as those he'd read on the telegrams. Clay pulled those from his pocket and compared.

The poster from Denver was a drawing depicting a bald man with a mustache. When Clay covered the top of the man's head with another paper, the eyes were Monte Morgan's. Sophie's claim hadn't really surprised him. He'd had a gut reaction to the man the first time he'd seen him. He just wished he'd been more convinced before he'd seen this proof.

Gabriella Dumont was another matter. He'd never suspected Sophie was anything other than who she claimed to be. Yes, there had been little things that he'd excused or overlooked now that he thought of it, but swallowing all of this at once was difficult. The artist had drawn the young woman as a beauty. The dark eyes were difficult to conceal, but her hair was different. Clay laid the pictures out on the floor and took a couple steps back to glance at them from another perspective.

Recognition was unmistakable. Without a doubt Gabriella Dumont was Sophie Hollis. Fugitive from the law.

Confidence shark.

Accomplice to murder.

Was he once again falling for a story? Had she been a willing partner? Her lack of emotion when she shared those things that she'd supposedly endured made her seem cold or insincere…or what? Definitely detached. Was that how she survived? How she kept her heart and her head from being torn apart? How did he know for sure she hadn't been a willing partner in those crimes? She could be playing a part in a long line of cons. But to what purpose?

If she'd wanted to convince Clay of a lie, she was an accomplished actress. She could have feigned a display of emotion to draw his pity. But she hadn't. She hadn't asked for or expected any sympathy.

But he credited himself with being a good judge of

character, and he'd never had the least suspicion she wasn't who she claimed. She'd matter-of-factly wanted to tell him those things—first so he wouldn't be shocked or disappointed in her lack of innocence, and later because she thought she needed to protect him and Amanda.

Amanda did need protection, that was for sure. Clay could take care of himself.

The proof was right in front of him; he had to believe this final story. But what was he going to do about it? Arrest them both and let them be taken back to Colorado for trial? He wouldn't have any control over the situation, and she could be sentenced and…hung. He'd seen men hung, and it was a disturbing practice. His imagination wanted to soar and picture Sophie with a noose lowering around her neck, but he banished those dark thoughts from his head.

Sophie had revealed Garrett for what he was. She'd given Clay everything he needed to set up the man. Catching him red-handed in one of his schemes would be rewarding. If Clay wanted to do that, how much more must Sophie want to see it happen?

Judging by the dates on some of those papers, she'd been a child when Garrett had gotten her in his clutches. Would a judge and jury see that she'd been too young and too afraid, that she'd feared for her life if she hadn't gone along?

He would check into her story of making restitution in several of those cases. That would go a long way to show her good intent.

Clay hadn't wanted to believe her involvement because he'd fallen for her. He couldn't deny her confession and this proof, but he couldn't arrest Garrett without arresting her, too. He imagined putting her in a cell himself, and his gut clenched.

He couldn't let either of them go free, but neither could he risk the chance that she might fall into Garrett's clutches again. She'd have no choice but to go back to what she'd been before.

He was being ripped in two different directions. His thoughts had jumped around so much he didn't know what was logic anymore. Guilty and playing him? Innocent and needing him? Neither. Both. It all came down to the fact that he *wanted* to believe her. He had to.

She had a crazy plan. A plan to catch Garrett redhanded. If Clay caught him in a crime right here in his town, he'd have more authority to influence Sophie's fate before the law.

And Sophie could prove herself by helping trap the man. Maybe her assistance would keep her from being tried and convicted in Colorado.

Clay picked up the posters, buried them along with the telegrams in his desk drawer and headed back out.

What choice did he have really? He loved her. He would never look at the world or meet a day without wanting to share it with Sophie. He would go along with her plan. Now he had telegrams of his own to send.

Sophie was going to try the same tactic with Amanda that she'd used with Clay. Proof. She feared the girl would refuse to speak with her, but she sent a note with a young boy and waited at a table inside the front window of Almira Wheeler's cozy pastry shop where tea was served of an evening.

She remembered the schedule well enough to know Amanda would be finished with her duties for the day. At six the blonde stepped through the doorway and glanced around.

Sophie waved to her, and, without a smile, Amanda joined her at a table.

"Thank you for coming. I didn't know if you would."

Amanda didn't say anything. She looked uncomfortable being there and didn't meet Sophie's eyes.

"I guess you were just curious about what I wanted."

Amanda's gaze finally rose, and Sophie recognized hurt and betrayal. "I'm hoping you want to apologize."

Sophie took a breath. "All I ask is that you listen." She took posters from her reticule and flattened them out on the tabletop. "I know you don't want to believe me. I understand. Garrett is convincing and can be as charming and attentive as he needs to be. But this is him."

She pointed to the wanted papers she'd received that day. "And this is me."

Amanda looked from the drawings to Sophie's face with disbelief.

"I'm not going to ask you to forgive me or beg you to understand and be my friend. I'm pleading with you to spare yourself any further danger."

She gave Amanda a brief explanation of how she'd come to know Garrett and the way he'd controlled her. Amanda needed to know enough so that she would believe he was dangerous and that her safety was at risk.

Amanda's expression showed that the explanation was sinking in and making sense. She raised her fingers to her temple and rubbed as though the thought process gave her a headache. "This is so hard to believe."

"I know. All I want is for you to be safe, and you're not safe while he's still here."

"So you traveled with Monte? Ever since you were how old?"

"About eleven or twelve," Sophie answered.

"He took care of you?"

"I ate well, had nice clothing, studied with tutors if that's what you mean. He never behaved like a parent. I was like a dog trained to fight or a horse raised to win races. I was like a pet who made money for him."

Amanda was obviously taking it all in. "Are you turning yourself in so that he'll be caught?" she asked.

Maybe down deep Amanda had suspected that Sophie was telling the truth, but she hadn't been able to accept it. "I've already confessed everything to the marshal," Sophie told her. "I want to set a trap to catch Garrett, but you have to be gone. You can travel free, and Mr. Webb knows you've been waiting to go to your cousin Winnie when her baby comes. He'll accommodate you taking a leave to see your family. I know he will."

"I've been hoping to hear something any day," Amanda said, the subject distracting her.

"You didn't go early because you couldn't afford to lose the pay." Sophie took an envelope from her reticule. "Take this. Don't worry, it's not stolen, it's the money I earned giving dance lessons. You've sent most of your pay home, and I've been saving mine. I won't need it where I'm going."

Amanda frowned and then recognition dawned. She blinked in surprise. "You're going to *jail?*"

"I'll be okay."

Amanda stared at the envelope. Tears welled in her eyes. "This is all true, Sophie? You weren't trying to get Monte for yourself?"

"His name isn't Monte," she replied. "You don't have any reason to trust that I wouldn't do something like that to you. But he has an evil heart and you have to trust me on that for your own good. I've wanted nothing more than to get away from him since I was twelve years old." She covered Amanda's hand on the table. "I don't think you'll be seeing him because we made a deal, but if you do, you mustn't tell him you know anything or that I told you."

"I'm going to talk with Mr. Webb as soon as I get back to the Arcade," Amanda said. "I'll get my ticket and be out of here by tomorrow."

Sophie felt as though a boulder had been lifted away from her.

Amanda raised her hand to squeeze Sophie's. "I'm sorry I got so angry."

Sophie shook her head. "No apologies. I would have been thinking the same way if I'd been in your place. Don't sell yourself short, Amanda. You're going to meet someone deserving of you."

"I don't know," she said. "I feel so stupid. What's wrong with me to get caught up with a phony like him?"

"There's nothing stupid about you," Sophie assured her. "He's a *master* at using people. You want to be loved and needed, and he zeroed right in on that need. He's good at what he does, so don't ever think differently or feel like it was your fault. It wasn't."

Amanda took a lace-edged handkerchief from her pocket and wiped her eyes and nose.

They ordered cups of tea and Amanda filled her in on the latest gossip and shared details about Mrs. Winters's cranky attitude the last few days. Finally, Amanda gave Sophie a hug. As though reluctant to let go, she held Sophie's hand as she backed away, then released her and headed back to the Arcade.

A burden had been lifted, but there was much to happen yet. She couldn't imagine where she'd be six months from now. The thought was daunting…frightening. But she had her mind set to do the right thing from here on out. She intended to enjoy her last days of freedom and see Garrett get what he deserved.

That evening most of the lights in the buildings along Main Street had been extinguished, but several remained bright. Late guests were arriving at a hotel across the street, and Sophie enjoyed her new vantage point from her window. She could still hear the train whistles and the bursts of steam as the engines halted in front of the depot, but she couldn't see the crowds or hear the voices.

She'd enjoyed another quiet dinner alone in the hotel dining room. The manager and the staff treated her well. A man in a gray serge suit had asked if he could join her for dinner, but she'd politely declined.

Telling Clay the whole truth and withstanding his reaction had been a torturous mix of relief and disappointment. Either he refused to believe her or he was angry with her. Or both. Since she hadn't seen or heard from him, he was obviously disappointed. And disgusted. His hasty rejection hurt, but she understood.

She didn't have many choices left. She'd taken her

best shot in confiding in him and coming up with a plan. She was finished lying and she was done running. After tomorrow Amanda would be safely out of Newton, so if Sophie didn't hear from Clay by then, she would go to the jail and turn herself in to Marshal Vidlak.

Garrett would be their problem after that. She'd be tucked away in a cell. She'd never allowed herself all these raw emotions before. She'd never dealt with feelings. Even though she'd been alone for most of her life, she was now experiencing loneliness in a new and acute way. Sophie needed someone to talk with.

Pulling on her walking shoes, she exited her room and locked the door. It was a fair distance to the doctor's home, but she remembered the streets and enjoyed the walk. Lights shone from the windows of the two-story house as she approached. The home, she corrected. The sound of a child's laughter reached her and found a place inside that remembered family. Dredged up a long-lost feeling of security.

It had been many years since she'd felt safe. Never once since the day she and her mother had been captured.

She'd never felt more like an outsider than she did standing at the gate in front of the Chaney home. She didn't know what she'd come here for. There was no magic cure for what ailed her.

"Hey! Miss Hollis!" Out of the darkness, a small figure dashed from beside the house and ran to where she stood. She recognized Ellie Chaney's youngest brother as he drew close holding a jar filled with flickering lightning bugs. "I 'member you. Come in. Ellie will be glad to see you."

"I wouldn't want to bother her. I was just out walking."

"At night? C'mon. She made cinnamon buns today."

She let him lead her toward the house and up the porch stairs. He set down his jar, then opened the screen door with a creak of hinges.

"Ellie! Miss Hollis is here!"

The doctor's wife entered the foyer from the comfortably furnished room at front of the house. "Sophie! How nice to see you. Please, come in."

"I was just out walking. I don't want to interrupt your evening."

"Don't be silly. Come in and have a seat." Behind her the doctor was playing on the carpeted floor with the baby. He called a greeting to her.

"Hello, Dr. Chaney," she said, then more softly to Ellie, "Really, I was just passing by."

Ellie touched her arm. "Don't move. Stay right there."

She spoke to her husband a moment, then took Ellie's arm and led her out the front door and around the side of the house.

In the darkness, Sophie made out a wooden swing on a frame in the side yard.

"Have a seat," Ellie told her.

Sophie sat and Ellie perched beside her before setting the swing in motion.

"Did everything work out all right at the Arcade?" Ellie asked.

"I got myself fired."

"Oh, no!"

"On purpose."

"Why?" Ellie's question held a note of compassion.

"It's quite a long story. And it probably doesn't have a happy ending."

"Caleb will put the children to bed. You have my undivided attention. I promise you can't shock me."

"Oh, I don't know. Your hair might stand on end."

"Sophie." Ellie took a deep breath. "My mother was a drunk and a prostitute. We lived in a shack with no heat. My brothers and I had no clothing or food except what we stole or the church ladies gave us. After Flynn was born whenever my mother had a baby, she buried it. Once I saw a dog dig one up."

Sophie stared at the other woman. "Oh, Ellie."

"Still think you can shock me? I can't remember how old I was when my mother took money to let a man have sex with me."

Sophie felt the helpless urge to cry.

"When I found out I was pregnant I tried to hide it from her. I gave birth to a baby girl alone and was terrified for her life. I ran out in the night and left her on a back porch. I stayed hidden until the couple came to the door and I saw them take her in."

Sophie's chest ached and tears welled in her throat.

"When my mother died, I tried to take care of the boys, but the state took them and put them in a foster home where they suffered another kind of abuse."

"What happened?" Sophie managed.

"I got a job as a Harvey Girl to earn enough to get them back and take care of them, but I broke my arm and couldn't work. Caleb doctored me and asked me to take care of Nate. Caleb was recently widowed. He taught me to trust. He showed me love and care, but it took a long time. My past was a wall around my heart. He even took me to see my little girl so I'd know she was happy and well-cared for."

"And she is?"

Ellie smiled. "She is. She doesn't know I'm her mother, but I visit her every so often. It's a sad-sweet joy to know her. Her parents are wonderful people. I did the right thing."

"What about…?" She couldn't bring herself to ask.

"The man who fathered her was killed."

Sophie accepted that information with a nod.

"Benjamin did it. The man tried to abduct me."

Sophie couldn't hold back a little gasp. Ellie and her family seemed so happy and normal, it was nearly impossible to believe the things Ellie had just shared with her. What courage the woman possessed! What an enormous amount of love it had taken to heal.

All the fear and rejection and regret she'd stifled for a lifetime boiled over the surface of Sophie's emotional reservoir, and her throat ached with silent sobs.

"Let it out, Sophie," Ellie told her. "It's okay to feel the hurt and the pain. It's okay to hate whoever did this to you. It was wrong and you deserved to be taken care of and loved."

Sophie nodded. "I—it was wrong, wasn't it?"

"That's what Caleb always told me."

"And you finally believed him?"

"I did. Just like you will. You'll believe you are a good person. A person worthy of love."

Sobs took over and Sophie's whole body quaked from the force of them. Tears poured from her eyes, and her shoulders shook. Ellie just held her, comfortingly rocking the swing back and forth in a gentle soothing rhythm.

Sophie cried until her throat hurt, until her eyes burned and she was emotionally exhausted. Her breaths became shudders, but eventually the tears subsided and she collected herself. The hem of her dress was soaked from holding it to her face.

"I'll bet it's been a long time since you did that."

Sophie wiped her nose. "Never." She sat up and looked at the other woman's kind face. "Thank you. For your honesty. For knowing I needed to hear those things."

"I just wanted you to know you could talk to me," Ellie said, her voice soft.

So Sophie told Ellie about her childhood. She revealed the things that brought her the most shame and regret. And she told her about Amanda...and about Clay.

"I've never loved anyone before," she said. "I don't want him hurt, but I'm afraid it's too late. How can he love me after all I've done? After the lies I've told—even to him?"

"Love doesn't keep count of offenses," Ellie told her. "Love is bigger than mistakes, bigger than our pasts. That's what Caleb taught me. You can believe it, too."

Ellie rubbed Sophie's shoulder. "The marshal is a good man. He'll know the right thing to do. The best thing for everyone. Have a little trust in him."

"All right," she said with a nod. "I love him, Ellie. The only reason I'm afraid of going to jail is because I'll lose him."

"You're very brave. I'm going to believe that this is all going to work out for the best."

Sophie looked at the young wife and mother beside

her. "I think I knew all along that you were someone I could talk to. The girls at the dormitory are kind and caring, but I'm so different from them, sometimes I'm surprised we even speak the same language."

"I felt the same way," Ellie told her. "Like an imposter."

Sophie shrugged. "I've always been an imposter, so I've never known anything else."

"I used a made-up name, too."

At that Sophie started to laugh. She threw back her head and let the laughter roll over her and from her.

Ellie joined in, and they laughed until they cried, then they laughed again.

Finally Sophie wiped her eyes on her already soaked skirt. "You don't know how much I needed this."

"I think I can guess. Want to come in for a cold drink now? I made lemonade earlier."

Caleb had put the children to bed. Benjamin sat at the kitchen table with a book. Sophie remembered what Ellie had told her, and her heart went out to the young man and this family.

Caleb joined them for a glass of lemonade, and then he insisted that Benjamin walk with her to the hotel.

"Your sister is a very special person," Sophie said to him.

He nodded. "She's the only mother Flynn ever knew. She was more of a mother to me than the woman who birthed us."

"How do you handle that, if you don't mind me asking?"

He shrugged. "I dunno. Mostly I don't think about it. I think about the people who care about me."

"You're a wise young man. And you want to be a veterinarian."

"Yup."

"You'll be good at it."

"Here's your hotel, Miss Hollis."

"Thank you for accompanying me. Good night."

He turned and ran back the way they'd come.

Sophie watched him go, then entered the lobby and climbed the stairs to her floor. The unknown was still disturbing, as was the fear of losing Clay. But she had the satisfaction of knowing she'd done things right. Finally.

If she had to go turn herself in tomorrow, she'd always know he'd cared for her. There simply was no way things could have been different for them. She was who she was. She'd lived the experiences she had through no choice of her own—and made the best of it.

A pitcher of water stood outside the door. She carried it in, lit one of the lamps and undressed. Brushing out her hair, she made a point of noticing her roots where her hair was growing in a lighter brown. No need to touch up those again.

Sophie wet a cloth and raised it to her face. A movement in the mirror caught her eye, and her heart stopped. Dropping the cloth with a splat on the wood floor, she turned.

Garrett moved forward from the shadowy corner, and his gaze raked over her. "Some things haven't changed, Gabriella."

Sophie grabbed her wrapper from the screen where she'd hung it and pulled in on. "Nothing about our agreement allows you to be in my room," she told him.

"Couldn't have anyone seeing us together without you in disguise, so I stopped by."

"Picked the lock, you mean."

He grinned. "I'm still the best."

"What do you want?"

"I noticed you cutting all your ties, and I wanted to warn you not to be obvious or make a spectacle of yourself. The less attention you draw the better."

"It doesn't matter anymore what people think of me," she told him. "Once we pull off this job, they'll never see me again."

"You should have kept your disguise at the Arcade."

"Easy for you to say. You've never had to wait tables or be polite to every person who comes through the door."

He moved closer, and Sophie's heartbeat accelerated.

"I'm no longer a naive young girl," she told him. "I've joined you in this scheme of yours and I will work the craft as you taught me, but I make the decisions about who shares my bed."

A scowl creased his forehead, and he pierced her with a contemptuous look. "Don't think too highly of yourself and your ability to make that choice just yet." He moved forward, grabbed the front of her wrapper and jerked her up to face him.

She turned her head so that his nose grazed her cheek.

"You conceited, ungrateful little bitch. What do you think you'd be without me? I made you into a woman men lose their heads over. I gave you your abilities and talents. You don't tell me who makes decisions, or have you forgotten the punishment for displeasing me?"

With a determination and courage she hadn't known she possessed, she yanked her clothing away from his grip and faced him with a fierce glare. "I haven't forgotten your abuse for a moment, not for a second. But I've put it behind me and washed myself of the taint."

Garrett's expression revealed his shock and anger.

"I'm old enough now," she said, "wise enough to know there are worse things than being coerced or manipulated, and one of them is the loss of respect. Not respecting myself. I'll scream and fight or I'll jump out that window before I'll ever submit my body to you again."

He straightened his shirt and tie. "Think more about that, Gabriella. Consider other people who might have more to lose in all this than you."

Clay. Amanda. She'd already considered. "You said you'd leave them alone if I went along with your job. If you want to trust me to do what you ask, don't go back on your word now."

"We're not finished," he told her. "Not nearly finished. Once we've moved on and you don't have your friends and your marshal, you'll see things my way."

Sophie'd said enough. She held back anything more she might have spewn at him and asked, "How much longer will it be?"

"Any time. He's ready. Be prepared." He took a few steps toward the door and pointed to a liquor bottle she hadn't noticed sitting behind the door. "He likes brandy…and blondes."

Sophie's heart hammered long after he'd left and she'd locked the door. She leaned against it, thinking what tissue-thin protection a locked door was.

Finally, she moved. Noticing the wet rag on the floor, she picked it up and rinsed it out. Her skin was hot and clammy, so she washed before donning her night-clothes, then extinguished the lamp.

She sat before the window and concentrated on thinking about her meeting with Ellie. Garrett had stolen much of the relief she'd felt, but she wasn't as lonely as she'd been before.

As bad as all this was right now, Ellie had survived worse. She remembered Ellie's advise and made up her mind to trust Clay no matter what.

She had nothing to lose.

A knock startled her. Jumping at the sound was fool-ish. Anyone who meant her harm wouldn't knock. Garrett certainly wouldn't bother. She padded to the door in the dark. "Who is it?"

"Me." His voice.

Chapter Eighteen

Her heart slammed against her ribs with joy at hearing Clay. She opened the door and ushered him inside. "You came."

She stepped to the bureau and relit the oil lamp, then another on the writing desk. He looked so good, so tall and handsome, his skin burnished from the sun, his thick dark hair unruly as though he'd run all the way in the wind. He smelled like fresh air and safety. She wanted to run to him, press herself against him and never let go. But she didn't.

"The posters came today," he said.

She studied his expression. And waited.

Seeing her took away Clay's breath as it always did. She looked like the same woman he'd fallen in love with, maybe even softer and more lovely in her green satin wrapper and bare feet. Her dark hair was spread over her shoulders in shining waves. Was she the same woman he thought he'd known? Was she who she said she was?

"I think your plan will work. I'll let the others know and have the men at the ready."

Sophie rushed forward and flung herself against him. "Oh, thank you, Clay!"

He was so surprised, he didn't make a move to respond, and she drew away as though she'd been struck. She backed into the center of the room. "I'm sorry. I don't have any right to do that."

Her eyes expressed such uncertainty and fear, he could barely stand to look. He took a long forward stride to reach her and pulled her into his arms. She didn't let herself relax against him.

"I don't know what's gonna happen, Sophie," he told her. "I had hoped—well, it don't matter what I'd hoped."

Sophie took a step back and looked up at him. "It matters to me what you hoped. Tell me."

Before he'd heard the rest of her story he'd hoped that she'd decide she wanted to marry him. He'd even voiced it, but she hadn't responded. "I had a pipe dream that we could start a family."

The first real emotion he'd ever seen displayed crossed her features. Regret filled her lovely dark eyes. "He stole my life, Clay. He's the reason I can't have friends or a husband or a family. I've never been free, and now I'm going to jail."

The disappointment and hurt in her tone sounded real. She didn't seem afraid, just…sorry. "Garrett's gonna pay," he assured her. "He's gonna hang for that killin'."

He thought he saw relief cross her features.

"He couldn't steal my love or my dreams," she said.

He ached to hold her. To believe in her.

"Amanda is leaving in the morning to visit her family for a while," she told him.

"Good."

"Telling the truth spared her, didn't it?" she asked.

"You spared her."

"You think less of me now, don't you?" she asked.

"Not less. It's just…I thought I knew you, but I didn't. You're not the person I thought you were."

"Yes, yes I am," she argued in a quivering voice. "I'm the same Sophia who went riding with you and shared a picnic lunch. I'm—" her words caught, but she finished "—I'm the same woman who smoked cigars in your bed."

Her mention of that day hurt like a surprise punch to the gut. That had been one of the best days of his life. Hers, too, he'd thought. "You've closed up."

She shook her head. "I tried to barricade myself from having feelings again, but it didn't work. It's just…" She crossed her hands on her breast. "I thought I had so much to lose. Freedom. Self-respect. You. None of them were ever mine anyway."

Maybe she truly had risked everything to tell the truth. What purpose would a lie serve now? He'd been as angry with himself as he'd been with her. He'd felt like a chump, falling for her while she'd been lying to him. "Thinkin' over your options in all this, I see how you thought you had no choice but to do things the way you did. You went out of your way to avoid the law. To avoid me."

"I'm sorry you got pulled in, but I'm not sorry about a single minute I spent with you," she told him. "Not a minute. I lied about my past, Clay, but I never lied about the way I feel about you. It wasn't fair to let either one of us think there was a chance for anything more, but the woman you were with that day was me. The real me."

He stepped forward to wrap his arms around her.

This time she folded into his embrace and laid her head against his chest. She was small and soft and the wonderful scent he couldn't forget filled his head.

As though she'd just thought of something, she looked up. "You didn't let anyone know you were coming here tonight, did you?"

He shook his head. "Don't want Garrett to know what we're up to."

"And you can't let anyone see you coming here or let them know you're more than the city marshal to me." Her eyes were a deep dark umber in the lamplight.

Her words restored his hope. "Am I?"

"You're the only good thing that's ever happened to me," she told him. "You're what I never even let myself dream about or imagine. But you and I can't happen. You'll meet a woman who deserves you."

The thought was absurd. "Do you really think I'd want anyone else now?"

"Time makes a difference," she assured him. "Once I'm gone you'll find someone to make you a good wife."

She believed she was going to jail, and he couldn't tell her differently. "I can't think past what we have to do," he told her. "Can't see past the woman in front of me. All I want to consider is you in my arms right now."

Sophia rested her head against his chin. She didn't

want to think past this moment either. At least not yet. She had so few good memories to take with her. Selfishly she wanted more. Enough to fill her heart for all the cold lonely hours that would be hers soon enough.

"I have some first-rate cigars," she told him. "I'd be glad to share."

"Hold that idea," he told her.

He stepped away and twisted the key in the lock, then unbuckled his holster and hung the guns on the back of the door.

Sophie waited expectantly.

He took off his boots and moved toward her. "What is this?" he asked, untying the ribbons over her breast.

"My nightwear."

"Mighty fancy nightwear for a Harvey Girl."

"No uniforms at bedtime," she informed him with a smile.

He spread the front apart and let it fall down her arms. Sophie tossed the wrapper on the foot of the bed.

He fingered the satin edging above her breasts.

Her skin tingled everywhere he touched her.

Clay glanced toward the bowl on the washstand.

"Go ahead," she offered. "It's cold by now though."

He unbuttoned his shirt. "I won't notice."

She backed up to the bed and watched him wash, appreciating the smooth contours of his back, the play of muscle in his shoulders and arms. He was a pleasure to look at, pleasure to touch. Even the sound of his voice was a pleasure she wanted to engrave into her memory forever.

She wanted him with her forever, too. The thought that he might forget her and assign his affections to another woman was almost more than she could endure. He was hers. Hers for tonight. Hers for right now, anyway.

And he *would* remember her.

Chapter Nineteen

She hurried to tug the curtains closed over the open window and turn down the wick on the nearest lamp before folding back the covers on the bed. Sophie removed her nightgown while he was still occupied with a towel. The summer air kissed her skin.

Clay draped the towel over the brass holder, extinguished the lamp and turned. His expression would be in her memories for all time. He didn't move, just studied her with hooded eyes. The breeze sucked the curtain out the open window and blew it back in.

"Beautiful Sophia," he said at last.

Her heart ached with loss already. She took bittersweet pleasure in the way his gaze glided from her body to her face and hair. He was everything she wanted and nothing she deserved.

He moved forward to capture her lips in a kiss of possession and purpose. She didn't need to breathe again because he was her air. Her heart never had to beat again; he was the life force that sustained her. His kiss was her nourishment, his groan of desire a cleansing drink.

Whatever happened, she would have this. She had trusted him to make the right decision regarding Garrett. Now she was trusting him with her heart. It wasn't fair to say it to him, so she showed him her love with kisses and touches that came from her soul.

She hoped that a month from now, a year from now, he would still feel she'd been a risk worth taking.

She wanted to kiss him hard and keep him with her forever. She wanted to let him go before it hurt more than this, before he could be hurt more. But she was selfish enough to want this night.

His kiss was so tender, she would have cried if she hadn't already purged every tear earlier. He unbuttoned his trousers, dropped them to the floor, and eased her onto the crisp sheets. His lips trailed down her neck, blazing a path between her breasts. "So beautiful…soft everywhere…smell is in my head…"

He cupped her breast and kissed her.

She arched toward him, eager for his touch, famished for tenderness, for the sheer joy of each intimate moment in his arms.

"Sophia," he said on a gruff sigh. "I can't get enough of you. Sophia. Yes, kiss me like that."

How was it he could wound her with words of love and kill her with tenderness when another man's cruelty had never pierced her armor? She clung to each kiss as though it could be the last, carved his face and body into her memory with her hands. He would remember her; she would see to it. She wanted to love him so well and so thoroughly that she would be a part of him forever.

When he joined their bodies, she was so overcome by the sheer beauty and inconceivable goodness that her throat constricted and tears welled in her eyes. She gulped them back, but an emotional flood had been unleashed, and there was no restraining it. Her chest heaved with her feeble efforts to hold back, and a wail escaped her lips.

"Sophia?" he asked, holding her gently, pushing her hair from her face with one hand.

"Don't stop," she said. "Please d-don't stop."

"But you're cryin'."

"Yes. And it's s-so good. It's such a relief to feel."

Clay pressed his lips to her wet cheek, tasted her tears, kept his movements slow and easy. From that moment on nothing would ever be the same. She'd never voice it, but she loved him. Loved him enough to want to protect him. Loved him enough to open herself up to him. Loved him enough to cry.

Her eyes fluttered closed when he wanted to see them, wanted to know what she was thinking...feeling... He wanted more. He wanted promises. He wanted forever. The desperate way he wanted her hurt.

"Look at me, darlin'."

Her eyes were dark and wet with tears that still flowed.

He'd wanted more than physical possession. He wanted her to be his. Not in the way Garrett had wanted to own her, but in an intimate, almost spiritual way.

With an ache he needed to ease, he drank at the sweetness of her lips, threaded his fingers into the silken texture of her hair. He forgot she'd never said the words because her demonstration spoke to his heart.

He loved to say her name, loved her reaction when he did.

"Sophia."

She trembled.

"Sophia."

She kissed him, openmouthed and tasting of tears.

Was this her goodbye then? "You cryin' because it might be the last time?" he asked.

She cradled his cheek. "I'm crying because it's the first time," she answered.

He had never expected to experience the hollow ache of loss again, but here it was, a claw ripping at his gut. He wouldn't lose her. He'd do whatever it took to keep her with him.

She met him kiss for kiss as he realigned his mouth over hers. He rolled her with him so they lay on their sides and eased her thigh over his hip. She became impatient with his leisurely lovemaking and moved to straddle him, surprising them both, releasing a soft gasp, and then discovering her position of control.

In the nearly-diminished glow of the lamp, she fulfilled all the dreams he'd ever had. Her expressions were real, her inexpert movements endearingly erotic. She wasn't crying now. She was concentrating, her breathing telling him she'd found her way.

He caressed her breasts.

She caught her lip and dropped her head back.

Her thighs trembled.

He cupped her bottom and helped her.

This wasn't the last time. He wouldn't lose her. She was everything he wanted. He would find a way, and he would make her happy for the rest of her life.

With a series of delicate gasps, Sophie collapsed on his chest. He turned her beneath him, shuddered in release, then held her protectively in his arms.

"Please stay with me," she whispered.

She'd never asked for anything that he could remember. "I won't leave."

Moments later, her soft breathing told him she slept. He wondered how she could when her future—*their* future was questionable. She had developed so many other protective instincts, perhaps learning to close off fear and uncertainty was another survival instinct she'd perfected in order to stay sane.

He woke during the night with her head on his chest, his arm still around her. The wick had burned out and moonlight highlighted the curve of her hip, the length of her leg. He wanted to pick her up and carry her away where no one would ever find them. He wanted them to live out the rest of their lives in a place where the past and the future didn't matter. If only there was such a place.

Sophie woke at the sound of a buckboard on the street below. Clay's solid warmth told her he still held her. Lifting her head, she discovered the tenderness in his blue eyes. "Did you sleep?"

He nodded. "Some."

She sat, pulling the sheet to her breast, but away from his torso. He didn't seem to mind and neither did she. "Thank you for staying the night."

"My pleasure."

He didn't looked pleased. He looked the way he had the night he'd told her he'd buried old Sam. He'd spent the night because she'd asked.

She almost wished he was asleep, so she could look him over without embarrassment. She placed her palm against the flat plane of his belly. Over the place on his broad chest where his heart beat beneath. The heart of a kind, strong man.

She'd never seen him show fear. Never seen him act rashly or in anger.

She'd seen him arrest a man. She pretty near knew everything he ate. She knew he danced fairly well.

He closed his eyes and she looked her fill. Skimmed her fingertips over his muscled arms and the taut brown circles of his nipples.

This man had run along a riverbank and waded into a river for her straw hat. She could still see him, feet bare, denim trousers darkened and saturated to his thighs. The image would always make her smile.

She knew all about his kisses and the tender way he made love.

"What're you thinkin'?" he asked.

She lifted her gaze to his. "I'm saving everything I know about you."

He frowned. "Sayin' goodbye?"

She blinked back the sting of tears. Once she'd given in to them, she could barely keep them at bay. "No."

She found her wrapper at the foot of the bed and slipped it on.

A knock at the door had them exchanging a look.

Clay got up and found his pants on the floor. Sophie called out. "Yes?"

"Message, ma'am." A youthful voice.

"Just a moment." She got a coin from her bureau drawer, unlocked the door to ease it open a couple of inches, then took the note and handed the young man a tip. He thanked her and she closed the door to tear open the envelope.

On Strong Hotel stationery she read Garrett's distinctive handwriting. "Tonight. Eight-thirty. The Silver Spike."

She glanced at Clay to ask, "Gaming hall?"

"Fancy one."

She folded the note and looked at him.

"This is it then," he said.

She nodded.

"I've already rented the rooms on either side of yours."

"Good."

"You will not take any chances," he said firmly.

"I'll do what I do. I'll bring the man to this room. Garrett will give me about five or ten minutes and then he'll show up. He'll pretend to be my offended lover and blackmail the man with a threat to tell his wife."

Clay cast her a curious glance. "It won't make any difference this time, but what would happen if the man didn't care and told him to go to hell?"

"It's never happened. Garrett knows people's weaknesses. He wouldn't use this scheme if the man wasn't a prime candidate. He'll be someone who thinks highly enough of himself to believe he can seduce me. It will all look like his idea. He will also be a man who will want to protect his marriage."

"I guess I'll be interested to see who it is." Clay sat at the edge of the bed and Sophie picked up his shirt for him. He didn't take it, but instead just looked at her. "How did you ever keep from thinkin' all men were alike?"

She held the shirt open and waited for him to stand. "The chief who took me in was a good man. Over the years there were men who couldn't be conned into our schemes. I saw some with integrity, so I knew they existed."

Clay stood and turned away from her to place his arms in the sleeves of the wrinkled shirt.

"Make sure you go out the back way," she told him unnecessarily.

He buttoned up, tucked the tail into his trousers and buckled on his gun belt.

"Thanks for staying," she said.

He found his hat and adjusted it on his head in that familiar way she found endearing. Without a word, he snagged her around the waist and drew her against him in a bone-crushing embrace.

Sophie was comforted by the steady beat of his heart beneath her cheek, the strength of his arms around her, and the knowledge that she was loved. Whatever happened from here on out, she had that.

Clay released her. Backed away and turned without another look. Opened and closed the door, shutting himself away from her.

Sophie stared at the back of the door, her chest aching with loss. Emotion that had been buried for so long welled up, and she flung herself on the bed. The sheets smelled like him, making her cry harder.

Minutes passed. An hour. The sun had risen hot, and the room held the promise of another sultry day. She lay on her back, drained. This was it. Her sad-sweet day of liberation.

Her determination in place, Sophie rose and began preparations. There was much to do to be ready.

* * *

Clay looked up from the discussion he and the other marshals were having when two women entered the jail. Two grim-faced lads followed at reluctant pace.

"May I have a word with you, Marshal Connor?" the taller of the two women said.

Clay handed Owen a list he'd been holding and guided the citizens to his desk, where he cleared a stack of papers from one chair and a pair of spurs from another. With a quick swipe of his hand over the seats, he gestured for them to make themselves comfortable. The boys remained standing, one on each side of who he assumed were their mothers.

"We've come with some disturbing news, Marshal," the taller woman said. "I'm Grace Hadley and this is my boy, Quentin."

"Prudence Saddler," the other woman said by way of introduction. "This is Lawrence."

"Pleasure," Clay said, hoping they'd hurry with whatever they'd come about so he could get back to the tasks at hand.

"I'm not sure you'll find it such a pleasure when you learn why we've come," Mrs. Saddler said.

The two women looked at one another, then at their sons.

"Quentin and Lawrence have something to tell you," she added.

Clay narrowed his gaze and leveled it at one lad and then the other.

"Quentin?" his mother warned.

"Din't mean no harm, Marshal," the boy said, his face

flushed and damp. "We was trying some of Larry's pappy's tobacco."

"Could you come to the point, son?" Clay asked.

"We was smokin' behind the jail—the old jailhouse that is. Thought we wouldn't get caught there."

"Quentin was the one what dropped the match," Lawrence finally piped up.

"But you brung the tobacco an' matches," Quentin accused.

"Newsprint don't work so well for rollin' smokes," Lawrence added. "Burns too fast."

What these boys were stammering to confess became clear and Clay rose to his feet. "It was you two that caught the jail on fire?"

The boys cringed back and toward their mothers. "Weren't on purpose!" Quentin shouted.

The other marshals caught the drift of the conversation and came closer to hear the rest.

"I only learned this yesterday," Mrs. Hadley told them. "I went to Pru and we decided to bring the boys here for you to decide their punishment."

Clay was decidedly relieved to have an explanation for the mysterious fire that had burned the jail to the ground and started the rest of the recent events in motion. The fact that the culprits were two mischievous young boys was easier to take than any of the other, more sinister, possibilities that had crossed his mind.

"It's a serious act," Clay told the boys. "Even if it was an accident, you should have stayed and owned up to it."

Tears ran down Lawrence's cheeks. "I'm awful sorry, Marshal. My Pa already done whupped me good, an' my Ma ain't givin' me no desserts for a month."

Quentin's hand strayed to his backside as though re-membering a tender spot from the encounter. He looked fearfully at Clay. "Are you gonna lock us up now?"

"I guess we'll have to talk that over." Clay motioned Owen and Marshal Vidlak across the room where they remarked about the confounded luck of havin' a couple kids burn down their jail.

When the men came back, the boys appeared thor-oughly shaken. "We've decided not to press charges," Clay said, though they'd never even discussed the pos-sibility. "You'll be doin' your time sweepin' floors and hauling wood and ashes for the next six months. I don't think that can even come close to payin' for the new building, but you'll learn the value of a day's work and of takin' responsibility for your actions, mistake or not."

"Yes, sir."

"Thank you, sir."

He directed the boys to wait outside while he briefly spoke with their mothers. The women were grateful for his decision.

"You're a fair man," Mrs. Saddler said. "It's going to do Lawrence good to work around here."

Clay made arrangements for the boys to begin work-ing off their debt and wished the women a good day.

At least the fire was one thing he didn't have to con-cern himself with any more. If only the rest of the mess he faced could be solved so easily.

At eight o'clock she stood before her mirror. The room was straightened, but with a few dispensable items remaining visible so the room appeared lived in. She had packed her belongings and stashed the bags beneath the bed so it would look to Garrett as though she was ready for the quick getaway.

Despite her dark eyes and brows Sophie'd always been able to pull off blond wigs. She simply stained her skin a shade darker and played up her lips.

She wore a blue satin dress that bared her shoulders and dipped dangerously low in the front. With so much cleavage showing, men never spent much time analyzing her eye color. She checked the delicate watch she usually wore on a chain around her neck but had tucked into a pocket she'd designed on a garter.

She wore pearls at her throat and on her ears. Classic. Sophisticated. She had twenty-five minutes left, and this morning she had timed the walk. It would take ten to get there.

There was a tap on the door.

She opened it to discover Marshal Vidlak. She gave the man credit for keeping his eyes on her face. "Clay said to make sure you knew we was right next door," he told her.

"Thank you, Marshal. I don't expect to leave the Silver Spike until after eleven. You'll be watching?"

"We have two men watchin' the Spike. Soon as you leave, one'll follow, the other will run ahead t' let us know you're comin'."

"That's reassuring. Thank you."

He touched the brim of his hat and backed away. She stared at the door, wondering why Clay hadn't come himself. He was busy getting things ready, she assured herself.

She knew what Garrett was doing now, playing a friendly game of cards with his new best friend, making sure the mark barely broke even or lost a little. He was creating the atmosphere, buying drinks and swapping stories.

Sophie had done this more times than she could count. There was always an anticipatory tingle of nerves which Garrett had taught her was good. That little jolt that said she wasn't complacent, that she wouldn't be taken unaware by anything that transpired.

Waiting had never felt quite like this before, though. There'd never been so much to lose.

Much as she regretted it, she was still a professional. Sophie calmed her nerves, breathed slowly and evenly and dabbed on flowery cologne. She was ready.

The walk took nine minutes. She entered through the double doors into the foyer of the Silver Spike. Since it was a gaming hall and not a saloon, the appearance of a woman drew less attention. Men often brought wives and female partners to these fashionable halls. And there were a few women, widows mostly, who frequented the tables without male companions. Sophie pretended to be one of those women.

Garrett had known about what time the games would break and when the tables would change, and he'd been sitting with their mark the entire evening.

She leisurely surveyed the tables, working her way to where he sat with three companions.

"Mrs. Saxton!" Garrett pushed back his chair and rose to greet her. "I didn't know you were arriving today."

"Just this morning, Mr. Morgan. You may recall that a cousin of my late husband is employed at the Sante Fe's Western Union. I accepted an invitation to accompany his daughter on a trip, so I'm here to meet her."

"How nice for you. I'm thinking of setting up an office here. I've found one or two investors."

"Well, you are in the business of multiplying money, and this is an excellent place to do so. You're looking well."

"Thank you. Please, you must meet some friends of mine. Frank, meet Mrs. Saxton. Frank Wick here."

The man pushed back his chair and stood. "Pleasure, Mrs. Saxton."

"You may call me Elizabeth. Any friend of Mr. Morgan's is a first-name friend of mine."

With a smile, Frank showed his true pleasure over that comment.

"This is Rudy Jacobson, Max Cline, and over here John. Never caught your last name, John."

The man nodded to Sophie. "Just call me J.J., ma'am."

Garrett turned to acquire an empty chair from another table. "Do sit in and be my good luck this evening."

"That's not fair," Frank interrupted. "Mrs. Saxton should sit by me."

"You've been winning all night, you hardly *need* her," Garrett objected good naturedly.

Sophie detested this role, but she was in it come hell or high water now. "I'll sit *between* you two gentlemen," she said with a laugh. "And the winner may take me to breakfast tomorrow morning."

Garrett feigned a look of jealousy that he quickly hid.

She settled onto the chair, and Frank parked again, his attention momentarily riveted by her display of cleavage when she sat forward to smooth the wrinkles from the skirt beneath her. She deliberately jiggled herself into a more comfortable position.

As usual, Garrett had done his work well. Frank Wick had an eye for the ladies. And, because she knew Garrett so well, she also knew Frank had a bank account as big as his appetite. It was a given that he had a respectable wife and a batch of little Wicks at home.

"What are you playing?" she asked.

"Texas hold 'em," Frank replied. "Little game us ranchers like to play."

"You have a ranch?" she asked, wide-eyed. "With cows?"

"Decent spread," he replied. "I run a couple thousand head."

"I'm impressed. Do you ride a horse around your ranch and everything?"

He grinned. "I do."

She strategically placed a hand at her breast and sighed. "There's something breathtaking about a handsome man astride a horse."

Frank Wick was a shoe-in. He puffed his chest out and reached into his vest pocket to withdraw a cigar. Sophie didn't let herself watch Frank light it and puff importantly. She'd have been tempted to yank it out of his hand. How ungentlemanly that he hadn't offered her one. "What did your husband do?" J.J. asked.

"Boring bank work," she replied. "He owned the Seattle Merchant Bank and a couple of others. He was a dear man. A good husband, even though he never rode a horse. *City slicker* I guess you men would've called him."

"Come now, Elizabeth," Garrett said lightheartedly.

"That boring bank business is what afforded you the lifestyle you enjoy today."

She laughed. "I said it was boring, I never said it wasn't wise…or profitable. And my Herbert was a very generous man."

"Would you care for a drink?" Frank asked.

"Why, yes, a glass of sherry would be delightful, thank you." *And fork over one of those cigars while you're at it.*

Sophie wanted to check her watch. This couldn't be over soon enough. But she was in character now, and the wheels of deception were moving smoothly. Two hours, she assured herself. Two hours, give or take a few minutes, and this whole chapter of her life would have come to an end.

Old resentment rose up inside her, the conviction that men like this deserved to be deceived because they were pigs. She corrected her thinking this time. No one deserved to be deceived, and this man was being lured by his own weakness. Everyone had weakness, and she had no room to stand in judgment, especially since she goaded them on. She'd changed her thinking, changed her goals, changed her life.

What was left of it anyway.

An hour dragged by. She sipped her sherry while Frank downed several snifters of brandy and finished two cigars.

He was still plenty coherent, plenty aware of her, but his judgment was now conveniently impaired.

She worked her chair closer to his.

"You and Morgan," he said in a low voice. "You, uh, you have strings?"

"He'd like to think so," she replied in the same conspiratory tone he'd used. "I choose my friends as I see fit, however." She slanted him a flirtatious glance. "And you look like a *very* good fit to me."

He couldn't keep his eyes from the neckline of her dress, and after a while she had a struggle keeping his hand away from her thigh under the table.

Garrett was letting him win. J.J. won a few hands, but all in all, it was Frank hauling the dollars across the table. He was feeling on top of the world, Sophie thought, showing off for her, feeling important and in no pain.

Another hour passed. She excused herself to use the outhouse behind the gaming hall and glanced past the path lit by gas lamps, wondering if Clay's men were watching her. On her return, she checked her watch, then tucked it back into her garter. It was time.

"I'm feeling rather tired," she told the men several minutes later. "I had a long trip. I believe I'll head back to my hotel. Perhaps we'll see each other again?"

She looked at Frank deliberately.

"Where are you staying?" Garrett asked as a prompt.

"At the Enterprise Hotel. It seems quite sufficient so far."

"Well, Elizabeth, you shouldn't walk all alone," Frank said right on cue. He turned over his cards and swept his money from the table into his pocket. "I'm out for the night."

"I'll feel safe with *you* walking me home," she told him, and linked her arm through his.

Garrett exchanged a look with Rudy, but shuffled the cards without comment.

Now Frank Wick was thinking she'd chosen him

over the dapper Monte Morgan, and his ego was full to bursting as planned.

She'd worked this routine a hundred times, she could do it again. She didn't have to sleep with the man. He only had to *think* she was going to.

They exited the hall and she kept her arm tucked through the crook of his. It was safer that way. He wasn't free to touch her, and she was in the position of control.

She didn't look to either side or check behind her, but she sensed Clay's man following. Perhaps Clay himself? She wasn't afraid of the man beside her. Frank wasn't the criminal here. She was.

"I didn't ask if you wanted to take along somethin' to drink," he said, his words slow and deliberate.

"I have a bottle of brandy in my room," she answered smoothly. "Would you like to come up?"

"I would indeed."

Ten minutes seemed like hours. The risk was always in the mark sobering up from the walk and the fresh air, but she didn't sense that Frank had walked off much of his brandy.

He seemed reluctant to approach the front door of the hotel. "I—um—wouldn't want to tarnish your good reputation," he said.

He couldn't care less about her reputation; he was concerned about someone recognizing him.

But she played along. "Why don't you walk around to the back door? I'll make sure no one is paying any attention, and then I'll open it for you." She steeled herself to flatten her hand over the front of his shirt and look up at him suggestively.

"I'd feel better 'bout that," he said with a loose nod.

He reached for her, but she slipped away and walked toward the front entrance.

Chapter Twenty

The man who worked the night shift was dozing in the leather chair behind the counter as she passed. His soft snores followed her along the hallway and through the dark dining room until she reached the kitchen. She eased back the bolt and opened the door.

Frank must have been leaning against it, because he lost his balance and fell inward. She caught him with both hands on his chest, helped him steady himself and relocked the door.

"The night clerk is sleeping," she told him. "But we'll bypass the front desk anyway."

Frank kept up and climbed the back stairs behind her.

She glanced at the dark space under the door next to hers, found her key, and unlocked her door. The rest shouldn't take longer than ten minutes, she thought, the quiver of nervous anticipation sharpening her wits. She lit one lamp, but left the curtains parted.

She opened the brandy and splashed generous portions into two white hotel coffee cups.

"To new friends," she said, raising her cup to Frank's.

"New friends." He swallowed deep, then glanced around, taking note of the dressing gown on the screen. Sophie filled his cup again.

He was probably Garrett's age, maybe not yet forty. Lines had formed at the corner of each eye from working in the sun. He was average height, his waist not thick. His wife probably truly loved him. His children were no doubt handsome. His family attended school and church and activities right here in this town. What would happen once Garrett was caught and the story of what had taken place here got around?

Sophie had never let herself think about the blackmailed men left behind to explain their financial losses to their families and the community.

"They can afford it. They deserve it," had been Garrett's philosophy. Sophie simply hadn't wanted to question—to have to feel guilty. To face her part in tearing apart lives.

She filled his cup again. He'd made himself at home on the end of the bed.

He was playing right into her hand, but she resented his forwardness anyway. She'd always felt that way. Detested the men who were so willing to be led to destruction.

"Goodness, it's warm up here tonight. Maybe you'd like to take off your jacket."

He smiled a lecherous smile. "Would be cooler, now, wouldn't it? Are you too warm, Elizabeth?"

She gave him a fetching smile. "I have something cooler I can slip into. Would you mind unbuttoning my dress?"

"Nah."

She held up her "hair," careful not to dislodge the blond wig. Frank fumbled with the row of buttons, finally ripping a couple off in his clumsy haste. "Sorry 'bout that. I'll get you a new dress if you'd like."

"You *would?* I love gifts." She moved away to step behind the screen. "Go ahead and make yourself comfortable."

She peeked around the side and mentally readied herself. "We could just skip these awkward steps if you'd like."

He sat on the edge of the bed and looked at her.

"The male body doesn't offend me. Go ahead and get yourself ready and get into bed."

She didn't wait for his expression. She removed the dress, making sure to toss it over the screen where he could see it, and pulled her wrapper on over her undergarments. She listened, waiting for the sounds that told her he was incriminating himself item by discarded item.

When she heard the bedsprings, she breezed out from behind the screen. He was propped on the pillows, his chest naked above the sheets. It was plain he wore a shirt out of doors, because his chest was white against his face and neck.

"I'll open the window to give us some air," she said, and slid it open.

She turned out the lamp and walked to the end of the bed.

"I have a little secret to share with you," she told him in a coy tone. "Since we're going to be such good friends and all."

"You can tell me anythin', little lady."

"Well, truth is I wanted one of your cigars all evening. It would have been improper to ask in public, but since we're alone, would you have another you could share?"

His eager expression faltered. Taking time for a smoke wasn't what he'd had in mind. "In my jacket pocket. Down there somewhere. Help yourself."

"I'll have to turn the light back on."

That was Garrett's final signal. He'd be crossing the street now.

She found a cigar and a match tin. "Do you want one?"

He shook his head. "Couldn't that wait until— Couldn't that wait?"

"Are you in a hurry, Frank?" She puffed on the cigar. Her heart chugged a little faster, knowing the marshal's men were ready to spring. Not knowing how Frank was going to react. Thinking of Garrett's reaction when he knew he'd been set up. The wisdom of this plan suddenly seemed in question.

She took off her wrapper, and Frank's expression fell.

She managed a dry laugh. "You didn't think I wasn't going to let you watch, now did you?"

She suggestively untied the strings that held the front of the corset together, and dealt with the fact that the lawmen were going to barge in and see her in her drawers.

The cigars Clay had given her were better than Frank's. "Sorry about this, Frank."

He blinked. "What?"

She drew back the sheet and got on the bed. "Nothing personal."

"Lady, this is pretty personal."

"Let's do away with the sheet," she suggested. Timing was everything.

Frank had that sheet off in record time. He reached for her, and she raised the cigar away. "I'd better set this down."

She turned and he grabbed her from behind.

Sophie was attuned to the sound of the door opening, though it took Frank's brain a minute longer. He was groping for her breasts when she turned directly toward the door as though in shock. "What's this? How dare you!"

Rudy Jacobson was Garrett's witness of choice, a man who probably had a bone to pick and was loving catching the other man at something unscrupulous. Rudy's eyes widened at the sight of a naked Frank and Sophie in her beribboned corset and drawers. Garrett was right behind him, having pushed Rudy in first.

"What have we here?" Garrett asked, coming to stand at the foot of the bed. "Mr. Jacobsen, did you have any idea what you were going to behold this night?"

Frank had to roll over the other side of the bed to grab for the sheet. "What the hell is this, Morgan? Get your ass out of this room or our deal is off."

"Oh, perhaps our dealings have only just begun." A sly grin tilted his lips.

Sophie stood and reached for her wrapper.

"Stay right there, Elizabeth," Garrett said to her. "I'll deal with you later."

She settled back on the mattress like a docile paramour.

"You've got a lot of nerve comin' in here like this,"

Frank said to the two men. "What the hell are you thinkin'?"

"I'm thinking we'd better send Rudy away now. I'll come to the Silver Spike shortly," Garrett told the man. "After I've had a word with Frank and I send Elizabeth packing."

"Yeah. Okay." Rudy backed out through the doorway. Sophie wondered how far he'd make it before a lawman detained him.

Garrett reached to take the cigar from Sophie's fingers and clamped it between his teeth. "Get dressed."

She stood.

"Margaret would be very disappointed if she knew what you'd been up to this evening," Garrett said to the other man. "What do you think she'd do if she knew you'd been caught in your altogether in a beautiful woman's hotel room?"

"How do you know about Margaret? And how would she find out?"

"I know everything I need to know. And she'd find out when Rudy and I went to your home to do the right thing and let her know that her husband is a fornicating bastard."

"You wouldn't." A nervous sheen of sweat glistened on Frank's face and chest. "Why would you?"

"I would if I didn't have motivation not to."

"You that sore of a loser, Morgan?"

"You're the loser, I'm afraid. Don't feel bad, though. There are only a handful of men alive who can resist Elizabeth's charms."

Frank looked from Garrett to Sophie. She shrugged. It all became perfectly clear in that clarifying moment, and his befuddled expression turned thunderous. "You son of a bitch! You set this whole thing up!" He turned a glare on Sophie then, and she looked away before he could call her names.

"Don't worry, we're going to work something out," Garrett told him. "You've just transferred all those funds from cattle sales."

"My investment money, you wanted it all along."

Where was Clay? Surely they'd heard enough by now. He was here, wasn't he?

Frank turned his fury toward Sophie. "You tramp! You set me up. You no good whorin' bitch!"

He lunged toward her, and Garrett jumped out of his way. Frank reached her as she turned to run. He grabbed for her and came away with a fistful of blond hair. His momentary shock gave Sophie time to move away to a safer distance. *Where was Clay?*

Garrett drew his pearl-handled gun and aimed it at Frank. "Don't make it any more difficult on yourself than it needs to be. Let's discuss money and leave her out of it."

This was going all wrong. Garrett had never pulled his gun on the mark before! Sophie's heart pounded at this unplanned development. She'd been eager for Clay to arrive, now she prayed he didn't.

Frank threw the wig toward Sophie as the voice split the air.

"Hands in the air, Garrett."

Clay was here.

He stood with his .45 directed at Garrett's back. "Drop the gun. Your game is over."

After a mere second of shock, Garrett cast Sophie a hateful scowl.

She cringed under the magnitude of his fury and sensed desperation take over his instincts. Slowly, he turned the barrel of his revolver so that it pointed to her chest. "Go ahead. Let's see who can shoot first, shall we?"

Marshal Vidlak and Deputy Owen Sanders flanked Clay inside the doorway, all three with weapons drawn.

Clay glanced from Garrett to Sophie and back again. A muscle jumped in his jaw. "Three to one is pretty good odds in my favor," he said, his voice a soul-deep reassurance.

Garrett turned slowly without changing the direction his pistol was aimed until he faced the three lawmen. "You're probably right."

Shit, shit, shit. This wasn't how it was supposed to happen. Sophie's heart was beating so loudly she was afraid it would drown out their words 'til she couldn't hear.

"You would probably kill me," Garrett said matter-of-factly. "But I'll kill *her* first. Any time you're willing to risk it, go right ahead." He used his thumb to cock the hammer, and Sophie could almost feel the air leave the room as the men all drew a breath. The thought of dying flitted through her mind, and she wondered if death would be quick or if she'd linger in pain.

Clay's eyes never left Garrett's face. A trickle of sweat rolled down his cheek. "Just put down the gun, and nobody gets hurt."

Garrett chuckled. "And you're the big hero, and I swing from a rope. Not an option for me, get it?"

They would hang him for murder. Maybe her, too. He would never give himself up, Sophie realized.

"Risk it." Sophie's words hung in the humid night air. "Shoot him, Clay. If he hits me, I might live. If not, it's okay. If he's a bad shot, don't let me suffer."

"Now, isn't that touching?" Garrett said. "When did you become so brave, Gabriella? You've always been stupid and ungrateful."

"*Shoot him,* Clay," she ordered. "Don't let him get away with it. With *any* of it."

Clay understood what she was saying. She was begging him not to let Garrett get away with what he'd done to her. She knew how livid Clay had been when he'd learned Garrett had taken advantage of her as a young girl. The stories Sophie'd told him were vivid images in his mind. *I submitted,* she'd told him. *I survived.*

The man before him had used her body and soul for his own gain. He'd manipulated and demeaned and controlled—but he hadn't broken her. She'd waited for the time and the place to escape him. She'd planned this whole fiasco to trap him and make him pay. Sophie needed to show Garrett he hadn't gotten the best of her.

"Her name's Sophia," Clay said. "Not Gabriella, not any of the dozen other names you've given her. Sophia."

"What the hell do *you* know?" Garrett asked. "You're one of the pawns she's using to get what she wants. I should know. I taught her how."

Garrett was a master at using people's weaknesses—some sixth sense had alerted him to Clay's internal struggle.

"Guess we'll just have to see who has the last laugh," Clay said. "After all, she set *you* up on this one."

Garrett's nostrils flared. He glared daggers at Sophie.

She figured poor Frank had probably peed himself and the sheet by now if he hadn't already jumped out the window. She didn't dare look.

"You're a revoltin' excuse for a human bein'," Clay told him. "You bought a young girl and used her for illegal gain. Used her just like you use everybody. But you couldn't turn her into you. And you couldn't break her spirit. She waited for the right time and place and she hightailed it away from you."

"I found her, though, didn't I? She didn't want to hide that badly."

"You didn't win, Garrett. She set you up. You thought you had her under your thumb, that you were settin' up this night, when all along, she was the one with the reins. She told me exactly what you'd do and exactly how to catch you. She used your own bait and trapped you."

The air in the room was static with tension.

Garrett's face was beet-red above his white shirt. "Guess I just have to kill her then."

This was it. Clay had no choice. If he told his men to stand down and let Garrett go, Garrett would take Sophie with him. Clay should have planned for something like this.

Sophie's words played in his head. *Risk it. Risk it.*

He'd told her once she was a risk he was willing to take. But not like this. Not risking her life.

Either way was a risk. This entire setup had been dangerous. A chance Sophie had been willing to take.

Clay wasn't sure who moved first. With a flurry of

green satin, Sophie flung her wrapper over Garrett's gun hand. A burst of gunfire exploded and she was thrown back on the floor. Clay fired. More gunfire erupted. Clay squatted and the men on either side of him ducked and rolled.

Garrett's body bucked from the force of the bullets pounding into it. He fell to his knees and his gun hand, encased in green fabric, fell to his side. With eyes wide open, his upper body swayed. The cigar he'd been holding fell. He collapsed forward with a slam.

Clay looked at both the other lawmen who immediately jumped toward Garrett's prone body. He scrambled to Sophie where she lay on the wooden floor and rolled her to her back. She clutched at her side, curling her body protectively. Blood pooled in the cracks between the floorboards and ran in a rivulet away from her body. The entire side of her white corset was soaked in crimson.

Chapter Twenty-One

He'd seen dozens of men shot. The sight had never affected him like this—as though the world spun out of control and his own life hung in the balance. He grabbed a towel from the washstand and pressed it against the wound in her side. "Go get the doc!"

Sophie was staring up at him, her dark eyes glistening. "Is he...did he?"

Clay glanced at Hershel who shook his head.

"He's dead," Clay told her.

She tried to turn to see for herself, but Clay held her down with a hand on her shoulder.

"Don't move. You'll bleed more."

She nodded and closed her eyes. Her breath was coming short and fast. "We did it."

"*You* did it, Sophie."

"Thanks," she managed. "For those things you said to him."

"Don't talk now. Dr. Chaney will be coming." He glanced at the doorway in panic. "You hurtin' bad, Sophie? Course you are. Damn."

"Get me a sheet or something. I'm in my underwear."

Clay stood and turned to Frank Wick, forgotten in the chaos. "Hand over the sheet and get your clothes on before anyone sees you here."

Frank just looked at him.

Clay jerked the sheet away. "Get the hell out!"

Clay covered Sophie while the man fumbled with his pants and shirt, then edged toward the door. No one stopped him.

Clay plucked away the pins that had held Sophie's hair in place under the wig and ran his fingers through the dark tresses. "You were brave."

She bit her lower lip against the pain. He didn't know what he'd do if he lost her.

It would be his fault for not foreseeing that Garrett wouldn't docilely be arrested and led off to trial. The man had no scruples; Clay should have known he wouldn't hesitate to turn a gun on Sophie to save his hide.

"Sorry," he said. "Should've known he'd do somethin' like that."

"Thank you for taking the risk," she said with a weak smile.

"I didn't. You moved first."

"I was mad." She closed her eyes.

"Stay awake until the doc gets here."

She blew out a couple of harsh breaths. "It hurts like the very devil."

He grasped her hand and held it to his lips. He'd never felt so helpless in his life. "The doc's comin'."

There was a commotion on the stairs and Caleb Chaney entered the room, carrying his bag. He paused over Garrett's body.

"He's dead," Clay said. "She's the one needs a doctor."

Caleb knelt over her. "They said she was *shot?*"

Clay edged over so the doctor could move in. Caleb pulled the sheet aside and raised the blood-soaked towel.

"Is it…is it bad?" Clay asked.

"There's so much blood, it's hard to tell." He looked at Sophie's face. He checked her pupils. "I think the corset is helping staunch the blood flow. Let's move her to my office before I take it off to examine her."

Dr. Chaney motioned to the men just inside the doorway. "Bring in the stretcher."

Clay lifted her upper body by grasping her under the arms.

"Shit!" she shouted.

They maneuvered her onto the canvas sling, Clay taking one end as Owen got the other, and carried her down the stairs.

By the time they put her in a wagon and arrived at the doctor's office, Sophie was unconscious.

"It's okay," Caleb assured him. "I don't think she's in shock. It's probably just her body's way of dealing with the pain."

"What can I do?"

"Go take care of things, make your report. I'll take good care of her."

"She might wake up and call for me."

"I'm going to make sure she's out, Marshal. She won't be in any pain once I give her an injection. I have to see how much damage the bullet did and whether or not it's still in there. You won't be any help to me."

Clay pursed his mouth in a hard line, hating the helplessness.

"Let me do my job," the doctor said finally.

Entrusting Sophie to the man's capable hands was the most difficult thing he'd ever done. He backed out of the building and stared sightlessly at the lights in the windows before turning away.

Sophie came to consciousness in a dizzying wave of pain that radiated from her left side. The sun coming in the window of the room where she lay was blinding.

Caleb Chaney looked into her eyes one at a time. "I'm going to give you something to let you sleep a while longer."

Thank God. She nodded.

"Before I do, the marshal would like to say something to you."

Clay was there.

"Sophie?" His hand was warm and large as he enveloped hers. "I have something for you."

"What?"

He held up a shining gold ring—a wedding band. Was he proposing? What an odd time to think about marriage. She didn't know if she was going to live or die, and if she did live, she wouldn't be free to be a wife.

"Garrett had it on him. It's yours, Sophie."

She blinked at him.

"Your mother's ring. It has your parents' names inside." Clay slipped the ring on her finger. It was warm from his skin. The weight was solid and satisfying. Tears formed in the outer corners of her eyes and rolled back into her hair. Clay wiped them with his thumbs.

She grasped his hand. "Thank you," she said, her voice hoarse.

He kissed the backs of her fingers.

"He's dead then?"

"He's dead."

Somehow she didn't feel this was over, couldn't shake the feeling that Garrett might appear at any moment. He'd controlled every second of her life for so many years, she couldn't shake the sensation that he was hovering just out of sight.

Her side throbbed.

"That corset saved your life," he told her.

She listened.

"Doc says the bullet glanced off a bone stay and tore a groove along the flesh. It's all stitched up, but it will heal."

"I'm not going to die."

She thought she saw a glimmer of moisture in his eyes before he closed them and whispered, "No, thank God."

Jail then…or a noose.

"You'll get well and there will be a hearing. I'm doin' everything I can," he promised. "I won't let anythin' happen to you."

What could he do? He couldn't turn back time. He couldn't change the things she'd done.

"Clay?"

"Yeah."

"I'm not holding out much hope."

"I'll hope for the both of us, then."

Oh, she loved this man. Loved him with all her being. If he was another casualty in her long line of victims, she would never forgive herself. It took a great deal of strength to raise her arm, but she wanted to touch him. She grazed her fingertips over his brow, along his cheek, pressed them against his lips.

He tasted her fingers with a kiss. "I love you, Sophie."

"You deserve better," she assured him.

"No. I deserve you."

"I want to sleep now."

He took her hand and tucked it under the sheet, then turned to where Caleb Chaney had been waiting. "Give her somethin' for the pain now."

The doctor swabbed Sophie's arm and she felt the prick of the needle. Delicious mind-numbing warmth flooded through her veins and she slept.

Sophie's identity had been revealed, and Clay's relationship to her was now common knowledge. He had a responsibility to uphold the law, maybe even more so to make certain there was never any question about his integrity. She wasn't going anywhere, but he still had to follow procedures. He assigned a deputy to stand watch outside the room.

Two days later, Dr. Chaney couldn't keep her in bed any longer. She was on her feet and had insisted on using the outhouse and sitting at a table for breakfast. "My side hurts, but I don't want any more of those shots. Thank you very much, I wanted them when I first got here…but I'm getting better."

"You have to let that flesh heal," he told her.

"I'm going to dress, and then I'm leaving," she told him for the hundredth time.

"All right, Sophie. I can't tie you up. Ellie went to your hotel room and brought you loose-fitting clothing. It's in the cabinet right there. If you need help dressing, I'll send for her."

"No, I can do it."

"Don't do any bending or stretching that pulls on those stitches. Come back tomorrow, so I can look at them. If you see any bleeding, send for me."

"Yes, Doctor. I promise."

"I'm ordering a buggy brought around."

She consented. Walking was too much for her today.

After he left the room, it took her a good fifteen minutes to get into her clothing. Ellie had thoughtfully picked out a loose chemise and shirtwaist. Sophie worked up a sweat bending over to put on her stockings and shoes, and almost quit twice, but resolved to be self-sufficient.

With her clothing in place and her hair in reasonable order, she exited the room.

John Doyle jumped up from the chair where he'd been sitting. "You can't go anywhere!"

"I'm not escaping, Deputy," she told him. "No need for handcuffs. I'm heading for the jail right now."

He fell into step behind her.

Dr. Chaney was sitting at the small desk in the next room.

"How much is my bill?" she asked.

He told her, and she promised to send the money the following day. He ushered her through the waiting room to the door.

Ellie's brother Benjamin was waiting for her with a buggy at the curb. "Miss."

He assisted her to the seat, and she sat with her hand protectively over her sore side.

"Where you headin'?" he asked.

"The jailhouse," she said.

"Which one?"

"Wherever Marshal Connor is."

"He's workin' in the new building," the deputy said from where he stood beside the rig.

Benjamin guided the shiny black horse to pull the buggy along the streets, and John Doyle followed on horseback.

"Bet you've never delivered a prisoner to the jailhouse before," she said.

"Ellie said some bad stuff happened to you," he answered. "Me'n Ellie, we know all about takin' care of yourself. Don't any of us Chaneys think less of you."

His compassion touched her deeply. "Thank you, Benjamin."

"Talk around town is you're a hero."

She waved that comment away.

They turned right from Main onto Eighth. The new jail did indeed look finished. "I'll check an' make sure he's here before you bother t' get down," Benjamin offered.

He tied the reins, climbed down, and disappeared inside the brick building.

Clay appeared a second later, his dark hair shining in the sun, a frown on his face. He took in Deputy Doyle where he'd tethered his horse and stood watching. Clay turned his face up to where she sat. "What're you doin'?"

"Help me down."

He and Benjamin both hurried to assist her from the buggy to the ground.

"Wait here, will ya?" Clay asked Benjamin.

The young man agreed with a nod.

Sophie walked toward the door and Clay followed. The inside was much larger than their old building; their desks were new, and the whole place smelled like freshly cut wood and varnish.

Hershel Vidlak sat with his feet propped on a desk, reading the *Newton Kansan*. "Afternoon, Miss Hollis," he said, sliding his feet to the floor.

A deputy she didn't recognize was screwing a rack of some kind to the back wall. At Marshal Vidlak's greeting he turned and nodded.

"Why are you out of bed?" Clay asked. He rolled a new chair with a brown leather seat and backrest toward her. "Here."

She ignored it. "I want to see him."

He got a crease between his dark brows. "Who?"

"Garrett."

Clay paused. "He's dead."

"I want to see the body."

"Why? Why put yourself through that? You've been through too much."

"I have to see for myself. I have to know. You've told me, and I believe you. My head acknowledges that he died that day. But I can't shake this feeling hanging over me. It's like he's still there, waiting…shadowing everything." Sophie searched his eyes for understanding. "I can't go the rest of my life, however long or short that is, without knowing for certain, for once and for all, *proof positive,* that he's gone."

Clay stared at her for a long moment. The familiar sound of a train whistle echoed in the distance.

"I'll be takin' Miss Hollis to the undertaker's," he said finally, speaking to the other men. Clay grabbed his hat and led her to the door.

"Reckon I don't need to follow," John Doyle said.

"Got it covered," Clay told him and led her out. "Mind givin' us a ride to George Monday's place on Main?" he said to Benjamin.

"Ain't he the dentist?"

"Yup." Clay was careful not to touch Sophie's side as he helped her back into the buggy, but she gasped and placed her hand over the spot anyway. Her face was too pale.

"You can lock me up after this," she said.

He climbed up beside her. "You should have stayed at the doc's."

"I couldn't. I had to come here."

"Cells aren't ready in the new place yet," he told her. "We aren't set up for prisoners. And I won't put you in the temporary jail. No privacy. You're gonna hafta stay at your hotel. Your things are all still there."

She glanced at him with a hopeful expression in her dark eyes.

"I'll post a guard during the day and take the night shift myself."

Her smile revealed a mixture of relief and expectation.

"Don't go thinkin' I'm gonna risk hurtin' your wound."

She simply shrugged as though they'd discuss that subject when they got to it.

Benjamin pulled the rig up in front of a small copper-roofed building. The shingle outside the door read George Monday, Dentist, Undertaker.

"Wait here." Clay climbed down and entered the building. After a few minutes, he came back and helped her down. "Meet us 'round back in a few minutes."

"What are you going to do?" Sophie asked.

"He's in the ice house. We'll bring 'im out."

Sophie glanced at the watch around her neck. She fingered the ring on her finger for assurance, smiled nervously up at Benjamin.

"You okay, Miss Hollis?"

She nodded. "I'm fine."

She checked her watch again.

Finally, she made her way around the side of the building.

Clay and a short heavyset man waited for her in front of a small structure. Before them on the ground was a long form draped in white cloth.

"Keepin' 'im on ice 'til I hear what I'm supposed to do with 'im," the man said. "Too hot to leave 'im out."

Sophie stared at the profile beneath the sheeting.

Clay handed her a handkerchief.

Monday bent and folded the drape down and away from the body.

He'd been washed and groomed and dressed in a three-piece suit with a green sheen. Obviously something they'd found in his hotel room, because it was his flamboyant taste and style.

Sophie had expected to gaze fearfully upon a sleeping man who looked as though he could sit up and reclaim her at any moment. She hadn't expected this person's shrunken appearance. His eye sockets and cheeks were sallow, and under his lips and cheeks, it looked as though his teeth were too big for his mouth.

His skin was a sickly gray, and the hands folded over his chest didn't even look real.

It was Garrett, though, his hair and features unmistakable.

Clay seemed to be waiting for her to crumple or fall apart. Sophie walked forward without a second's hesitation and gave Garrett a solid kick in the side.

No sound. No movement.

She glanced up.

Clay was watching as though he saw this kind of thing every day. The undertaker wore an expression of horror, however. Her need to prove to herself Garrett was dead may have been extreme, but she didn't care.

"This is it then," she said simply. "Thank you, Mr. Monday."

Side throbbing, Sophie turned and headed back for the buggy. She needed to lie down.

It only took another week for Judge McNamara to arrive in Newton for the scheduled hearing. A lawman stood watch outside her door during the day. Clay spent every night in her hotel room with her. Each night he held her and told her he loved her, and each night she withheld words of similar sentiment that wouldn't be fair.

Ellie came to visit her two different mornings. Emma stopped by on her day off, bringing chestnut pudding made fresh that day, and Rosie brought her a sampler the girls had worked on together. The cross stitch held a friendship sentiment.

Sophie prepared for the hearing with a clean conscience and a fresh resignation to handle whatever came her way. She'd made friends, she'd known love. And she was living her life as herself. Still, she couldn't pretend she wasn't frightened.

Clay came to escort her to the hearing that had been scheduled as the last appearance of the morning. She was scared to death. All the things she'd kept hidden were about to be public. The most shameful secrets of her past would be revealed. In one way baring that burden would surely be as purging as when she'd told Clay. But Clay had cared about her.

"Just the truth, Sophie," Clay told her, warming her cold hand between his comforting warm ones as their buggy was drawn toward the courthouse.

It was a square brick building, set back from the street and surrounded by well-tended shade trees and overflowing flowerbeds of red and white petunias. She walked the brick path to the door and waited for Clay to open it.

A bald man ushered them into a room, and Clay told her he'd be sitting with the other lawmen. He gave her hand a reassuring squeeze and took his place. She took notice to see that there were only one or two people besides the law officers there to observe. She moved to stand before the table where a white-haired man sat. Beside him a younger man waited with pen poised over a tablet.

Judge McNamara cut an impressive figure in his brown pin-striped suit. "You're the young woman all the fuss is about?" he asked.

"My name is Sophia, sir."

"Last name is Hollis?"

"I don't remember my real last name. I've been going by Hollis."

"Well, take a seat right here," he said, indicating a chair at the side of the table.

She sat gingerly, and the judge took notice of the way she favored her side. "I've gone over all the reports," he began. "Seems we have a bit of a dilemma here. It's your word against a dead man's."

Chapter Twenty-Two

"Judge McNamara." Clay's voice.

"Marshal," the judge acknowledged.

"Her name is Sophia Hollister."

Sophie turned and stared at Clay. The name resounded in her head, an elusive memory trying to focus.

The judge slid his glasses onto his forehead and studied Clay. "And how do you know this when she doesn't even recall her own name?"

Clay carried a stack of documents forward and presented them. "She's wearin' a ring there that belonged to her ma. I took it off the dead man. Two names are inscribed inside. The same names are on a passenger list from a wagon train that the man and wife traveled with. Records I found at army forts match the family's travels right up to the time and the area where reports say they were killed."

The judge shuffled through lists and telegrams, the rustling paper loud in the large room.

Sophie digested the fact that Clay had searched

records and hunted until he found her family and her real name. He could have mentioned this before. She gave him a dumbfounded look. He ignored it.

"Ward and Sela Hollister and their five children were reported killed by a Sioux war party," the judge said after review. "Miss Hollis's story fits this family's right up to that point in time. May I see the ring?"

Sophie took off the band and handed it to Clay who walked round the table and gave it to the judge. The judge used his glasses like a magnifying glass to read the tiny inscription Sophie hadn't remembered. She hadn't removed the ring since Clay had returned it to her.

The judge handed Clay the ring to give back to Sophie. Clay returned to his seat. "Okay, we know who you are. But you're accused of quite an extensive list of crimes. What do you have to say for yourself?"

"If you name them off for me sir I'll tell you to the best of my recollection whether or not I participated."

The judge raised an eyebrow in surprise, then held his glasses away from his face so he could read a list of names and the crimes associated with them through the lenses.

"Yes, sir. That was me. That one, too."

He continued, and she admitted responsibility for taking part in each one. "I'm not sure about those," she said at one point, "but that was one of our usual scams, so I can't deny it."

Ten minutes later the older man leaned toward her. "Young lady, you've just admitted to over sixty acts of crime. Do you have anything to say for yourself?"

Just the truth, she remembered Clay saying. She

swallowed hard. "Did any of those papers tell you that Garrett bought me? I was about twelve."

The judge's expression showed his surprise and interest. "*Bought* you?"

She nodded. "Yes, sir. I remember standing on a public street in the fall. It was a couple years after my mother had died. The Sioux were selling hides and jerky. I'd never been taken on one of their trips before. I had this ring with me." She fingered the band. "Hidden on a leather thong under my tunic. I wanted to touch it for comfort, but I knew I shouldn't let anyone see it.

"I saw the goods trade hands, but didn't realize what was going on right away. Whiskey. A rifle. And then I was being pushed toward the white man. The sun was warm on my face and head, and I remember the way he looked down at me."

Sophie paused. It felt good to have the truth about her life out in the open at last. "Could I have a drink of water, please?"

The judge's assistant got up and poured her a glass of water. She took a fortifying sip. "Thank you."

She told how Garrett had purchased clothing for her. How he'd paid for tutors and teachers of deportment. How he held his own session each day, coaching her to recognize people's weaknesses, how to play into those, how to play a role.

Occasionally Judge McNamara asked a question.

Sophie didn't leave out a single detail. Her explanation of when and how their relationship had changed made the men in the room uncomfortable. Sophie noticed they shifted in their chairs. But Judge McNamara looked right at her without flinching.

"How did you come to be here today?"

She went on to explain how Garret had killed the man in Denver and that she'd taken the money and run.

At that point Clay spoke up again. "Judge, there's someone who'd like to say somethin' now."

"Who is it?"

Clay gestured to a woman sitting in one of the rows of seats Sophie'd avoided looking at.

A woman wearing a homespun dress raised her hand tentatively, then stood. "I'd like a chance to make mention of what I know about Miss Hollis's character."

"What's your name, ma'am?"

"Gretchen Forrester."

"Come on up here, then." The judge motioned her forward.

The woman stood three feet from the table. "Miss Hollis or Dumont or whoever she is…" she pointed at Sophie. "She came to my home nearly two years ago and returned money that had been taken from my husband."

"How did your husband lose the money?"

"An investment of some sort that he told me went sour. He didn't wanna admit he gave it to a flim-flam man. But then when this lady came and offered it back, he told me what really happened. That was money I'd inherited from my father, and I intend to send my son to university with it."

"I hope your husband has learned his lesson."

"Oh, he has, sir. He has."

"You can sit down, Mrs. Forrester." Judge McNamara turned to Sophie. "What happened when the money ran out?"

"I saved enough back to see me through if I didn't find work. I was in Dubuque when I saw the advertisement for the Harvey House positions. So I came up with letters and references and traveled here."

"What did you hope to gain in coming to Kansas?"

Sophie took a moment to form her answer. "I wanted to live like other people. I had to lie to get the position, but lies were all I knew how to do. I figured if I could set aside a nest egg, I could start my own business eventually. I'd be independent. Most of all I wanted to be in control of my own destiny. That's all I ever thought of really."

The judge looked to Clay. "How'd you find Mrs. Forrester?"

Clay stepped forward. "Once I started tracin' Sophie's trail, the Pinkertons caught on. They'd been lookin' for Garrett. We shared information, and I got names of people she'd visited."

Clay glanced at Sophie before addressing the judge again. "What I'm hopin' you'll see, Judge, is that Miss Hollis—er—that Sophie was a scared kid doin' what she had to just t' survive. She got away. And when she did, she paid back many of the people they'd taken money from."

"Paying back stolen money with more stolen money doesn't right the wrong," the judge replied.

Clay's expression was grim at that remark.

The judge leaned back in his chair. "I'm beginning to see something here. Have you done all this research into Miss Hollis's background purely as your official duty?"

Clay looked uncomfortable with the question, and

she hoped it was because he didn't want to comprom-
ise the facts and not because he was embarrassed about
their association. "No, sir, I didn't. It's more personal
than that."

"Did you ever wonder, Marshal, if she was pulling
a con over on you?"

Clay nodded, regret evident in his posture.
"Wouldn't be human if I hadn't. I had feelin's for her,
and as a lawman I wondered if I was lettin' those shade
my judgment." He glanced at her. "Sorry, Sophie. We're
tellin' the truth today."

"It's okay," she said.

The judge looked at her again. "Sophia, did you use
the marshal?"

She felt like she'd been struck. She couldn't catch her
breath for a moment and her ears rang. Used Clay?
Used him?

"Well, I—I guess in a way it would seem I did. I mean
I knew he cared for me and that he wanted to help."

"Have you ever asked him to do anything for you?"

"Yes, sir, I have."

Clay frowned at her, but she went on.

"I asked him to help me trap Garrett. And—" She'd
asked him to spend the night with her, but she couldn't
say that, even if it was the truth. She raised a hand as
she thought of something else. "I asked him to let me
see the body once Garrett was dead."

"So, Marshal, the plan to catch Garrett in one of
these blackmail schemes was entirely Miss Hollis's?"

Clay shifted uncomfortably. "It was."

"But you agreed to go along with it. Care to explain why?"

"Had no idea the man would be killed, o' course," he answered. "I thought once he was caught right here in Kansas, there'd be a better chance of a trial here, rather than escorting him directly to Colorado."

"And what did you hope to gain by holding his first trial here?"

"I was hopin' Sophie'd stand a better chance of pardon."

Clay moved to pick up another stack of letters and telegrams and handed them to Judge McNamara. "More people want to say somethin' on Sophie's behalf."

The judge gestured with a sweep of his arm. "Where are they?"

One of the other marshals went to the door and opened it. One by one a dozen or more men and women filed into the room and took seats.

Sophie stared, recognizing some of them as either people she'd returned money to, others as girls from the Arcade. Louis Tripp was there, and even Mr. Webb had come! Her heart could hardly contain her joy that so many people cared and believed in her enough to speak on her behalf.

Clay sat down and one by one the judge let each person say their piece from where they sat. A Pinkerton agent shared his findings. Citizens thanked her for her honesty in bringing them their stolen funds, others shared her kind deeds or her work ethic. They would've been passing out lemonade in hell if Mrs. Winters had shown up, she thought.

The door opened again and Caleb and Ellie Chaney entered.

"Dr. Chaney, I suppose you wanted to say something about Miss Hollis's character, and I suppose too that it would all be glowing."

"It would."

Ellie gave Sophie an encouraging smile and Sophie's throat tightened with humble appreciation.

"One more, Judge," Clay said.

Deputy Sanders strode to the door. A young woman accompanied him back. Blond hair. *Amanda!* Sophie covered her trembling lips with her hand.

"I'm Amanda Pettyjohn," she said. Her cheeks were bright with color. "Your honor, Sophie is a dear and loyal friend. She taught me to dance. That's not why you should let her go, though. You should let her go because she saved me from getting mixed up with Monte—I mean Tek Garrett. She risked our friendship and a lot more to tell me the truth. And then she gave me money she'd earned so I could go home when my cousin Winnie had her baby." She turned a beaming smile on Sophie. "It's a girl!"

Sophie smiled through tears.

"Thank you, Miss Pettyjohn. Take a seat."

Amanda sat two chairs away from Deputy Sanders.

The judge laid his glasses on the tabletop. "I don't see much sense in taking this any further."

Sophie anticipated the worst.

"I pretty much had my mind made up after reading the reports and the documentation, little lady. But your marshal here and all your friends intrigued me, so I listened to them. Not all my days are this interesting."

He looked at the people occupying the chairs. "Sophie was a child when this Garrett got hold of her. He purposefully corrupted her to his way of life and used her."

Sophie listened, hope growing.

He turned his attention to her again. "I'm of a mind that whatever wrongs you may have participated in before, you had no plans for any further con work."

"No, sir," Sophie assured him. "I wanted to put those days behind me."

"And you risked your life to catch the true criminal."

This was sounding more hopeful every minute!

"Marshal, you will notify the proper authorities that Tek Garrett was killed while carrying out a criminal act. Also alert them that Miss Hollis has been cleared of all accusations subject to my authority and that I am petitioning a federal judge to make certain she is absolved of her part in any and all charges not included here today."

Sophie stared at the man in disbelief. "You mean I'm free? I'm not going to jail?"

"You're free, Sophia. Punishing you would just be more cruel and unfair treatment, which you've already endured. Go. Create that destiny you've wanted for so long."

Sophie stood. "Oh, I will, Judge. I will! Thank you. Thank you."

She turned her attention to Clay. He was smiling from ear to ear. She rushed forward and he opened his arms to enfold her, careful of her tender side. "It's over, Sophie," he told her. "You're free."

Sophie's friends and acquaintances gathered around her to give her gentle hugs and share their support and pleasure in the judge's findings.

Sophie made a point of finding Judge McNamara and thanking him before he left. The judge's assistant picked up papers and folders, and followed the older man from the room. Others were filing out, too, now.

Clay hadn't left her side. She turned to embrace him. "Why didn't you tell me you'd done all that?" They hung behind to speak privately. "Why didn't you tell me you knew my real name?"

"You said you didn't want to get your hopes up. I wasn't even sure how much good my efforts would do. I just had to try."

"You risked your reputation as a lawman for me." She leaned back and looked up into his clear blue eyes.

"Said it before. You're a risk worth takin'."

Oblivious to their surroundings now, without thought to anyone left in the room, Sophie cupped his jaw and raised her face for a kiss.

Clay obliged her, telling her with searing passion that it had all been worth it to hold her like this, to know she was in control of her own life from here on out.

Sophie leaned back to say, "Today is all about the truth."

His gaze steadied on her lips.

"There's something I have to tell you now," she said.

Two tiny lines formed between his black eyebrows.

She hadn't meant to stab him with concern. "I love you. I couldn't say it before. I didn't have the right, and I wasn't free to. Now I can tell you. I love you, Clay Connor."

His arm tightened across her back. "I love you, Sophia Hollister." He kissed her gently. "You only just found out that name an' all, but before you go getting used to it, I was hopin' you'd be willin' to change it one last time. For good this time."

Hope surged in Sophie's heart. She'd never anticipated anything this good, this right being hers. She closed her eyes to remember this feeling. She never wanted to forget the way her heart felt as light as a butterfly.

"Open your eyes and say you'll marry me."

Her smile came from her soul. She opened her eyes and had to blink back tears of joy. "Only if you promise to kiss me like that forever."

"I can do better than that."

"Can you love me forever?"

"I will."

"Can I smoke in bed?"

He chuckled and she loved the sound. "Only if I'm there with you."

"In that case I trust you with my heart's destiny, Marshal."

He kissed her well, proving his word that he could do better.

"Let's go celebrate," he suggested. "I heard cheesecake's on the menu at the Arcade today, and I haven't been there since you quit."

They drew apart, but held hands as they walked toward the doorway. "Good idea," she agreed. "I have a few bridesmaids to share the rest of our good news with."

He drew a face. "Just how many would that be?"

"Is twenty too many?"

He laughed and wrapped his arm around her. "Funny, that's how many *children* I was countin' on, Sophie."

Her laughter echoed throughout the empty room.

* * * * *

Happily ever after is just the beginning...

Turn the page for a sneak preview of
A HEARTBEAT AWAY
by Eleanor Jones

Harlequin Everlasting—
Every great love has a story to tell. ™
A brand-new series from Harlequin Books

Special? A prickle ran down my neck and my heart started to beat in my ears. Was today really special?

"Tuck in," he ordered.

I turned my attention to the feast that he had spread out on the ground. Thick, home-cooked-ham sandwiches, sausage rolls fresh from the oven and a huge variety of mouthwatering scones and pastries. Hunger pangs took over, and I closed my eyes and bit into soft homemade bread.

When we were finally finished, I lay back against the bluebells with a groan, clutching my stomach.

Daniel laughed. "Your eyes are bigger than your stomach," he told me.

I leaned across to deliver a punch to his arm, but he rolled away, and when my fist met fresh air I collapsed in a fit of giggles before relaxing on my back and staring up into the flawless blue sky. We lay like that for quite a while, Daniel and I, side by side in companionable silence, until he stretched out his hand in an arc that encompassed the whole area.

"Don't you think that this is the most beautiful place in the entire world?"

His voice held a passion that echoed my own feelings, and I rose onto my elbow and picked a buttercup to hide the emotion that clogged my throat.

"Roll over onto your back," I urged, prodding him with my forefinger. He obliged with a broad grin, and I reached across to place the yellow flower beneath his chin.

"Now, let us see if you like butter."

When a yellow light shone on the tanned skin below his jaw, I laughed.

"There…you do."

For an instant our eyes met, and I had the strangest sense that I was drowning in those honey-brown depths. The scent of bluebells engulfed me. A roaring filled my ears, and then, unexpectedly, in one smooth movement Daniel rolled me onto my back and plucked a buttercup of his own.

"And do *you* like butter, Lucy McTavish?" he asked. When he placed the flower against my skin, time stood still.

His long lean body was suspended over mine, pinning me against the grass. Daniel…dear, comfortable, familiar Daniel was suddenly bringing out in me the strangest sensations.

"Do you, Lucy McTavish?" he asked again, his voice low and vibrant.

My eyes flickered toward his, the whisper of a sigh escaped my lips and although a strange lethargy had crept into my limbs, I somehow felt as if all my nerve endings were on fire. He felt it, too—I could see it in his warm brown eyes. And when he lowered his face to mine, it seemed to me the most natural thing in the world.

None of the kisses I had ever experienced could have even begun to prepare me for the feel of Daniel's lips on mine. My entire body floated on a tide of ecstasy that shut out everything but his soft, warm mouth, and I knew that this was what I had been waiting for the whole of my life.

"Oh, Lucy." He pulled away to look into my eyes. "Why haven't we done this before?"

Holding his gaze, I gently touched his cheek, then I curled my fingers through the short thick hair at the base of his skull, overwhelmed by the longing to drown again in the sensations that flooded our bodies. And when his long tanned fingers crept across my tingling skin, I knew I could deny him nothing.

* * * * *

Be sure to look for
A HEARTBEAT AWAY,
available February 27, 2007.

And look, too, for
THE DEPTH OF LOVE
by Margot Early,
the story of a couple who must learn that
love comes in many guises—and in the end
it's the only thing that counts.

This February...

Catch NASCAR Superstar *Carl Edwards* in

SPEED DATING!

Kendall assesses risk for a living—so she's the last person you'd expect to see on the arm of a race-car driver who thrives on the unpredictable. But when a bizarre turn of events—and NASCAR hotshot Dylan Hargreave—inspire her to trade in her ever-so-structured existence for "life in the fast lane" she starts to feel she might be on to something!

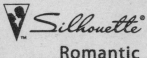

Silhouette®

Romantic
SUSPENSE

Excitement, danger and passion guaranteed!

Same great authors and riveting editorial
you've come to know and love
from Silhouette Intimate Moments.

New York Times
bestselling author
Beverly Barton
is back with the
latest installment
in her popular
miniseries,
The Protectors.
HIS ONLY
OBSESSION
is available
next month from
Silhouette®
Romantic Suspense

Look for it wherever you buy books!

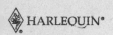

E V E R L A S T I N G   L O V E ™

Every great love has a story to tell ™

Save $1.⁰⁰ off

the purchase of
any Harlequin
Everlasting Love novel

Coupon valid from January 1, 2007
until April 30, 2007.

Valid at retail outlets in the U.S. only.
Limit one coupon per customer.

5   65373 00076 2   (8100)0 11302

HEUSCPN0407

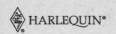

EVERLASTING LOVE™

Every great love has a story to tell™

Fall from Grace
Kristi Gold

Save $1.⁰⁰ off

the purchase of
any Harlequin
Everlasting Love novel

Coupon valid from January 1, 2007
until April 30, 2007.

Valid at retail outlets in Canada only.
Limit one coupon per customer.

52607370

HECDNCPN0407

REQUEST YOUR FREE BOOKS!

Harlequin® Historical
Historical Romantic Adventure!

2 FREE NOVELS PLUS 2 **FREE GIFTS!**

YES! Please send me 2 FREE Harlequin® Historical novels and my 2 FREE gifts. After receiving them, if I don't wish to receive any more books, I can return the shipping statement marked "cancel." If I don't cancel, I will receive 6 brand-new novels every month and be billed just $4.69 per book in the U.S., or $5.24 per book in Canada, plus 25¢ shipping and handling per book and applicable taxes, if any*. That's a savings of close to 15% off the cover price! I understand that accepting the 2 free books and gifts places me under no obligation to buy anything. I can always return a shipment and cancel at any time. Even if I never buy another book from Harlequin, the two free books and gifts are mine to keep forever.

246 HDN FEWW   349 HDN EEW9

Name	(PLEASE PRINT)

Address	Apt. #

City	State/Prov.	Zip/Postal Code

Signature (if under 18, a parent or guardian must sign)

Mail to the **Harlequin Reader Service®**:
IN U.S.A.: P.O. Box 1867, Buffalo, NY 14240-1867
IN CANADA: P.O. Box 609, Fort Erie, Ontario L2A 5X3

Not valid to current Harlequin Historical subscribers.

Want to try two free books from another line?
Call 1-800-873-8635 or visit www.morefreebooks.com.

* Terms and prices subject to change without notice. NY residents add applicable sales tax. Canadian residents will be charged applicable provincial taxes and GST. This offer is limited to one order per household. All orders subject to approval. Credit or debit balances in a customer's account(s) may be offset by any other outstanding balance owed by or to the customer. Please allow 4 to 6 weeks for delivery.

Your Privacy: Harlequin is committed to protecting your privacy. Our Privacy Policy is available online at www.eHarlequin.com or upon request from the Reader Service. From time to time we make our lists of customers available to reputable firms who may have a product or service of interest to you. If you would prefer we not share your name and address, please check here. ☐

HH07

COMING NEXT MONTH FROM

HARLEQUIN®
HISTORICAL

- **BEAU CRUSOE**
  by **Carla Kelly**
  (Regency)
  Society's opinion matters not a whit to Susannah Park, happy with her son and her memories of love. Then into her quiet, settled life comes James Trevenen, shipwreck survivor and man of action!

- **INNOCENCE AND IMPROPRIETY**
  by **Diane Gaston**
  (Regency)
  Rose O'Keefe's beautiful singing voice has made her a sensation among the pleasure-seekers of the night. She reminds Jameson Flynn of the world he left behind. But can he save her from becoming another man's mistress?

- **MUSTANG WILD**
  by **Stacey Kayne**
  (Western)
  Tricked into signing a marriage document, Skylar Daines is relieved when her "husband" says he will fix the marital slipup. But then she realizes that Tucker Morgan can offer what she yearn for most—a home.

- **CRUSADER'S LADY**
  by **Lynna Banning**
  (Medieval)
  Marc de Valery is charged with escorting King Richard the Lionheart from Syria back to England and finds himself saddled with a young servant boy who turns out to be a beautiful, provocative young woman!